Be with me.

"Run to me, Em. I will not turn away from you, I promise."

His mouth feathered over hers in a soft kiss. Emily closed her eyes, marveling in the firmness of his lips against hers. Raphael's hands held her steady as he deepened the kiss, his tongue coaxing her to open to him. She parted her lips and he slipped inside, tasting her, his tongue plunging and retreating, brushing the roof of her mouth, tracing every part of the moist cavern of her mouth. Emily sighed and shyly met his sensual advances. Breath escaped her as he lightly nipped her lower lip.

Raphael pulled away, his chest heaving, his eyes darker than the blackest night. Her own pulse beat frantically as she struggled to breathe, feeling the delicious flush of heat suffuse her entire body.

She knew now what it meant and knew what he wanted. He wanted to mate, but waited patiently for her.

Emily was ready now.

Books by Bonnie Vanak

Silhouette Nocturne

The Empath #30
Enemy Lover #51
Immortal Wolf #74

BONNIE VANAK

fell in love with romance novels during childhood. While cleaning a hall closet, she discovered her mother's cache of paperbacks and began reading. Thus began a passion for romance and a lifelong dislike for housework.

After years of newspaper reporting, Bonnie became a writer for a major international charity, which has taken her to destitute countries such as Haiti and Guatemala to write about famine, disease and other issues affecting the poor. When the emotional strain of her job demanded a diversion, she turned to writing romance novels. Bonnie lives in Florida with her husband and two dogs, and happily writes books amid an ever-growing population of dust bunnies. She loves to hear from readers. Visit her Web site at www.bonnievanak.com or e-mail her at bonnievanak@aol.com.

BONNIE VANAK

IMMORTAL WOLF

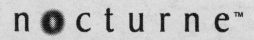

Silhouette Books

nocturne™

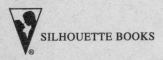

SILHOUETTE BOOKS

Recycling programs
for this product may
not exist in your area.

ISBN-13: 978-0-373-61821-7

IMMORTAL WOLF

www.silhouettenocturne.com

Printed in U.S.A.

Dear Reader,

Come with me and dare to enter the dark, dangerous world of the Draicon werewolves.

Meet Raphael, the leather-clad, Harley-riding immortal Draicon. He's a courageous fighter; a ferocious, yet tender lover; a loyal brother, and he will do anything to protect those under his care. He's given up hope of ever finding his true mate. Until he meets Emily—the werewolf he must sacrifice for the survival of the entire Draicon race.

Everyone Emily touches with her hands she kills, or so she thinks. Her blood can restore life, yet the tenderhearted Emily doesn't dare reach out and embrace any other living creatures for fear of hurting them.

Emily's been abandoned by everyone she loves and lives in isolation. Now Raphael must convince her to trust him, the one she trusts least. Together they have to find answers to save Emily's life—and prevent the spread of evil.

So if you happen to run into Raphael in the woods of eastern Tennessee, beware. Raphael is an immortal wolf who is extremely protective of those he loves!

Bonnie Vanak

For my chapter, Florida Romance Writers, thanks
for all your support and being such a great team.
And to Joan Hammond and Julie Sloane, who
encouraged me from the very beginning. Also,
special thanks to Meri Aigner for her knowledge
of Harley-Davidson motorcycles, and my friend
Maureen "Mo" Fries. You guys rock!

Prologue

Once she restored life. Now she brought death with her touch.

Emily Burke brushed a tender hand across the cold marble gravestone. Beneath it lay Helen, her favorite aunt. Around the stone, daisies planted in loving care were withering and dying on their frail stems.

Never had she felt this forlorn. Not since she'd killed her father a year ago.

Sunlight dappled fading gold-and-red leaves on the canopy of trees. Stray beams drifted onto the small clearing in the deep woods. Here and there, rounded markers etched in the Old Language marked the places where family eternally rested. The Burke pack had ruled this section of eastern Tennessee for generations, living and dying on these same three hundred wooded acres.

If her people had their way, soon her gravestone would join the others. Then the curse haunting her would be broken at last.

A shiver skated down her spine as a cool breeze caressed her cheek. In a few days, the most revered of all Draicon, the Kallan, arrived to prepare her for the rite of *trasna*. The ritual passage to the Other Realm required formal meditation, farewells and anointing. Though fairly young, the Kallan was renowned. Females whispered of his legendary sexual prowess. Males lowered their heads in respect for his tremendous power.

Without the Kallan, her own pack would be forced to execute her.

Stretching out her hands, she studied the chamois men's gloves that covered them. She pulled off the right glove and the thin latex sterile glove beneath it. Emily touched the gravestone again, relishing the feel of the hard surface, cool marble. Just to feel…anything.

I can touch you now, Helen.

A daisy plant drooped by the gravestone. Emily swallowed hard. She glanced around and picked up a sharp rock. A sharp swipe across her palm and she winced.

She held her bleeding palm over the plant. One, two, three, four drops of crimson, her life's fluid, dripped onto the flower.

Emily allowed the cut to heal and watched the daisy with faint hope. The white petals unfurled and the lemon-yellow center glowed with health. Once more, she'd brought back life. The last descendant of the pureblood Draicon, she could restore life with her blood.

Emily had healed many, including the animals of the forest who lay sick and dying.

Yet for a year, her touch now killed her own kind.

Oh, to be cursed with the touch of death and the blood of life. Why? Did the goddess curse her because Aibelle saw Emily as vain?

"What have I done?" she whispered. "Please, tell me how I can amend it. I did not abuse this gift I was given at birth. I only wanted to heal."

A year ago in a dream, the goddess Aibelle mysteriously told her the balance of life and death was within Emily. And the next day, Emily had touched her father and…

Tiny crescent marks gouged her palm as she squeezed, her nails digging into tender flesh. Swallowing hard, she covered her hand. Both gloves had been purified in sage smoke and bathed in a rich mixture of spices and herbs before drying. No matter. Her hands killed her people.

She had killed her father after touching him. Killed her aunt Helen as well. Now she must pay the price, before her curse spread to other Draicon.

She had one hope. Recently, she'd telepathically found her dracairon, her destined mate. Amant. His deep, sexy voice in her mind didn't hint of origin, and it sent a thrill through her. Worried he might have heard of Emily, the cursed one, she'd given her nickname of Erin. She imagined him as big, powerful and slightly threatening to anyone who dared to hurt her.

Even the Kallan, the Draicon who would execute her.

Amant was her knight, who would charge to her rescue. If Amant knew of her fate, he would do anything to save her. It was his duty. Instinct would drive him to risk all to keep her safe.

Emily closed her eyes and mentally reached out to call out to her white knight.

Help me.

Raphael Robichaux sped toward Bourbon Street on his Harley toward his favorite bar for one last prowl through his turf in New Orleans. Miles away, a female awaited him to deliver her to death. A quick death, but death nonetheless.

The big bike purred as wind whipped his ragged shoulder-length hair. Riding the Harley gave him the only true freedom he knew. But as Raphael neared Bourbon, a voice called out in pained insistence.

Kallan. Kallan. I have need of you.

Raphael turned the bike around, toward the weak, hopeful sigh. In a shadowed alleyway littered with paper bags and the stench of old vomit, a male sat against the exposed brick wall. Even as he slid off the Harley, Raphael knew it was an elder Draicon in great pain.

Yellowed, sharp fangs flashed in the alley. Morphs. Former Draicon who turned evil by killing a relative, they could shapeshift into any life-form. The pair licked the blood streaming down the elder's temples, tasting death and the Draicon's fear to gain energy.

One swiped at the helpless male, swiping bloody furrows across his chest. The elder gasped.

Raphael stood at the alley's entrance. "Go pick on someone able to fight back." Challenge rang out in his voice.

Growls greeted him as they backed away from their

prey. The Morphs straightened. Energized by the elder's terror, they shifted into rats, cloned themselves and then chewed on the elder's arms and hands.

The elder screamed.

Absolute calmness came over Raphael. He never lost sight of the original two, their markings, their movements. He lifted his hands to create a veil of protection, much like an electronic fence, around the elder. Shocked by the pure magick, the rats squealed and dropped off, before turning on Raphael.

He was ready. Waving his hands, he divested himself of clothing and shifted into wolf.

Focusing on the original pair, he sprang forward to attack. They squealed and shifted into their true form. As they did, their clones vanished, denied the energy necessary to maintain them.

Just as quickly Raphael shifted back into his human form, clothed himself. Daggers materialized in his hands. He twirled, punched, acted. The two Morphs gave low howls and dropped to the ground. In a minute, they vanished into ashes.

Raphael went to the elder, who was holding his stomach as if trying to keep his guts stuffed inside. His mouth went dry as he scanned the Draicon's injuries.

"Please, help me end this. I can't…cross." The elder, at least 1,500 years, wheezed. Pain radiated from him in great waves. "Just let me go."

Raphael hedged, torn between wanting to give the honored elder solace and the agonizing decision to end it for him. But the male's burning plea nudged him forward. It was time.

Closing his eyes, Raphael laid his hand on the

other's shoulder. Concentrated, pulling back to the Other Realm of peace and no pain. He uttered words in the ancient tongue.

His eyes flew open as he removed a short, golden dagger strapped always to his waist. The blade had a magick anesthetic. With a low murmur of sacred words, he stabbed the elder in the heart.

Death was swift, merciful and painless. Light faded from the Draicon's gaze, but a small, serene smile rested on his thin lips. With reverence, Raphael closed the elder's eyes. He wiped blood off his sacred Scian with a small cloth tucked into his back pocket. Then he replaced the dagger, fished out his cell phone and made a call.

Five minutes later, four of his former pack arrived. They wrapped the body in a long length of oriental carpet and discreetly carried it to the waiting truck to take the elder to the honored burial he deserved.

Raphael closed his eyes, wishing he didn't feel so damn alone right now. As much of a rush killing the Morphs gave him, dispatching one of his own into the peace of the Other Realm made him feel empty. Dark inside.

He was the Destroyer, the bringer of death.

Bringing the solace of crossing over to the Other Realm was an honored vocation. Screw it. He was a damn death dealer. He was the Kallan, the only one who could terminate the life of a fellow Draicon without consequence.

Minutes later, he parked the bike in front of the Full Moon bar. Music poured down the street in an acoustic tidal wave; soft, cool jazz and hard, pounding rock. A few women lounging on the sidewalk and sipping hurricanes gave him the twice-over. Wind teased the pure white streak of hair at his temple, played with the gold dagger earring dangling from his left ear.

A collective female sigh, soft as a Mississippi River breeze, drifted toward him. He angled his famous half-smile at the staring threesome. "Evening, ladies," he drawled.

Three in one night. Nothing new. Hard, fast female company, the bliss of quick, anonymous sex and the energy it brought pushed back the loneliness a little. The tallest had a lush figure, with enough flesh on all the right places he loved to caress. He adored females. Even human women, who were too frail to absorb the rough sex Draicon males sometimes relished.

But sex with anonymous strangers never touched the empty space inside him. Raphael gave the women a charming smile and walked away. Behind him, their murmurs of disappointment buzzed like mosquitoes in the bayou.

He headed toward the scratched wood bar and grabbed a mug of beer. Male and female Draicon nursing drinks stared. "That's him," he heard one female whisper. "The Kallan. They say he was appointed because he killed eighty Morphs in one day when they were about to slay a pack in California."

Sometimes the story boasted over a hundred Morphs, and the pack of Draicon were from New England. It mattered not, for the legend shadowing him was far bigger than reality.

"He's also the only mixed-blood ever to become Kallan. Who would have thought a Cajun mongrel could have entered the ranks," a male murmured.

Raphael stiffened.

Too often he felt as if he were dancing atop a paper pedestal erected by his people. When would he fall off because his blood wasn't pure enough? Only his family treated him normally.

He snorted. Normal? He was immortal. Normal wasn't part of the package.

Being a Kallan required strength, physical prowess but most of all, emotional detachment tempered with compassion and spiritual purity. A Kallan did not relish dispatching his own people. He saw his role as a guide to the Other Realm, who prepared them for crossing over. Those transitions, even if they committed crimes against their own kind, were treated with dignity and compassion.

He had never dispatched a female before. Raphael hoped he'd have the strength and emotional detachment to execute the cursed Draicon.

Two of his brothers shouted a hearty hello. He was crossing the distance between them when a voice spoke in his head.

Amant? Are you there?

The whisper made him halt. It was her, the one he revered above all others. Raphael held up a hand in greeting to his brothers. He retreated to a solitary table.

Erin. I'm here, he reassured her.

Her voice sounded shaky, as if she tried disguising her fear. But something deeply worried her.

I thought I'd lost you. You haven't spoken to me since yesterday.

Hush, little one, he soothed. *I'm right here, as I have been. What troubles you, chere?*

I just missed you, that's all.

I missed you, too, he admitted, pulling out a chair and propping one booted foot upon it.

One month ago, he had been preparing crayfish for the family barbecue when he'd heard her. His draicara seeking him out. Raphael had gone still at the sweet purity of her voice, the low melodic tones. He'd felt bathed in serenity and yet sharpened by sexual need.

It was the most erotic thing he'd ever experienced, and yet she'd spoken but one sentence.

Since then, they'd talked nearly each day. He wisely did not press her and allowed her to seek him out. He'd called himself the nickname bestowed on him by his brothers—Amant, the French word for "lover." He didn't want to frighten her or have her overcome with awe at the legendary Raphael, the most feared and respected Draicon.

Where are you now? What are you doing? Erin asked.

In a bar. Talking to you.

He leaned forward, placing both feet on the floor. *What's wrong, Erin? You sound sad. Are you alone?*

A tiny sigh went through him like an arrow. *Where I am, I am always alone.*

Where was her pack? Her Alpha?

I must go. It isn't safe here. I have to go someplace safe.

He picked up her anxiety, like little hairs brushing against the nape of his neck. Raphael frowned, wishing he could see her. *Your people—are they near? Do you feel threatened?*

It's just some males from my pack walking nearby. I can't let them see me.

His hackles rose at the suggestion of someone daring to touch his draicara. Automatically, he flexed his muscles, his protective instincts rising. *If they try anything with you, they will pay.*

Don't worry. They won't come near me.

They'd better not. You're mine and mine alone, he couldn't help rumbling.

She gave a light laugh, as sweet and airy as a songbird. *I can take care of myself. Trust me. I have for a while now.*

It's my job to take care of you.

Her voice deepened. *You're so good to me, even if you aren't here. I cherish our times together these past weeks. When can I see you?*

Raphael blocked away thoughts of the task awaiting him. *Soon. I have an assignment, then I will come to you.*

Promise? Despair punctuated her voice. Troubled, he sent her waves of reassurance, soothing images of forest and glen, the deep quiet of the green woods. He felt her tension ease.

How I wish you could kiss me now. Kiss me and tell me all is well.

Her admission sent waves of erotic heat through him. He would kiss her, inch by sweet inch. His body tightened with need. He wondered what she looked like and wished she would allow him to see her reflection in a mirror.

I am eager for us to meet. I can't wait to touch you, he admitted in a husky, sensual whisper.

No!

Her distress screamed in his mind. Raphael frowned and speculated. Even if she were a virgin and scared of her first time, such fear wasn't normal.

Has someone hurt you? He didn't mean to make his voice so sharp, and softened his tone. *Tell me, so I may help you, chere.*

I will be fine. Her wistfulness gave his heart a twist.

Let me help you. I'm your dracairon. It's my duty to care for you, and see to all your needs, be they large or small.

You sound as if I'm an invalid who needs assistance getting out of bed, came the tart reply.

Raphael gave a small, amused laugh. It might come to that. He blocked the thought from her of the sexy image of Erin lying languid and flushed in bed, dazed by the pleasure he'd given her. *Of course not. But I am your mate, and it grieves me to know you are in such distress. Tell me what you need.*

You. She went silent a few heartbeats and added, *Do you want me?*

Her deep, sultry voice sent lust spiraling through him. Raphael gripped the chair's armrests. Want her? *You have no idea how badly I want you.* Mentally he sent her an image of an enormous bed, two bodies tangled together between rumbled silk sheets. *All that and much more,* he said softly.

Oh! Oh. I didn't realize, I've never...um...

Silent delight filled him at her charming, blushing innocence. *Don't worry, chere. It's your first time, and I will be gentle. You have nothing to fear from me.*

I'm not afraid of you. I could never be afraid of you.

Satisfaction poured through him. He would cherish her and be mindful of her innocence at their first joining. The ecstasy he'd deliver would erase any pain of taking her virginity. Raphael licked his lips, envisioning part-

ing her soft thighs with his hands, lowering his mouth
to her core and flicking his tongue…

There?! Shock vibrated through her voice. Raphael
laughed softly.

*There, and many other places. Trust me, you will
enjoy it.*

I wish I could touch you.

The absolute sorrow in her voice gave him pause. His
heart twisted. *Soon,* he promised.

Out of the corner of his eye he spotted two men strut-
ting toward him. Both solid as linebackers. Deep frowns
scored their faces. One sported a knife scar across his
cheek. Trouble. At the bar, his oldest brother, Etienne,
shot him a questioning look. *Need help?*

Raphael shook his head. *Erin, pardon me for a
moment,* he told his draicara. He stood, stretching out
to his full six feet, four inches.

"Gentlemen," he offered.

"You're the ugly bastard who screwed around with
my woman last month," Big and Scarred announced.

"Your ex," he countered.

"We was gonna make up," Scarred said. Glass shattered as he brought his beer bottle down on the table.
He held the jagged edge out.

"I doubt it, judging from the bruises you left."
Raphael narrowed his eyes. "Women should be treated
with courtesy and respect. All women. You need man-
ners." He felt power rising in him, the itch to slam this
bastard into place.

"And you're an ugly mongrel dog," Scarred's
friend chimed in.

Violent anger rolled through him. He masked it. "Never call me a mongrel," he said pleasantly.

Raphael coldcocked one with a fist and sent the other toppling to the floor with a bare shove. Beer splashed over the table as bottles toppled downward. His reflexes were so fast they'd had no time to blink.

He sat down again, placing a boot upon Scarred's unconscious body.

My apologies, Erin. I had to take out the trash. Just a little business that took me away from your delightful company. Where were we?

What business?

Two men who didn't like the looks of my face. He studied his knuckles. Not even a scratch.

Are you hurt? Sharp worry tinged her voice. Raphael felt unexpected wonderment fill him. No one ever worried about him fighting before. His family assumed that the Kallan could fight all battles. His friends knew he could.

You must be a very strong warrior.

I do what I must. He gave a little shrug, toed at the unconscious form on the floor.

You're also quite modest. I can feel the humility radiating from you.

Again he laughed in delight. For the very first time, he wished he were not the Kallan and could speed to Erin's side. His draicara had need of him, but his duties as Kallan came first.

Chere, tomorrow I must leave you. I cannot contact you. I have a duty to perform that requires absolute concentration.

For how long?

An eternity. Three weeks.

It's all right. I understand. She gave a tiny sigh, sounding suspiciously like a muffled sob. *Maybe...I will see you. In some other place. Someday.*

Erin. He tried reaching for her, but she'd vanished like mist seeping through the bayou. Raphael sat back, slightly troubled. He didn't like the sound of her goodbye.

It sounded almost like farewell.

He set aside his concerns. After, he'd find Erin and give her all she needed. For now he must focus on what lay ahead.

His brothers, Etienne and Gabriel, drifted over. They studied the two prone bodies at Raphael's feet. "Couldn't you have played outside?" Gabe asked.

"They didn't want to share my sandbox." He joined them at another table and signaled the waitress, who slapped a cold longneck on the table. Raphael tilted his head back and drank deeply.

Etienne turned a chair around, straddled it, leaning his long arms on the back. "When are you leaving?"

"As soon as I finish the next one." He backhanded his mouth.

"What is it this time? Where?"

Raphael drummed his fingers on the table, overcome by a sudden chill. "A female."

His brother's mouth turned down. "Bad business. What happened?"

His mind sifted through the details with impartiality. "I'm told Emily is the cursed one, doomed by Aibelle the goddess. She was cursed a year ago by Aibelle with the death touch because of her vanity. All Draicon Emily now touches she kills. The ancient prophecies foretell Emily will bring about the end to our people if she is not sacrificed by midnight of the next full moon. If she isn't, the curse shifts to the entire pack and beyond."

Etienne whistled as Gabriel shook his head. "Seems unfair," Gabe said. "Where is she?"

"They told me she's ready, elderly and will be glad to cross. She's in eastern Tennessee." Raphael didn't add he was relieved his victim was older. Bad enough she was female. Most he dispatched saw his services as a relief. In his forty years as Kallan, he'd only disposed of five very unwilling prisoners, who had killed innocents and were about to turn Morph.

Gabriel gave him a pensive look. "The Draicon in that area are the Burke pack. You're not saying they're…"

At Raphael's brief nod, both Gabriel and Etienne's eyes widened. "Whoa. Burke pack. Better mind yourself, Rafe. They're very traditional and stick strictly to custom," Etienne warned.

Like I don't know it. The invitation with its fussy handwriting had arrived on crisp parchment (no e-mail for the Burke clan). The beer in his mouth soured. He swallowed hard.

"No cable for you, *t'frere.* No Internet, no Wii, nothing modern except the phone, basic utilities and cars. Keeper of the records of Draicon, the Burkes are direct, purebred descendants of our forefathers. Guardians of the Old Ways. Royalty." Gabriel gave Raphael's leather jacket a nod. "The last Kallan even dressed in ceremonial robes to please Urien, the Burke alpha. I heard Urien was upset you became Kallan because you're not—"

"A purblood like them? Like all the other Kallans

before me?" Raphael's fingers squeezed the beer bottle, cracking it. Foam oozed out of the sides.

Silence draped the air. Etienne exchanged uneasy glances with Gabriel.

Urien can kiss my leather-clad butt. Resentment filled him. The purebreds, always with their traditions, customs and superiority complex. They didn't want a Kallan who was a renegade, a Cajun and a mongrel in their eyes. Tough. He was all they had.

"I'm not going there to make a fashion statement. Just to honor their request."

Respect shone on his brothers' faces. Gabe shook his head. "I don't know how you do it, Rafe. I certainly couldn't perform *trasna* on a female. I hope you find the strength."

"You'd better hope, Gabe. You have a lot riding on this assignment." Raphael set down the beer, his look grim as he studied his brother. "Just hope that she is older and ready to die. Because if she isn't and I have a conflict on hand, remember the code? You're the one whose life is forfeit. And there's not a damn thing I can do to stop it."

Gabriel removed a legal-size paper, a knife and a quill from his pocket and set them on the table.

"You don't have to do this, Gabe."

"If I don't, then who will?"

The time-honored tradition bothered him, but he could not break it. Each time his services as Kallan were requested to terminate the life of another Draicon, he signed a binding contract. A male family member was required to sign as well, putting his life on the line as collateral should Raphael back out of the agreement.

The contract ensured Raphael would proceed with

the execution or those requesting his services would kill his relative. No Kallan had ever reneged, and over time the document became more a formality than a reality.

Still, Raphael felt queasy over the idea of giving the Burke pack the authority to end Gabe's life should he fail to dispatch Emily.

A nagging thought chased itself around in his head. He dismissed his worry. Discipline, not emotion, was needed for his upcoming duty. But this particular transition presented other challenges. The last time he'd had a brother sign a blood oath, Etienne had been unmated, and the transition was an elder longing for the peace of the Other Realm.

Never a female.

A very delicate, tough assignment.

Gabriel made perfect sense. Since Etienne had been mated, he was forbidden to sign a blood oath. Alexandre, who had lost his mate and daughter, had expressed a desire to join them and might even hinder the ritual of *trasna* in his eagerness to do so. Indigo and Damian, both adopted as blood brothers, were not related kin. Besides, Damian was mated now to Jamie and had a pack of his own. Indigo, well...

Purebloods considered Indigo an abomination because he was a Changling—half-vampire, half-Draicon. The Burke pack would ban him from offering his life.

Only Gabe remained.

His brother's eyes, dark as his own, regarded him evenly. Gabe pointed to the paper. "I read over everything. Shall we?"

So be it. "Take the knife, cut your hand and sign your name in blood."

Gabe picked up the sharp blade with a wry look. "Did I ever tell you I faint at the sight of blood, especially my own?"

"Faint after signing, *mon frere*. I might even catch you."

With a slight wince, Gabe cut his hand and signed his name. Raphael stared at the crimson signature. A small dot of blood, like a tiny teardrop, stained the parchment.

"What's wrong? My signature not legible?" Gabe joked.

Raphael made no reply, staring sightlessly out the window. The premonition was before him, dark and hovering like gray shadows. Blood staining his brother's shirt. Gabriel lying still.

Death.

But for whom, he couldn't say.

Chapter 1

Today the Kallan arrived. The male who would end her life. If she didn't find a way to stop him.

Emily paced before her cottage. She couldn't wait and walked silently to the farmhouse.

On the way over, she heard the steady roar of a motorcycle as it crested the quiet hill before the farmhouse. Despite every instinct that urged flight, she advanced toward the sound. She needed to see the one who would end her life. She crept through the yard by using the thick pine trunks of the trees that flanked the drive from the cottage to the farmhouse to shield her.

Her pack had gathered on the gravel drive. With a cough, the big motorcycle's engine died and the pack drifted toward the male on the bike. Emily gave him a grim smile. Maybe the others went meekly. She'd give him the fight of his life. Her life.

He removed a gleaming black helmet. Shoulder-length dark hair fell about his head, curling at the edges. One lock of hair was pure white at his right temple. Dressed in a black leather jacket, black T-shirt and black leather pants, he looked tall and imposing even while seated.

The rider slid a firm thigh over the saddle and stood. Emily put a hand to her throat, feeling it tighten. He towered over her family. He was breathtaking, with his fine bone structure, high cheeks, full, sensual lips and determined chin. Power radiated from him, and he exuded a sense of authority.

His dress was as different as his height and muscled body. Her people wore the clothing of the Old Ones. Simple wool vests in dark green or blue, broadcloth shirts and trousers for the men. Women were always clad in long dresses, some laced up front with a full skirt and formfitting bodice. Traditional. This Kallan's leather-clad body made her feel tingly and caused wicked thoughts to race through her mind. What would he look like without the covering?

She hadn't expected him to look so sexy, so young. The Kallans of old in the Book of Records were ancients. The last Kallan had been a graybeard who wore dignified clothing, like the long emerald robes her Alpha wore at ceremonial celebrations.

Tight leather covered his long legs, molded to his bottom. A hot flush rose to Emily's cheeks as she stared at the prominent bulge between his legs. The Kallan swaggered with easy grace, gravel crunching beneath his booted feet. Never had she seen such a display of raw masculinity. He sucked up all the open space with his presence. A dangerous Draicon, formidable. Emotionless as well. Had to be, to do what he must.

A small fear shook her. He looked like a fierce hunter who would flush out prey and never stop. Any thoughts that she could outrun him, outwit him, shattered like brittle glass.

Suddenly he looked up from greeting those around him. His attention shot straight to the trees hiding her. He seemed affixed to her position as his eyes narrowed.

Her heart galloped as she stumbled backward. This was not how she would meet him. Not cowering and lurking, but chin up, face forward.

Not yet. She needed to gather the fragments of her tattered courage first. Emily slipped away, her bare feet making no noise on the soft grass.

Later, when dusk fell and shadows cloaked the land, she would march up to the farmhouse and introduce herself. Kallan or not, Raphael would never best her. She would show him.

Instead of the animosity and superior attitude Raphael expected, the Burke pack welcomed him with vigorous handshakes. Immediately he donned the unemotional mask necessary for his duty.

Amid the glad-handing and introductions, Raphael scented her. Emily, the transition.

Wildflowers, a hint of lavender. His attention whipped over to a small stand of pines. She hid behind them.

Her scent spoke volumes to him. Fear twined with anger and tremendous strength. Underlying it was a strong femininity that flooded his body with sexual heat.

Raphael stared. It must be Emily, the cursed one, but why was her presence so enticing? He scanned the Draicon around him. None seemed to sense Emily was nearby. No one acted affected. Except him.

A small nagging tugged the back of his mind. But the sweet, sensual fragrance of Emily faded. He turned on his charming smile, the one reserved for uncomfortable situations. This pack didn't seem anxious or upset as expected with his arrival.

They seemed relieved.

"Greetings, Kallan. We are most happy to have you. I will see to whatever needs you have in regards to Emily's transition." Bridget, the Alpha female, gave him a wide, welcoming smile.

This Emily. Yeah, he had need. A strong need to hunt down and flush out that alluring scent. Emily. Strong, fragrant. Not weak, as they'd told him.

Urien, the Alpha male, was short, slim, with red hair, blue eyes and a strong chin. He stared with the usual arrogant, domineering look of a purebreed. Raphael refused to lower his gaze. He fixed his coolest look on the Draicon. To his surprise, Urien glanced away and stepped back, clearly surrendering.

Most Alphas, engaged in such a bristling display of dominance, would step forward, give a small nod to acknowledge Raphael's own position of power and shake hands.

"Where's Emily?" he asked, searching their faces.

The pack shifted, shuffled their feet. "She is not welcome here," Urien said bluntly. "It's not important for you to meet her at this moment."

Raphael hid his angry bemusement. The Alpha pair

refused to smooth over this very difficult time for Emily? What could be more important?

He remained silent in his disapproval as they escorted him inside. They treated him with the usual reverence, but damn, they were all so cowering, refusing to look him in the eye.

What the hell had happened here? Had the earth goddess's curse taken hold of more than the doomed Emily?

Bridget let him on a tour of the big, rambling Victorian farmhouse. She explained that the home housed the entire Burke pack but he could find no evidence of Emily.

As he followed her up the staircase, Raphael stopped. He cocked his head, listened. Silence.

"Your offspring, your young. Where are they?"

Bridget looked uncomfortable. "We have none."

"None at all?" He was incredulous.

"Our pack has lived and thrived here for decades, but breeding outside the pack and mixing the bloodlines is forbidden. As a result, our females have become barren. We have been unable to conceive for decades. Now if you'll follow me…"

"When was the last birth?" he demanded.

Panic flared in her eyes, then she glanced away. "A female, a forbidden birth, some years ago. Emily. Liam sired her on another outside the pack. Urien accepted her because Liam is his dearest brother and we needed a little one. But now Urien regrets not banishing Liam for the pack's good."

"You told me she was an elder who was glad to cross." Raphael's dismay grew. "Why did you lie?"

"It is hard for us. Emily was our hope. And now to

have to sacrifice her for the good of the pack? It breaks our hearts."

"Where is her father?"

Her expression went blank. "Dead a year ago. Emily killed him. Accidentally, when she touched him."

Her own father? Pity surged through him, along with mounting suspicion. "What happened?"

"Emily had dreamed the goddess Aibelle appeared to her and said the power of life and death was within her. The next day, Emily asked her father and me what Aibelle meant. She grabbed her father's hand, squeezed it. Liam gasped and dropped to the floor. I told Emily to fetch Urien from the fields, but it was too late. By the time he returned, Liam was dead from Emily's touch. She is the one foretold by the prophecies to bring an end to our people."

Bridget wrung her hands. "You must understand how difficult this is. Urien loves Emily, but she killed Liam, and then six months later his sister, Helen. We must follow the ancient prophecies and dispatch Emily before the curse spreads. The fate of the entire Draicon race rests with you, Kallan. How many more of our people must die?"

Raphael's heart sank. "What about these ancient prophecies? I want to see them for myself."

Not that he could read them. Any knowledge he had of the Old Language he'd memorized when he became Kallan.

"It is forbidden for those outside our pack to read them, those who are not pure of the blood."

Her voice was soft and the tone apologetic, but if Bridget had spat in his face, she couldn't have insulted him more. Raphael gave her a long, cool look and they resumed the tour.

When they reached the upstairs bedrooms, Bridget opened a door to a lavish suite. "This is your room. We hope you like it."

"Where does Emily sleep?"

After some hesitation, she said Emily lived in a cottage in the woods. There were several cottages in the forest, but after Emily killed her father, everyone else moved to the farmhouse. No one wanted to be near her.

"Emily is too dangerous," she insisted. "It's best this way. Emily likes living in the woods."

Did she? He wondered if it were Emily's choice or if they forced her into it.

Raphael closed the suite door and leaned against it. He gave Bridget his most intimidating look.

"I want to stay in the cottage next to Emily."

Bridget started to protest. He remained silent. Finally, she sighed. "I'll see to it. But, be careful. She's dangerous."

"I'll deal with it." Raphael stared her down. "Now take me to my quarters."

Raphael. The powerful, mighty warrior who would kill her was named Raphael. They said he was swift, merciful and gave the person a dignified end.

His dagger was honed with magick from the Old Ones.

Those subjected to an ending by his sword were even accorded dignified names. The transitions. They transitioned to the Other Realm, with Raphael the Kallan aiding their journey.

Noises had drawn her to the cottage next door.

Emily stood now behind a pine tree, peering into the living-room window as she watched Raphael stretch his long body.

Fascination stole over her. Smooth tanned flesh flexed over strong biceps. Emily ducked out of sight as he turned.

Footsteps sounded inside. She peeked again. Raphael tugged his black T-shirt over his head and off. Now he stood at the bathroom door. Certainly the view was admirable. She felt a tingle rush through her body as she gazed at his body.

His fingers reached for the front of his black leather pants. Coloring, she ducked down again. When she lifted her head, sounds of the shower began.

Curiosity overwhelmed her. Emily crept around to the cottage's side. The bathrooms were designed to let in natural light and give the feeling of being outdoors while in the shower. A wall of glass looked out to a curtain of pine trees. Sneaking between the glass and the pines, she watched.

In the glassed shower, Raphael stood beneath the twin jets, his back to her. Damp, ragged black hair hung in strands to his wide shoulders. Smooth, golden flesh covered his muscled backside, and his bottom…

Emily stared at the rounded firmness of his buttocks. When he turned around, she released a startled gasp. Her shocked gaze roamed from the dark hair on his firm chest to the rippling muscles on his abdomen, down to the thick hair at his groin and the…

Her gaze whipped back up to his other end to find two dark eyes regarding her with amusement.

Emily squeaked, fleeing into the safety of her forest.

* * *

Emily was curious to see him. Well, she'd gotten a good look at him. More than an eyeful, Raphael thought with a grin.

But would she spend the next three weeks running away?

He dried off, dressed and went onto the porch. Sitting on a wood rocker, he listened to the peaceful cheep of tree frogs, the distant lowing of a cow left in a pasture. Twilight draped shadows over the stretch of grass marching down the gentle slope toward the forest.

What kind of life was it for Emily when her entire pack feared even the tread of her steps on the stairs?

Something about his charge bothered him. Not her absence. That was normal. But the feelings she evoked in him, powerful and overwhelmingly sexual. He'd never felt like this before around a transition.

His feelings were equally intense regarding her pack. Something was off, especially Bridget. He couldn't gauge them, probably because of their pure blood and lineage.

Old resentments flared, but he set them aside. He leaned back in the rocking chair. Raphael closed his eyes, scenting a delicate aroma of lavender and female. The fragrance heated his blood and he gripped the rocking chair's armrests to steel himself against sudden arousal.

"Emily, come out. I'm Raphael, the Kallan. I know you're there, watching me. I'd like to meet you. Don't be afraid."

Silence filled the air. Then a strong, sweet voice spoke into the gathering darkness.

"Afraid? You're the one who should be afraid, Raphael Robichaux."

Her voice deepened with a slight menace. "Very afraid. Because I carry death with me wherever I go. And my hands, judging from the way they are itching right now, tell me you are next."

Something tugged at his conscience. Her voice with its slight Southern accent seemed familiar. Emotions crowded him. Most overwhelming was a deep feeling of utter sorrow, as if part of his very soul were to die.

It was his distress at her youth and growing anger at her pack's deception that marred his perception. Nothing more. Raphael dismissed his inner feelings. Emotions were dangerous and clouded his judgment.

He opened his eyes, staring at the sunlit dappled oaks and maples. "Good. Then come forward. If you wish me harm, then have the courage to show yourself."

"Why should I? I've already seen you," the reply came, followed by a small sniff.

Delight filled him at her snappy attitude. "Seen a lot of me, have you? Let's look at each other face-to-face and not through the bathroom window."

Her gasp made his grin widen.

Movement snapped his attention to the left. Raphael half closed his eyes, waiting.

A figure emerged from the woods. His senses sprang to alert. The approaching female walked with quiet grace. Light from the porch showed hair the color of an angry sunset drawn up tight in a bun like the other Burke females. Damn.

Young. Much younger than his 105 years. Barely a decade past her first change into wolf. Much more disturbing was the wild cascade of emotions tumbling through him. Fascination. Thrill. And a reckless feeling of intense arousal.

As if he wanted to spring forward, take her into his arms and kiss her senseless. Strip off her ugly, ankle-length dress, lower her to the green grass and ravish her until they both lay panting and spent with pleasure. With her oval face, wide green eyes fringed with red-gold lashes, pert nose and rosebud mouth, she resembled a fae wandering from the safe haven of a forest. Even the ugly, shapeless dress she wore didn't disguise the ethereal beauty and delicate features.

Raphael closed his eyes, shutting out his initial reaction. *Emotions are dangerous.*

He drank her in through his other senses. A small smile touched his mouth. Despite the myriad of feelings pushing at him, he could read her spirit. Defiant and not willing. He faced a big fight.

She would not go gentle into that good night, but kicking and screaming. And part of him relished her anger. After all the times he'd dispatched his own kind, he wanted someone to fight him. Someone to tell him to piss off, instead of beg for death with dull, pain-glazed eyes.

The air around him shifted. A chill dropped over him as if winter breathed hard and fast across his body. Raphael suppressed a shiver. His warm Cajun blood howled at the icy blast.

It emitted from her.

Death lingered in her, but not her own. Her touch killed.

Waiting, he reached out to assess her. She smelled absolutely delicious—strong and very alive. He tasted the cold fury in the chill she threw off. Yet he burned with desire as he sensed her drawing nearer.

Raphael waited, rocked and remained silent.

"You can't be the Kallan. You're much too young."

The accusation made him smile. Opening his eyes, he studied her approach, graceful as a wood nymph. The last rays of sunlight glinted her hair, making it look as brilliant as the setting sun.

"So are you. I was told by your Alpha you're elderly." He didn't hide his anger. Raphael sat straight, his thighs splayed, hands on knees as he regarded her.

"I'm twenty-two." She hesitated, and her voice seemed sad, oddly familiar. "I feel as if I am an ancient."

A frown touched his mouth as he scrutinized her appearance. "Have we met?"

She laughed, the sound like gurgling water cascading over stones. "Doubtful. You'd remember me, for I don't shake hands. Ever."

Emily held up her hands, displaying thick, ugly mustard-yellow gloves. They were a grim reminder of the lethal threat she carried.

"I could kill you with a single touch," she said, her dulcet voice contrasting with the ugliness of her words.

"I doubt it. Come, sit beside me. It's a lovely evening." He patted the empty rocker next to him.

She narrowed her eyes as if he invited her to sit on a pile of rattlers. "Sit and do what? Talk about the weather?"

"If you wish. I want to get to know you better, Emily Burke."

Gloved hands went to her rounded hips. Emily stared him down. "I know your purpose. You're here to execute me. Don't waste your breath on flowery prose or eloquent speeches about how lovely the Other Realm is, and how I will be at peace or this nonsense about getting to know me better. Let's get one thing straight, Kallan. You're my enemy. Period. We'll never be friends. Period."

We will be lovers.

His thought materialized out of nowhere. It startled him, and as he studied her, it became very appealing. His body responded to the idea, imagining removing the pins from her hair, releasing it to spill in a cascade down to her waist. Emily naked as he feathered tiny kisses over her pale skin, enjoying her whimpers of excited pleasure as he fastened his mouth over a reddening nipple and then nudged her legs open and settled his hips between them…

Merde! What the hell was wrong with him? *She's your transition, imbecile!* He'd been thinking of her as if she were his alone. He had a draicara, Erin, and he was lusting for a female he must dispatch.

Raphael dragged in a deep breath, disturbed at his traitorous thoughts. What sort of Kallan was he? Viciously he wished Emily were a 1,200-year-old male, with warts and bowed legs, eager to end it all. Not this vision of springtime beauty, as ethereal and lovely as a delicate blossom.

"Hello?" The vision waved her gloved hands before him. "You deaf? Did you get my message? I can kill you."

"You can't kill me," he noted calmly, glad to see all emotion fled his voice. "I'm immortal."

"But you're not immune to pain. I can make you suffer."

Probably more than you know. Again the thought flashed before him, filled with heavy sorrow.

Her smile turned nasty. "Have you felt your body weaken and your magick leaking from your body?

That's what I do, Raphael. And that is what I will do to you if you dare to come near me and preach about the afterworld or dying for my people."

The inflection of her speech told him all he needed to know. She bluffed. Beneath the nasty words and threats was a dark thread of pure fear. Not for herself, but him.

For all living things she might harm.

Raphael smiled gently.

"I don't know any speeches. I don't preach. But I do like to eat, and I'm sure at some point you do as well. Will you join me for dinner?"

"As your guest or the main course?"

Raphael threw back his head and laughed, delighted with her spunk. "Depends. Sprinkled with a few Cajun spices, you might do."

And I know exactly where to sprinkle the spice. His body heated with erotic conjecture, Emily on the table like a feast for his hunger…

He stood, the rocker banging against the wall. "Come, Emily. I hate eating alone."

As he walked down the stairs, heading for her, she froze. "Stay away from me, Kallan. Just stay away."

Then she fled into the gathering shadows like a frightened deer.

Raphael sighed, ran a hand through his hair. This time he'd not let her go. He jumped off the porch and inhaled. Easy enough to find.

Tracking her delicious scent, he followed her into the woods.

Emily drew closer to the oak tree and the vine of sacred mistletoe twining around the strong limbs.

Though the moonlight tonight would be too dim, she must pick the berries.

She needed answers from the sacred texts her aunt Helen once guarded.

Six months ago, Helen had taken her to the garden alone, telling her she had to share a confidence about the pack. Helen, keeper of the sacred texts, had told her where they were hidden. "If anything happens, Emily, find and decipher them. They will provide the answers you need."

Helen asked if she could still restore life and pointed to a dying rose. Emily had removed the thin glove covering her hand and pricked her thumb on a thorn. Four drops of her blood caused the petals to unfurl and renewed their crimson blush. Helen had become extremely emotional.

"I knew it, Emily. You have the gift of life within you still. There is something I must tell you. You need to know the truth about your gift."

To her horror, Helen had touched her hand. Her uncovered hand. Emily had screamed as her aunt dropped to the ground. Terrified, Emily ran off to tell Urien, who ordered her confined to her cottage. An hour later, Urien grimly told Emily that Helen was dead from her single touch.

He'd banished her for good that day.

The texts were a last hope. Ever since she was informed of her impending death, she'd poured over them, desperate to translate the prophecies foretelling her death. If she were to die to save her race, then she wanted proof. Helen said the texts would provide all the answers. But to discern the words, she needed to be calm and unemotional.

Impossible. The only alternative was smearing ripe

mistletoe berries over the parchment. The berries would make the words clear to her, even if she became too upset.

Footsteps crunched the leafy undergrowth. Emily went still, like a deer scenting the enemy. He approached with deliberate announcement of his presence.

She fled.

"Emily, come out. Stop playing games. Sooner or later, we must talk."

The deep, husky voice sounded familiar. No, it was this Kallan. He played games with her, trying to coax her to his side. Raphael possessed powerful magick. He could disguise his voice, making it sound familiar, and loved to encourage a transition to welcome death with open arms like a lover.

Emily squeezed her eyes shut, clapped her hands over her ears to shut away the deep, sensual tones of that voice, as soothing as an old friend. She had no friends.

I am alone.

Maybe this time she'd finally work up the courage to escape. Leave the property she seldom left since her birth. Flee into the night.

Driven by instinct, Emily cut back into the sheltering woods. Her bare feet, accustomed to the rough undergrowth, raced over the covering of dead leaves and twigs. Behind her she heard Raphael call her name.

Call all you want. You'll be talking to air, peabrain.

Thinking of the mighty Kallan as a peabrain gave her small comfort. Emily continued on through her beloved forest, exiting into a sloped meadow. Dewy grass sloshed beneath her feet as she ran.

The property's edge was within reach. Freedom. Emily ground to a halt, instinctively knowing the boundary. She stared at the dirt separating the Burke's land from the outside world.

Her gaze whipped over to the crest of hill before her. Beyond the property lay freedom. If she worked up the courage, she could escape. Flee her fate.

Her overprotective father and Urien rarely allowed her to venture outside their territory, warning of great dangers. Morphs with talons ready to shred delicate skin to ribbons. Their fangs were long and yellowed, their greed for Draicon flesh very great.

Her heart raced with fear.

If she fled, where would she go? What if her touch killed humans as well? Emily's heart wrenched at the thought of taking another innocent life.

Something moved in the darkening shadows. Shapes. Restless, pacing back and forth as if caged. Nothing but a band of coyotes. Urien had been wrong. The outside world presented little danger. Not compared to the larger, taller threat silently stalking her.

She stepped onto the roadway.

A stench like feces and rotting garbage filled her nostrils. Terror squeezed her heart like a strong fist. Emily recognized the forms as they came closer to the property's edge. Close enough for her to smell their hot, fetid breath. Close enough for her to see the flash of black in their eyes.

Morphs, the ones who feasted on Draicon flesh.

Emily screamed.

Chapter 2

Raphael tore down the pathway, alarmed at the distressed cry. There, from the woods' edge, near the property line. Emily. Something threatened her.

Instinct took over. He ran, waving his hands and eliminating his clothing as he did so, changing into wolf.

She stood in the gathering darkness, gloved hands to her mouth. Trembling as if a mighty wind shook her.

Just on the other side of the small, narrow dirt road he saw them.

A line of Morphs staring her down. As if they wanted her dead and would devour her heart.

While it still beat inside her chest.

With a snarl, Raphael leapt onto the road, charging the Morphs staring at Emily.

"Stop! They won't come here!"

Stark fear in her voice snapped him to a halt. His

paws skidded in the loose gravel. The Morphs inched backward, their hunched, shriveled bodies twisting, talons outstretched as they hissed at him.

Raphael growled at the enemy. Wanting to snap and tear and destroy, every instinct rising to attack. But his charge was his first concern. He wouldn't leave Emily alone, facing danger.

The Morphs shapeshifted into wolves, loping off silently. Raphael trotted back to Emily and shifted back to human form. A cold wind brushed against his naked skin, chilling his bones. He clothed himself with a wave of his hand, looked at her terrorized face.

"Are you all right?"

Emily stared after the Morphs. "They won't come on the property. Urien said it was the magick shield on the land, but I think it's me. They fear me."

Raphael sensed her inner turmoil and challenged her. "Then why not leave?"

A frown creased her lovely face. "I should. I could, but in the past, Urien said they'd attack in packs, cloning themselves and sacrificing the clones to kill me. They would strip the skin from my bones and eat my heart to ingest all the magick I have. I know I'm going to die, but I don't want to die like that."

Anguish tinged her voice. Raphael's heart dropped to his stomach. Damn, this was going to be tough. All this time he'd been Kallan, he'd never faced such a challenge.

Think of her, not yourself.

"Emily, let's get back. You're shivering," he said in his gentlest tone.

Raphael shrugged out of his leather jacket and went

to drape it about her slender shoulders. She jerked back as if he were a hot iron. "Don't touch me!"

"I was only going to offer you this."

"Then you'd have to destroy it after I wore it." She backed away. "You're supposed to be wise. Everything I touch is contaminated. My own people can't stand being within ten feet of me. They won't let me touch anything. Even the livestock. I can't feed them, water them, care for them. I'm unclean."

Raphael's heart twisted.

"Stop looking at me like that. I hate pity. Damn you."

With a swirl of skirts, she spun around and stormed off toward her cottage. Raphael gazed after her. He'd leave her alone for now. Come morning, they had work to do.

Once Emily had loved the dark. Now it brought only fear of the night and terrible dreams chasing her through sleep. Last night's had been particularly gruesome. Long, yellowed fangs ready to sink into her flesh, eager to rip and tear.

Emily hooked a band of hair behind her ear. Before sleeping last night, she had managed to calm herself enough to decipher a snippet of the sacred texts.

"The Destroyer has been sent to kill her. The Chosen One surrenders herself to the Destroyer." Two sentences having a vague interpretation. But what if she did surrender herself to the Destroyer? What then?

She had become too upset, and the words blurred to nothingness before her eyes.

Emily poured herself a cup of coffee, donned her gloves and took the cup outside to enjoy the morning air. Distress filled her as she spotted Raphael sitting on the rocker on her porch. In a dove-gray T-shirt, jeans and boots, his powerful body tensed, he stared into the woods.

"Why are you on my porch?" she demanded.

Silence met her. She tracked the line of his gaze and saw a small deer peacefully cropping dewy grass. "What are you looking at?"

"Prey." His voice was low, intent.

His back to her, Raphael stood and tugged the shirt over his head. Muscles rippled beneath his smooth, tanned flesh. Her mouth went dry as she stared. He reached for the waistband of his jeans.

"W-what are you doing?"

"I'm going to hunt. I haven't eaten deer in months."

"There are no deer where you're from?"

He glanced over his shoulder. "Where I come from, we eat nutrias. Rodents bigger than small dogs. They look like mutant beavers."

Fascination stole over her as she watched him shed his clothing slowly and carefully. Emily suspected he did it on purpose to get a reaction.

She reacted.

She had seen naked men when her pack males shape-shifted into wolves. But not this beautiful. His legs were long and sturdy, his bottom taut with muscle. His broad shoulders tapered down to a lean waist and hips. Fascinated, she studied the rippling muscles of his tanned flesh. An odd marking in blue ink decorated his strong left bicep—a dagger that had intricate runes like the Sacred Scian thrust through a heart.

Iridescent sparks started to shimmer around him, then faded. "Aren't you joining me?"

A ripple of pleasure went through her. Her pack

hadn't invited her to run with them in years. Emily leaned back, sipping her coffee.

"I don't hunt anymore."

"Why?"

She fell silent, reluctant to tell him why. He seemed to struggle with a decision. His large shoulders slumped as he heaved a sigh. "Ah, it wouldn't be much of a challenge. Like fishing with C-4 explosives."

Raphael waved a hand, clothing himself again. Relief swept through her, and bemusement. Most others would ignore her and pursue their hunger.

"Your refrigerator should be fully stocked," she said, setting down her coffee. The Sacred Scian hung in a sheath on his belt. Emily swallowed hard.

"It is, but I like the thrill of the hunt. I am, after all, a big, bad wolf."

A charming grin touched his mouth, melting her a little. He seemed friendly. Open and willing to talk with her as if she were just an ordinary Draicon.

She wasn't. Emily squeezed her hands.

"Why do you wear those clothes?"

He shrugged. "It's what I like. I never follow other people's style."

"Style? I don't know of style, but I do know it's important to be like everyone else in the pack."

"So that's why you wear that sackcloth?" he drawled.

Emily fingered the shapeless dun dress with its long sleeves and coarse material. "It's tradition. Our people embrace traditional clothing."

She stared at the small gold dagger dangling from a loop pierced through his left ear. "Our males do not wear earrings. We wear no decorations upon our bodies."

Raphael leaned against the railing. "The earring is more than a decoration."

He tugged at his left ear and the tiny gold dagger dangling from it. In a flash, the golden blade on his belt vanished and appeared as a second dagger in the earring. "I keep the Sacred Scian close to me at all times. The earring gives me the freedom to walk armed into places where humans forbid weapons." He flashed the charming grin again. "Much better than setting off metal detectors at airports."

She felt her breath escape her as he tugged his ear again and the Scian reappeared on his belt. The sacred dagger, carried only by a Kallan, would end her life. He wore the blade as he wore his clothing, with a casual indifference that belied his role. Fear skittered through Emily. Other Kallans had been purebloods, with long robes and gray beards, and kept the Scian hidden. They revered their dress and the Scian, and ancient texts painted them as mystics. They chanted ritual words, worked spells and possessed great magick.

This Kallan was a warrior. Beneath the amused dark gaze lurked the intent of a true hunter. Raphael would not easily be fooled as she might have fooled the elderly Kallans.

"You're so cavalier with the Scian. Why do you wear it on your trousers at all? The pureblood Kallans of the past always kept it guarded in a tortoiseshell box."

Amusement fled his eyes, replaced by a flattened expression. Emily backed away, sensing the rising anger, the ruthlessness of purpose.

"I wear it how I wish. I'm not of your people, but I revere my role and my duties as Kallan as much as the

Kallans of old. My Scian is a weapon and never leaves my sight. I'd say I'm much less *cavalier* with it than the old ones." Raphael removed the blade, flipped it into the air and sheathed it.

"We've never had a Kallan who wasn't a pureblood. You're a mixed-blood, so different."

His jaw tightened to flint. "There's a first for everything. I worked hard to become Kallan and passed the test. That's all your people need to know."

Sunlight glinted off the dagger's fine gold hilt. Emily hedged. If he were to kill her with the blade, then she wanted to see it closer. Touch the knife that would end it all. She stretched out her gloved hands. The covering would protect the blade from contamination.

"May I see the Scian? I've never held one before."

"No." His voice was curt.

Hurt, she retreated to the end of the porch. Raphael stared out at the woods. "Come, Emily. Walk with me. It's time to begin your lessons."

"I'm not a good pupil." Anger roiled within her.

"All transitions learn. It's my job to teach you, to prepare you for your journey to the Other Realm."

"A journey I won't easily take," she whispered.

His gaze softened. "Then let's walk, a simple walk through the woods. Show me your woods, Emily."

Given no choice, for he seemed determined to shadow her, she headed for the forest, the Kallan giving her plenty of space. Leaves drifted lazily downward, brushed by a cool wind. Emily scuffed her bare feet in the thick padding of dead leaves, moss and grass as they entered the woods. The path she used was wide enough to admit two, but Raphael trailed behind her.

Sunlight filtered through the tall oaks, pines and maples. The welcoming scent of forest and earth wrapped about her senses. She breathed deeply, smiling. Here was home, a sacred place where she felt most comfortable.

"Do you always go barefoot?" he asked.

It's the only part of me I feel free to bare. "When I can."

When they approached the small glen, she tried to quickly pass, not wanting him to investigate. But Raphael halted.

A frown creased his forehead as he gazed about. "This is a sacred place, with much ancient energy. I feel a heaviness in the air as well. It's coming from over there."

She gazed in the direction of his pointing finger and her heart dropped.

"No, you shouldn't."

Raphael left, heading toward the direction where he'd pointed.

"Don't. It's nothing you need to see," she called after him.

But as she raced forward, it was too late.

Raphael entered the small space with its uncommon quiet. No songbirds chirped here, and though the trees were not as thick, the air seemed dense.

He stood before the stone altar and touched the ancient rock with a solemn look.

Emily fisted her gloved hands. He was here to kill her. She didn't dare trust him or anyone else. Raphael was her executioner. No overtures of kindness, treating her with respect and talking with her and staving off the constant loneliness would change that.

The stone altar served as a granite barricade between them. Raphael shifted, putting a hand on his hip.

A stray beam of sunlight flashed off the solid gold dagger hilt at his waist. He caught her staring at the dagger.

"Oh, Emily," he said softly.

With a strangled sob, she turned and ran blindly through the forest, away from the grim reminder of what was to come. Finally she reached the haven of her cottage. Emily squeezed her eyes shut and, with all her emotions and thoughts, called out to the one destined for her. He'd told her he'd be out of reach for a few weeks, but her need was urgent.

If Amant could not help her, no one could.

Raphael walked through the forest, deeply troubled. Faint energy emitted from the stone altar where Emily would be executed to end the curse. The sight had not bothered him, but he sensed something of tremendous importance had occurred there. Yet the altar held no tinge of death or sorrow. He could not make out the energy patterns.

Pity surged through him, banishing the earlier resentment. Emily thought he wasn't as good as the other Kallans because of his mixed blood. Unworthy. Old memories flashed through him. Walking to town, to the Vieux Carre, from his simple bayou home to get supplies. Other, more pure Draicon taunting him, throwing stones and laughing.

Dog. Mongrel.

Would old prejudices against his Cajun blood never cease?

Raphael shoved aside the bitter past and concentrated on Emily. His transition came first. He must find her, get her to calm down again if they were to work together….

Amant?

The voice inside his head startled him. Raphael leaned against a tree, sighed. *Erin, the time isn't right….*

Please, Amant. I'm sorry for intruding. I have such great need of you, otherwise I'd never have contacted you. Help me.

The terror in his draicara's voice alarmed him, along with a horrible suspicion cresting over him. Raphael tried pushing back all the emotions crowding his mind, her panicked fear, his guilt that he could not attend to her needs.

If you can't come to my side, tell me what I can do. You're a great warrior, I sense this about you, a wise one who has fought many battles. He will hurt me. Please, just advise…

Who is threatening you? he demanded. *Tell me and I will take my dagger and cut his heart out. I will ask my brothers, and they'll come to your aid.*

You cannot stop him. No one can. He is one who is great, powerful. I cannot stop him, stop this. A sob broke out, echoed in his mind like shattering glass.

Hush, all will be well, he whispered, deeply distressed at her sorrow. How could he do this, be the Kallan and be apart from her? Time and again assignments would take him from her side, and his mate would not be his first priority. Yet every instinct inside raged to rush to her side, attend to her needs.

But Emily came first now. He must attend to her before easing Erin's fears.

For years, he quietly accepted that he'd never find his true mate, the missing half of his soul's magick. Others fortunate enough to do so experienced joy and fulfillment. Raphael assumed like the other Kallan before him that it was not meant to be. His duties came first, and he found small comfort in that.

Now she'd finally sought him out and he rejoiced inside. But *merde*—ah, the timing. He needed all his concentration and energy directed toward Emily. His transition came first.

Erin, listen to me. Do you have a weapon nearby? A small sniffle and he could feel her pulling together all her strength. *Good,* he said silently, proud of her courage.

Yes, a small, sharp knife.

Take it and arm yourself. Don't fear to use it on this male. Stab him, aim for the left quadrant of his upper chest. It will nick the heart and slow him, no matter how powerful this one is. Will you do this?

I can't kill!

Hush, he soothed. *You must protect yourself. It will incapacitate him. Now, get the knife.*

Worry filled him as he waited. After a few minutes, he heard her in his mind. *I have it. Are you certain this will work?*

Yes. Where are you? Are you in a confined place, a house or building?

Is that dangerous?

Get out. Less chance of being cornered, Raphael told her.

Silence, and then he heard her speak. *I'm outside, near some trees. I feel safest here.*

Raphael shook his head. *Now, do as I say. Find your family, your people, and stay with them. Even if the one threatening you is among them, he will not dare hurt you in their presence.*

Oh, Amant, she whispered, and hiccupped through her tears as if she laughed. *They're the ones who summoned him here.*

Raphael's heart dropped to his stomach. The delicious smell of lavender and wildflowers suddenly wafted on the chilling breeze. He moved away from the tree and began walking toward the scent, keeping the line of communication open telepathically as he did so.

Where are you, Erin? he asked. *Tell me.*

Waiting for her answer, he prowled noiselessly through the brush, entering the forest, stepping carefully as his wolf would, avoiding detection.

I can't talk. Panic threaded through her tone. *Someone's coming. I think… I think it's him.*

Abandoning stealth, he bolted through the forest, crashing through the undergrowth, his lungs working hard, his heart racing. Now the scent flooded his senses, a ribbon of hot desire pulling him forward in senseless need. He saw her now, backed up against an ancient oak, her body lush and tempting, her eyes wide in her fine-boned face.

Raphael cut off communication from Erin as abruptly as hanging up a phone receiver. He raced forward.

"Emily," he breathed.

Drawn to the female shrinking back from him, he leapt forward, trapping her against the tree with his body. He must know for certain.

Raphael pulled her to him in a crushing kiss.

Even as her lips opened under the pressure of his, he knew.

Even as his blood sang hotly in his veins and his cock grew to stone at her aroused scent, he knew.

His body screamed no, the cry echoing in his mind.

Raphael pulled back in abject shock and horror. No, not her, not this one….

Emily cried out, putting a gloved hand to her lips, blue eyes wide in her delicate face. Blue eyes turning rapidly to deep violet. "No! Oh, goddess, not you, it can't be…."

His throat closed up. Raphael couldn't speak, though he screamed inside his head.

Emily, the one he was to execute. No safe, anonymous stranger.

But Erin, his draicara, his mate. It wasn't possible.

Barely had the thought crossed his mind when an eerie, high-pitched scream, like that of an ancient banshee, tore out of Emily's throat. Raphael heard the snicking of the knife slashing through the air. Pain exploded in his chest as the blade sank deep.

He fell forward, landing face-first on the damp, welcoming earth.

Chapter 3

Emily had killed him.

The kitchen knife fell from her outstretched fingers. She stared in dawning shock, her heart racing. His kiss hadn't been a mere fusing of mouths, but a drugging, intoxicating kiss that drew in her very soul. It was fulfillment of all the desperate hopes, dreams and sensual yearnings she'd felt since finding him through their mind link.

He'd kissed her into silence, his own sexual hunger twining with a sorrowful knowing.

Emily brought her hands up to her face.

Blood soaked the chamois gloves.

A scream lodged itself in her throat as her gaze dropped to Raphael lying on the ground. She had killed him, the Kallan, her draicaron.

Her executioner was also her destined mate, the male who was supposed to save her.

Her hands, hands that killed, now shook violently. A cool breeze touched her cheek, soft as a gentle caress. It fluttered the hem of her skirts. Emily dropped to her knees, reaching out to touch Raphael.

She jerked back, her mouth opening and closing. Fisting her hands, she pounded them against her thighs.

"No, no, no," she croaked in a thin wail.

The pitch rose to a hysterical scream. She threw back her head and released her anguish to the sky. Emily struggled to rein in her emotions. Stretching out her hands, she thought quickly.

She could restore life with her blood.

Barely had the thought occurred when Raphael groaned and stirred. Blood no longer flowered on his shirt from the terrible wound she'd inflicted. Her gaze whipped to him, and she crab-crawled away as he sat up. His dark gaze regarded hers with a touch of wry humor.

"I see you paid attention to my advice. Good." He touched the crimson stain on his chest.

Relief over his recovery turned into grieved anger. "How can you jest over something like this? How can you do this?"

How can you be the one who is to kill me when you are supposed to be my mate?

Regret darkened his gaze. "I didn't want to frighten you any more than you already are." His mouth twisted. "I wish you'd stop looking at me like that."

"Like you are the Kallan?" she blurted out. "My mate?"

He stood, as whole and healthy as if being stabbed hadn't affected him. "Emily," he said softly. "Why did you tell me your name was Erin?"

"Why did you not tell me your true name?" she shot back.

"I didn't want my draicara to be afraid of the Kallan. I wanted her, you, to come to know me for who I am."

"My executioner," she said brokenly.

His eyes closed as he shoved a hand through his tousled hair, pulling free bits of twig and leaves. "Let's forget that for a moment. Tell me, Emily, why did you tell me your name was Erin?"

"Because it was my father's nickname for me, my favorite name. I didn't want you to know my real name. I was afraid—maybe you heard stories of Emily, the cursed one." She struggled to her feet, training her gaze on him.

Bitterness mingled in his wry smile. "I see we both had good reason for withholding our real identities from each other."

"But I should have recognized your voice, your accent." Emily touched a nearby oak, feeling comfort and strength from connecting to the sturdy, strong tree.

"Perhaps we both were blinded to the truth, until we were forced to confront it together." Raphael bent over, picked up the bloodied kitchen knife. A frown pierced his forehead.

"Stand back," he ordered.

Mystified, she watched as he dropped the knife and held out his hands. A streak of white light blazed from his fingertips, heating the metal, turning the blood to white ash.

Raphael retrieved the knife, formally held it out to her, hilt side. "I believe this is yours."

"Put it on the ground." When he did, she took it, reluctant to even let their fingers brush. Emily set the knife on a small stump.

"Why did you incinerate your blood?"

His troubled gaze met hers. "I'm an immortal, and my blood contains powerful magick, powerful enough to restore life, or make other beings, evil ones, immortal as well. If I am injured, I must do my best to destroy any droplets. I must not allow anyone to use it for their own purpose."

His blood as well? Faint hope filled her. "Power," she breathed. "You can restore life through your blood?"

If he could, their mutual problem was solved. Raphael could execute her and then revive her with his blood. She shared the thought, sending it to him using the unique telepathic connection shared between destined mates.

For a whisper of a minute, their minds connected, merged. She saw deep sorrow in his thoughts, a heart-rending grief.

"I am permitted that gift only once. I used it to save my sister-in-law, because I reasoned I would never find my draicara." Raphael's jaw tautened. "If I use it again, I will forfeit my own life, and the blood used to restore life will turn to poison in the person's veins."

For a moment, he looked away, his arms folding across his powerful chest. "Are you all right?" he asked quietly.

She knew Raphael was referring to her emotional state, which was rather precarious. His protective nature warmed her until she realized it was all futile. Emily touched the tree again for comfort.

"I'll be fine."

"There has to be a reason why this is happening. It makes no sense." He jammed his hands into his pockets. "Come back to my cabin. I'll get changed, make us breakfast and we can discuss it."

Emily felt her defenses rise. She couldn't dare trust him, the only Draicon she thought she could trust. The only Draicon who could save her would kill her.

She truly was all alone, and the thought sent her backing away with wariness.

"Find your own breakfast."

"Emily. Come now, we can't ignore the truth any longer. Eat with me, and let's try to find answers together as to why this is happening."

She could not answer. Emotion clogged her throat. Every cell cried out to take his outstretched hand, trust in his kind expression, go with him.

Self-preservation screamed against it. Emily shook her head.

"My touch kills, Kallan. Have you forgotten?"

She whirled around and darted back into the haven and security of her beloved forest.

No, I haven't forgotten. I can never forget.

Raphael's heart wrenched as he watched her slip away. He released a heavy sigh. He wanted to scream his anger and frustration. Debating on whether to follow, he inhaled her scent. Emily's unique fragrance was as clear as if he'd marked her himself. Didn't she realize he could track her through a forest filled with skunks and still find her? He resisted the instinct to give chase.

Instead, he roped in all his control and turned back toward his cabin. He needed energy, fast, from raw meat. The stab wound had nicked his heart, and even though it had healed, he felt drained.

Raphael suspected the deeper, more devastating emotional wound to his heart would take much longer to heal.

How could this happen? How could the one female he was to mate with, his other half, who contained the missing half of his magick, be the cursed one he had to kill? The rising sexual awareness of her and the desire riding him did not lessen. It made sense now, but he was helpless to control his body's reaction around her.

Until he made Emily his in the flesh, his sexual need of her would grow stronger, making him nearly animalistic in his drive to mate and claim. He hadn't wanted a mate. Always on the move, the race's death dealer whom most feared, he kept to himself but for family. Raphael had few friends, and knew a mate couldn't fit into his lifestyle.

He always suspected his would be a challenging mating at best if he ever found his draircara. He would have to soothe her fears and have a leisurely courtship to show her his gentler side. But this mating surpassed his darkest thoughts.

Anger rose up at her pack's deception. Had they been truthful, he could have avoided this. Raphael returned to his cabin, fished through the refrigerator and drew out two steaks. He ate the raw meat standing up, feeling the energy revive him. Through the lacy curtains at the window, he could see the edge of the deep forest where Emily hid.

He finished eating, dropped the bones on a plate, wiped his mouth and reached out with his mind.

Emily, where are you? Come to me. Stop running away.

Silence. His jaw tightened. She needed time, both to process what had happened and what she had done. His read was that she was a gentle soul, who loathed and feared her gift to kill. Stabbing him in the heart had emotionally taxed her, along with the knowledge that he was her draicaron.

He would give her the necessary space she needed for now. In the meantime, Raphael tossed the bones into the garbage with a grim look.

He had a much bigger bone to pick over with the pack's top dog.

Urien was friendly, invited him to join them for breakfast. When Raphael declined and confronted him about Emily, the leader stood his ground. "If I told you Emily was young and strong, not a weak elder, you would not have agreed to this sacrifice. And we could not bring ourselves to do it, but it must be done."

Raphael locked his hard gaze to the other male's. They sat in the expansive living room of the pack's house. In his traditional clothing of the Old Ones, a dun-colored vest of broadcloth, trousers to match and a forest-green, long-sleeved shirt, the Burke pack Alpha looked as if he'd traveled backward in time. Raphael had chosen the seat opposite him, facing the door. Never with his back to newcomers. Always on guard.

Now he wished he had been more careful before accepting this assignment. He did not tell Urien about Emily being his dracaira. Every male protective instinct inside him warned against it. Information would be exchanged only if Raphael thought it had a chance of saving Emily.

"It's not a sacrifice, but an execution. How do I know all you're telling me about Emily is the truth?" Raphael's mouth thinned as he glared at the other male.

"There are two gravestones in our cemetery that prove my words. What do you wish, Kallan? To see her actually dispatch another life?"

Beneath the bristling tension and aggressive words threaded an emotion Raphael could not identify. He sensed the male hid something. There was something else more ominous about Urien, but he couldn't place it. Raphael reached out with all his Draicon senses, inhaled the older male's scent.

He detected nothing but a slightly sweet fragrance. His gaze whipped over to the vases of fresh freesia and lilies on a polished round table.

If Emily was the cursed one, and her touch killed, there would be prophecies detailing her future. He leaned forward, his jaw tensed.

"I need proof, not of what she's done, but of the ancient words. Let me see the prophecies."

Urien relaxed and gave Raphael a pitying look. "I cannot. It is forbidden. Our ways are sacred and of the Old Ones, the purebloods. You, as a mixed-blood and a Cajun, are not allowed to see the sacred words. Besides, you could not interpret them, so they would be of little use."

Hairs bristled on the nape of his neck. Not understand. Always the snobbery, the division so clearly demarking his pack from the purebloods.

Raphael kept his thoughts guarded and offered a slow, calculating smile. "Then I will call my brother, my adopted brother, to my side. Damian is a pureblood Alpha, a descendant of the French Marcel pack. He has the authority to decipher the sacred words."

Alarm flashed in Urien's blue gaze, then vanished. Raphael detected the slightest scent of fear. "It would do no good. Helen, my sister, was keeper of the texts, and she hid them well and did not tell us where before Emily killed her."

How convenient. "Then if the texts are hidden, shouldn't they be found?"

"They are of the earth and its powers and too frail to be brought into the light this time of year. It is best to wait until winter, when the sun's light will not pierce them and perhaps fade the words." Urien gave him another knowing look. "Of course you would not know these things, as you are unfamiliar with the Old Ways."

He tired of Urien's games. "I am familiar with the new ways and a technology called artificial lighting. I can unearth them at night and then Damian can read with artificial lighting that will have no effect, since the lighting is not from the earth." Raphael watched Urien's face pale. "If your people are reluctant to do it, I will. If I have to dig up holes in every square inch of your property, I will."

"I am afraid your task is fruitless. Helen was a pure-blood Draicon, and her powers from the earth itself. She would have cloaked the texts with so many safeguards only the most ancient and knowledgeable of our pack could safely find them."

Doubt touched the male's face as he surveyed Raphael. "Our pack, not a mixed-blood pack, that is. Our past Kallans have also been purebloods, elders who had great powers and could accomplish such a feat. I am not certain if your powers are sufficient enough to uncover Helen's hiding place deep in the earth."

Urien's chiding tone grated on Raphael's last nerve. "I assure you, my powers are more than sufficient."

"Perhaps if I were to witness a test to be assured of this."

He was not a circus performer who performed tricks at everyone else's bidding, but if it erased the doubts in the Alpha male's mind and helped Emily…

He hated sacrificing his pride but would do so this one time for his draicara's sake. Swallowing his disquiet, Raphael stood, stretching his big, powerful body to its full height, emphasizing his larger, more muscled physique over Urien's shorter, almost delicate body. Red wolf. Smaller, agile.

Pureblood, who possessed knowledge Raphael had been denied, simply due to his pack's status in the Draicon hierarchy.

"What test did you have in mind? Uncover the earth with a wave of my hands? Singe the grass with a lightning bolt?" He gave his most intimidating stare, the one that froze the bravest Draicon in their tracks. Urien lowered his gaze. Still, Raphael wasn't satisfied, but disgusted.

He'd never met an Alpha Draicon who could not stand his ground. Small wonder the male wasn't willing to fight for Emily's life but chose to execute her as if she were a bothersome burden. Alpha males were supposed to protect all their pack females. Damian, a powerful and pureblood Alpha male, would lay down his life for a member of his pack and would never meekly back away from a confrontation.

No one was willing to fight for Emily. His temper flared. "Let's get this over with," he snapped. Raphael jerked a thumb at the door. "Outside."

In the pristine yard, with acres of meadow grass flowing down a gentle slope, he spotted a likely target. Raphael inhaled deeply, trying to get Urien's scent. He smelled earth and forest. Urien was Draicon.

Raphael turned and saw a face staring down from the upstairs window. Soon, footsteps on the farmhouse steps alerted him that they weren't alone. The other

Burke pack members gathered behind Urien. Raphael turned and looked at their faces. They resembled a crowd eager for a spectacle, anticipation shining on their round, pale faces.

Let's get this show over with, he thought in revulsion.

"There," he said, jerking a thumb toward a large boulder.

Raphael stretched out his hands and summoned the energy. Rock exploded into a shower of granite chips and loud gasps sounded behind him. He walked over to a fragment no bigger than a dime and tossed it at Urien.

"I trust that will suffice," he said with sarcasm.

"You are the Kallan. The Destroyer. You are permitted to search for the texts as you wish." Urien bowed his head slightly, but then his gaze was alert and watchful as he lifted it once more. Cunning. "I give you permission to search all our land. However, if you do not sacrifice Emily, you will violate the terms of the contract and forfeit your own brother's life."

A flash of grief and anger touched him. Raphael fisted his hands. "I won't violate any terms by obtaining proof that Emily is the cursed one foretold to bring about the end to all our race. All our race, purebloods and mixed. Know this, Urien. I will do what I must, but I will have the proof I need. I will not take an innocent's life."

As he started to leave them, he heard someone whisper, "This Kallan is not like the purebloods of old. He has much more destructive, dark power. He is the Destroyer."

No emotion showed on his face as he whirled around and went toward his cabin, but inside, his stomach churned the contents of his last meal.

* * *

Emily spent much of the morning sitting by her father's gravestone, searching within herself for answers.

"Papa, I wish you could hear me," she whispered to the cold gravestone. "I'm no coward, but I'm scared and don't know what to do anymore. If it's best that I die to save the pack, so be it, but how can my death at Raphael's hand solve anything?"

She didn't know whom to trust. Yet her father always stressed that pack was family and family was everything. Right now, she needed comfort from a familiar routine. The pack always had a big family-style breakfast. Once they had welcomed her at the table with hugs and kisses. Emily longed to belong once more.

Maybe this time, now that they knew she would soon die, they wouldn't shun her. The thought comforted her a little.

She stood and walked to the rambling farmhouse.

With a confident walk that disguised her inner trembling, she entered the house and stood at the doorway of the enormous dining groom. Her aunt, busy serving a platter of sausage, glanced up. Frozen horror stole over Bridget's face.

Gathering all her courage, Emily spoke. "I just wanted to join you for one meal, I can eat from a separate plate and destroy it after so I won't contaminate it, or you can even give me the leftovers you don't want…"

Her voice trailed off as the entire pack, her family, turned their heads. The repulsed looks echoed Bridget's. Urien pushed back from the table.

"Get out," he said tightly. "You are forbidden here."

Some tiny bit of stubbornness remained, gluing her

feet to the floor. She held her chin high, surveying them with what she hoped was a scornful glance.

"Fine," she said with dignity. "I'm not hungry."

Gathering the tatters of her shredded pride, Emily left, hoping they couldn't hear her protesting stomach. She did not run until she was certain the pack could not see her through the farmhouse windows.

Her footsteps made crunching sounds as she ran along the grand drive leading to her cottage. On the front porch of Raphael's cottage, the Kallan watched her.

Emily jerked to a halt, her heart thudding like a war drums. Her nostrils flared, catching his scent. Spices and an earthy, masculine scent flooded her senses.

She swallowed hard. She didn't dare trust him. She had trusted her own people to understand, to work with her, and they had turned their backs in her greatest need. But she had been alone for too long to reach out to anyone, even the one who was supposed to save her.

Emily started to pass, but his deep, commanding voice called out. "Emily, come here."

For a moment she hesitated, then she inhaled again, dragging in a lungful of his scent. It beckoned to her like an elixir, made her dizzy with sharp, sudden need.

Almost against her will, Emily found herself mounting the steps to his cabin. Raphael sat in one of the pine rockers. The chiseled edge of his profile showed in sharp relief.

She chose to stand by the railing, as far from him as possible without leaving the porch.

"Why do you keep running away to the woods?"

Her shoulders lifted in an attempt at insouciance. "I like the forest."

"So do I. It holds an aura of mystery, strength and power. Especially these woods." He cocked his head at her. "One of my favorite poems is about the woods. Robert Frost wrote it."

"Robert Frost," she realized. A Kallan who read poetry like she did?

"He was like you, in a way. He cherished the earth. You feel more at home in the forest, don't you?"

Emily fell silent, not knowing what to say.

Finally, he looked at her. His expression was blank, but she read steely resolve in his dark gaze. "I know this was a shock to you, as much as it was to me. But from now on, no more running from me."

"Who are you to order me?"

"Your draicaron. Your bonded mate. You can't run away from that fact, Emily." He leaned back in the rocker, his boots tipped upward. "I had a talk with your Alpha—"

"*My* Alpha."

Bitterness tinged her tone. Raphael gave her a thoughtful look and leaned forward, hands on his knees. She found herself staring at his long, powerful limbs encased in the blue jeans. Everything about the Kallan radiated power, control and pure male strength.

"I told Urien I want proof that the prophecies demand your sacrifice and that I will not go forward with the execution unless I have that proof."

She felt her shoulders release the tension she'd been holding. No one since her father had talked to her with this much forwardness and blunt honesty. Raphael did not mince words or make her fate sound glorious. It was an execution, and she was glad he stated it thusly. It softened her a little toward him.

Just a little.

Raphael slung an arm over the back of the rocker. "Did your aunt Helen ever mention to you where she hid the sacred texts?"

Like a deer spotting a predator, Emily froze. Motionless she stood, hoping she had not heard him correctly. How could he have known?

"Emily."

A statement, demanding answers. Emily lifted her gaze to his. "What concern is it of yours?"

"It is of great concern of mine, because it concerns you."

Deep inside, she wanted to trust him. She'd walked alone for a long time, shunned by her own people. But she did not dare. Once she had trusted her people, and they turned on her. Her life was at stake, and it was better to forge ahead on her own.

A gentle but insistent prodding touched her mind. Raphael.

Emily, talk to me. It's my duty to help you. Do you know anything of the ancient texts your aunt Helen hid?

Deliberately, she erected a mental barricade. It almost came as naturally as breathing.

Raphael quirked a dark brow. "Emily, what do you know of the ancient texts?"

Persistent. She lowered her guard for a mere instant and touched his mind. Feelings of concern, anger directed at Urien, resentment? And barely restrained sexual need.

Swallowing hard, she withdrew, slamming the door shut like a woman taking a peek into a dark, forbidden room.

"It doesn't work that way, Emily. You can't prod my thoughts and then shut me out. Now, tell me, what do you know of the texts?"

His voice was soft, yet steely. She moistened her mouth. "Why do you want them?"

"They'll have answers. Answers I need and will tell me if you are destined to die or if all that Urien says is a crock of camian dung."

"Camian?"

"Bayou alligator." Determination flared on his handsome face as he leaned forward. "I'll do whatever it takes to find the texts."

She fisted her hands in her lap. "I have the texts. They're safe. Urien doesn't know I have them, and I want it to stay that way."

His mouth relaxed. "Good. Now all we need to do is translate them."

"When did this become *we?*"

"The moment I discovered you're my draicara, and even before then. I take my charges as Kallan very seriously. Now, tell me what is needed to translate them."

Panic surged through her veins. She needed more time to find answers by herself. If Raphael discovered she had translated the first part of the passage, he might see it as a sign she was meant to die. She shivered.

"Let's go inside. You're cold," he said abruptly.

The inside of his cottage was as large as hers, but for the heavy, masculine pine furniture. The small kitchen had a table beneath a window. On the fireplace mantel was a collection of baskets containing pinecones. She peered through the opened bedroom doorway. The king-size bed had a hand-carved pine headboard and a sienna and forest-green quilt. She wondered if he even knew what color sienna was.

"Red." His tone deepened with languid sensuality. "Like your hair, sunset over the bayou, *chere*."

Raphael descended with grace onto the long leather couch, slinging an arm across the back. Leather creaked as he shifted his weight, planting one booted foot upon the square coffee table. "Come here, little one. I'm not so *dangereux*."

The slow, sensual slur of his voice sent a shiver of desire coursing through her. "Stop reading my mind."

"Stop evading my question. Sit." He patted a space next to him.

She ignored the invitation and stood by the fireplace. Her family had shunned her. Her entire world stood on the threshold of collapse. How could she trust him, a stranger who came to execute her, with her very life?

Guarding her mind, and steeling herself against the piercing pain of abandonment, she faced him. "You want answers. I'll tell you then. What is needed to translate them is none of your concern, Kallan. The texts are parchment, sacred and can only be translated by a select few like myself. I won't let you see them. It would be a violation."

She pivoted to storm out of the room, but not before catching the dark look in his eyes.

It would be a violation. Dog. Mongrel. Mixed-blood. He could hear all the slurs.

Raphael gripped the sofa's armrest so hard his fingers began to purple. First Urien, now his own draicara, deemed him unworthy to read the texts. His mixed blood sent him spiraling downward in their esteem as if he'd slid down a chute.

Straight into the trash heap of what purebloods like the Burkes considered impures. Raphael inhaled a deep breath.

His own draicara refused his help.

Not that he could read them anyway. He lacked knowledge of the Old Language, all because of his Cajun birth. He was considered impure. Mixed-blood.

Mongrel.

A distant memory surged. He tried pushing it down, but it surfaced with relentless force. He'd been in town, ambling through the French Quarter, enjoying the fresh air and looking to purchase fresh peaches, which he adored. As he rounded a corner toward the market, a group of purebloods spotted him. They knew who he was. What he was.

The names they called him weren't as bad as what they had done….

He had never again eaten a peach.

Though the marks were long gone, he absently rubbed his neck out of habit. Raphael scowled and stopped. He stood, pushing aside old, hurtful wrongs. He was no longer that weakling of ten, but a grown male with enormous powers and a draicara who needed his help.

Even if she thought he was incapable of providing it. He smiled grimly.

You'll see, chere. One way or another, I will aid you, like it or not.

The purifying sage was ready. The berries she'd picked sat in a plain wood bowl, as Helen had taught her.

Emily lit the sage and waved it over the ancient parchment on the table, focusing her energy toward the words. She tried to clear her mind, center herself amid the turbulent chaos of her thoughts.

She set down the sage, letting the smoke fill the room, and picked up the berries with a trembling hand. Emily stared at the parchment.

The words were pure gibberish. Her hand shook violently as she took a stone mortar and crushed the berries into a pulpy mixture.

Scooping her fingers into the mixture, she gently smeared it over the parchment. Emily blew on the crushed berries, then wiped them away.

She stared at the words. Hope filled her as they began to form before her eyes in the Old Language. She blinked eagerly, her finger tracing the passage.

"Destiny demands that the Destroyer will execute the Chosen One...."

Her mouth went dry as her heart raced in sudden panic and dread. Emily blinked hard.

The words faded.

"No, please, no," she cried out. Emily blinked again, but nothing appeared.

Tears filled her eyes. She slammed a fist down on the table, rattling the bowl holding the berries.

For so long, she'd tried to be brave, held all her emotions at bay. Now they poured out like a river breaking a dam.

The lone passage stated it in grim, ancient writing.

Raphael, the Destroyer, would execute her.

She was going to die at his hand.

Chapter 4

The heavy knock at the front door catapulted Emily out of her self-misery. She took in several calming breaths, inhaled the sage to cleanse her emotions.

Her draicaron must not see how upset she was. He'd question what she'd found and could use it against her to fulfill his duty. She dried her eyes, threw a cloth over her work and went to answer the door.

In his black leather jacket, jeans and black T-shirt, Raphael stood outside.

His stance was powerful, obstinate, and reminded her of her favorite towering oak. No wind, rain or the worst storm would fell it. Strong, sturdy and impenetrable. She could not run from him, or hide. He would find her.

Destroy her.

Emily clamped a barricade over her thoughts but couldn't stop shivering inside with fear.

"You're not shutting me out, Emily. It won't work."

She opened the door and stood aside as he walked into her living room. Raphael folded his arms across his broad chest. "My duties as Kallan require you to know about the Other Realm. I've decided to delay those lessons in favor of working with you to decipher the texts. If you will work with me."

"Come in. Sit down." She motioned toward the floral couch. She could not meet his gaze. Instead, she studied his feet, clad in tough leather boots. "I have a question."

"Go on." His tone was guarded.

"How many Draicon have you terminated as Kallan?"

He gave a heavy intake of breath. "Too many."

"Did any go willingly?"

Raphael headed for her largest chair. His big, powerful body seemed to suck up all the space in her tiny living room. "Some did. Some asked me to end it for them. Elders, who could not cross and were suffering."

"And those who did not wish to go? Did you teach them about the Other Realm as well?"

She raised her gaze to see him drag a hand through his silky, thick hair. "They were much harder. I gave them the basic lessons and then allowed them to spend the rest of their time conducting last requests, under strict supervision, of course."

"But you still killed them. What was it like? Did it hurt, because they did not want to go?"

She couldn't help the small note of worry.

"My Scian has a magick anesthetic. It never hurts," he said quietly.

Emily stared at the dagger intended to end her life. "Why are you doing this? Why did you become Kallan, even with all the power, if your only purpose is to kill our people?"

Raphael folded his arms across his chest. "It is my duty and responsibility to terminate the lives of our people who need the solace of death, or deserve it."

"And me? Do I deserve to die?" she blurted out.

His onyx gaze softened. "I doubt it. Which is why I need you willing to work with me to discover why your pack says you do. My duty is clear. It's not easy, and I will find answers first."

She nodded, seeing it from his point of view.

"Let's start with some basic questions." He gestured to the sofa. She sat.

"Tell me about your father, and how he died."

She related the details, and what happened with Helen, as well. Emotion clogged her throat as she relayed how she'd returned to find Helen lying on the ground. In their protective covering of heavy gloves, Emily fisted her hands, trying desperately to contain her feelings.

"They didn't even bury her in the earth she loved with the rest of our pack. She was so alone. They were too afraid her body, contaminated by my touch, would contaminate the ground. So they made a marker for her but they burned her body. I saw the smoke, but they wouldn't let me near. So much smoke. I waited until it was dark, and then I took her ashes and I buried them in the earth."

Suddenly her voice broke. Emily buried her head in her hands, her stomach twisted in knots as she bit back a sob.

She heard the chair creak, the soft tread of footsteps, and felt a warm body next to hers. Astonished shock rippled through her as Raphael slid a muscled arm about her shoulders. No one had dared to be this close since the goddess had cursed her with the touch of death. The comfort of his gesture and his inclination to draw near instead of away cracked the dam of her emotions. She longed to sink against his strong body and release everything she'd felt.

"Em," he said softly. "How much you've suffered."

His gentle compassion unraveled all her control. Tears sprang to her eyes, blurring her vision, but she jerked away, shuffling to the couch's far end.

"D-d-don't touch me," she choked out. "It's t-too dangerous. You'll get hurt."

Raphael headed for the kitchen and returned with a napkin. He held it out to her. She snatched it from his hands, careful not to allow any contact between them, and murmured thanks as she dried her eyes.

"Emily, I doubt you can hurt me," he said gently. "But until the time is right and you learn to trust me, let's take it one step at a time. Now, would you like to show me where you and Helen were working when she died? I need to see something."

The napkin crumbled in her hands. "It's just a garden."

"Yes, but I can sense energy patterns in the way a person died. I want to see Helen's."

Despite her misery, fascination stole over her. "Such a dark power to have," she marveled. "None of my people can do that."

A shadow crossed her draicaron's face. "Yes, very dark."

They walked outside through the forest until they reached an open meadow. Granite river rocks wreathed a small circular garden, once a lovely backdrop to the blue misty mountains ringing the valley. Emily hung back, studying the flowers, now dying from the approaching winter. Once snapdragons, petunias and pansies grew here in a colorful riot.

Since Helen's death, she hadn't the heart to return.

"We used to like gardening here. She took me here the day she died. She told me where the texts were, and she was going to tell me something else." Emily frowned, searching her memory. "I had the feeling it was very important, something about the pack."

She sensed Raphael's preternatural stillness. "Did she give you any clues before she died?"

"Just one thing. She said things were not always as they seemed, and destructive powers were not always meant to destroy good." Emily walked to the plantings where she and Helen had worked. "It was here. We were planting the pansies, the violet ones. They were her favorite."

He squatted by the garden's edge, touching the earth. Emily swallowed hard as she watched the muscles bulge in his long limbs. Raphael shrugged out of his leather jacket and dropped it on the ground. His shoulders were as broad as a doorway. Biceps bulged as he stretched his arms toward the earth. Closing his eyes, he sifted through the dirt. The tiny gold dagger earring swung from his left ear in the slight breeze.

Awestruck, she observed him seeming to hum with power, iridescent sparks shimmering about him. Unlike her magick, it turned dark and shadowy, as if shrouded by a dark fog. A shiver skated down her spine.

According to her studies, no other Kallans had performed magick like this. They had done their duties, and retired to their cottages to study the ancient texts, living a scholarly life. This Kallan had powers she had never heard of before, and it awed her with the implications.

Raphael seemed as if he could destroy life as she could, only not with a single touch, but with a single thought.

"Do you read anything?" she asked.

He stood, brushing dirt from his hands. "The earth has been recently turned and it's difficult to gauge. Have you gardened here since her death?"

"I never came back."

"Something has." He jammed his hands into the back pockets of his jeans. "An animal, perhaps. I detect raccoon scent."

"We have plenty of wild animals. I used to like watching them here."

"In the flower garden?" He quirked an eyebrow.

Her shoulders lifted in a delicate shrug. "It's nature. Deer usually come here, but I like growing plants, so I cultivated another garden especially for them. Now they leave it alone."

"You plant a garden for prey?" He sounded incredulous, his expression so outraged she laughed.

Emily stopped, surprised by the sound. "I haven't done that in a while."

"I'd like to hear about it."

His tender voice sent a funny flutter to her belly. Emily sidestepped the issue and gestured to the flowers. "It was my idea. Out of respect for the animals, who also gave their lives for our food." Her face fell as depression slid over her. "When I was still allowed in the pack, and allowed to contribute to farming game."

His expression softened. "It was a good idea. You have a natural touch with the earth and should be proud of it."

She shrugged. "I keep this garden for the butterflies. Peonies, asters, petunias, goldenrod, Queen Anne's lace, black-eyed Susans." Her lower lip wobbled tremulously. "Helen was fond of the black-eyed Susans. She used to pick them each morning and put them on the breakfast table in winter. They cheered her."

His gaze sharpened. "Flowers in the winter? Very odd. Or hearty flowers."

Emily swallowed hard, wondering if he suspected her gift. To distract him, she pointed to a nearby viceroy butterfly, its orange-and-black markings contrasting sharply to its perch on the dying pink petunia.

Extending her arm, she beckoned to the insect, hoping it would land on her finger. "They like to come to me."

"I don't blame them," he murmured.

Raphael stared at her with a hot intensity, so burning she felt as if he'd stripped her bare. Flushed, she turned away, feeling the flare of heat between them. The feeling was refreshingly new and made her feel tingly inside. Raphael didn't avoid looking at her as her pack did, or shun her as if she were diseased. How odd, and yet wonderful she felt uniquely free with him.

If only the feeling could last.

Raphael's insides knotted with hard sexual need as he studied her carefree expression. In her bare feet, her perfect little toes peeking from beneath the hem of the ugly brown dress, her body finally relaxed and color flushing her cheeks, she was lovely. Tendrils of curling hair escaped its ever-present restrictive bun. He jammed his hands into his jeans pockets, overcome with the urge to touch her hair, to release it from its confines and let it spill past her shoulders. An image flashed over him. Emily, her long hair spilled over his pillow, her face flushed with sexual arousal as he mounted her, her whimpers of pleasure echoing in his ears as he slowly thrust deep inside her welcoming heat....

He silently cursed in Cajun and stepped back, not wanting to alarm her with the intensity of his arousal. He was dealing with a female who had seldom interacted with another male outside her pack, and certainly not one as virile or vital as he was.

No, the Burke pack males all seemed pale imitations of Draicon.

That's what purebloods are, he thought in savage resentment. Yet his adopted brother Damian was a pureblood. Damian, the strong, vibrantly powerful male bore no resemblance to their pedigree.

It made no sense.

The butterfly fluttered near him, dancing in the air. Raphael studied it as Emily reached out. But it flitted away from her gloved hand, gently waving its wings. A shadow crossed her face, but she quickly recovered.

"It doesn't like my gloves. Hold out your hand and it will land on it. The butterflies are very tame."

He cocked an eyebrow at her. "I'm not a butterfly sort." But he did as she asked, only because the sadness on her face twisted his heart. He wanted to make her smile. Laugh again.

Raphael held out his hand. The viceroy landed delicately on his hand. A smile touched his mouth.

"Back home, I used to do this with the *zirondelle,* the dragonfly, in the bayou," he told her.

The insect was lovely, its wings gently fanning the air. It bent its head to his finger as if searching for nectar. Suddenly he felt a sharp pain.

Incredulity came over him as he stared at the crimson droplets welling on his skin. "It bit me," he marveled. "Son of a…bit me."

Emily stared at his hand. "They don't bite. How can it?"

He stared at the creature and saw a tiny mouth, with rows of sharp teeth. The butterfly started to fly away.

"Emily, stand back," he warned. He approached the winged insect with stealth, wolf stalking prey. "It isn't a butterfly." He pounced, capturing the creature in his hands. It struggled to free itself, tiny jaws snapping at his hands. Grimly he hung on, opened his palm and held it by one wing.

The jaws kept snapping. Raphael whipped his head about, looking to see if it were a clone and the original nearby.

"What are you doing?" Emily cried out.

"What I always do with the enemy," he muttered. With his fist, he crushed it, feeling it die. A small scream echoed in his head. Emily's scream, a keening wail lacing him with sorrow.

Raphael opened his fist, and gray ash spilled to the ground. His gaze met hers. Emily trembled, her gloved hands pressed to her rosebud mouth.

"You killed it, how could it be the enemy, it was just—"

"A Morph, Emily. The enemy. Trust me."

The way she stared at him twisted his heart. A heavy

weight sat on his chest. She stared as the others did, with a mix of horror and respect. His mate, who was supposed to be the one closest to him, looked at him as if he were the grim reaper.

"Morph, Emily. I don't know how it got on this land, past your pack's safeguards, but obviously the shields are thinning out and need reinforcing."

Or something far worse was at work. He gentled his tone, tried to make her see he was not the monster she imagined.

"Trust me, Emily, it was a Morph."

"Trust you. How can I?" she whispered, backing away from him. "You're supposed to be my mate, the one who saves me. How can you be the one who will kill me instead like you just did with the butterfly?"

When she fled for the safety of the woods, he did not immediately follow. Instead he brought his injured finger to his face, the bite already healed. If only the breach between them could be as easily healed.

Raphael rubbed his chin. He had to find her. Every instinct screamed at him to bring her closer, bond with her and save her. Even while his duty as Kallan was grimly clear.

He put on his jacket, waited a few minutes, scanning the territory, looking for more Morphs. Finally he hiked through the forest, following her delicate scent trail. Navigating the faint trail, he smelled fresh water and heard the ceaseless sweep of current rushing over rocks.

In a small meadow, a soft carpet of verdant grasses led to rocks guarding a raging river. The scent of pine and pure water and cleansing air filled his lungs. Raphael stopped, dragged in a deep breath. The scent was intoxicating to his wild wolf side, even more alluring mingled with the delicate fragrance of the female sitting on a rock, watching the water gush past.

Emily.

He approached, deliberately making noise. She did not turn around but tilted her head to one side.

"I knew you were coming here. I could sense you."

Delight at her awareness of him twined with caution. He carefully sat down on a rock a few feet away, studying the crystal-clear stream.

She rested her cheek on her bent knees. "It was truly a Morph, the butterfly?"

"I wouldn't lie to you, Em. I only wanted to keep you safe. I don't know how it slipped past the safeguards Urien put on the pack lands, but it did." Unable to keep from touching her, he rested a hand on the small of her back and began slowly stroking. "Don't run from me again. You're safer with me, until I can find out what's happening here."

Silence draped between them for a few moments. He drank it in with her scent, listening to a crow call overhead. A cool breeze danced against his face, and Raphael suppressed a shiver, but Emily glanced at him. Amusement danced in her eyes.

"You are not accustomed to our climate. I sense you are cold."

"Not as cold as I imagine I'd be in winter," he quipped. "But it's very peaceful and lovely here."

Emily picked up a stone and tossed it into the water. "This is my private place. Urien and the others don't come here, ever. I feel safe here."

"You feel safe even with me?" he challenged.

She stole another shy glance at him. "You don't look threatening now."

"It's because I'm too cold to feel threatening. I'm a warm-blooded wolf." He tipped back his head and released a low, mournful howl.

It worked. She giggled, and the tension between them broke. "Are you saying you're domesticated? I can't see it."

"Moi?" He wiggled his eyebrows. *"Non, chere,* I'm a wild wolf?"

"Very wild." She turned to face him, an impish gleam in her eyes. "Unlike that metal horse you ride, which is very tame."

Raphael drew back in pretended shock. "Are you calling my Harley domesticated?"

"It answers to your command and does your bidding like a real horse, so yes, I do."

He put a hand over his heart. "I am highly insulted you would call my Harley tame."

The giggle he'd coaxed from her made his spirits soar. Perhaps there was middle ground where they could reach out to each other.

"I have never seen such a machine," she admitted. "We have automobiles we use only for convenience, and they are practical and not pretty." She looked up at him from her incredibly long golden lashes. "Harley is pretty with its black and red and silver coloring."

He grinned. "She forgives you then, for calling her tame."

"She? His name is Harley."

"Her full name is Harley-Davidson Heritage Softail. All vehicles are called 'she.'" He picked up a rock, skipped it across a tranquil pool in the stream. "Probably because they are so touchy in the morning when you try to start their engines."

"We are not."

He laughed. "I'm teasing. It has nothing to do with starting their engines. It has to do with their temperaments." He reached over, tweaked a red curl escaping her tight bun. "Especially the red ones. Red's my favorite color."

She saw his expression and smiled. "You're incorrigible."

"That's what my mother always told me."

Emily hugged her knees. "Was it your mother who encouraged you to become the Kallan? Or your father?"

The familiar tightness squeezed his chest. "Neither. It was a decision I made on my own."

He turned his thoughts away from the painful past and surveyed the land. "This is a good place," he said quietly, tracing the black striations in a nearby rock. "It's of the earth and radiates with power. There are ancient, strong safeguards in place."

He rested his palm firmly on the rock and frowned, feeling the granite sing to him in muted harmony. "It's an ancient magick, of the earth but not of it. Something much stronger, and pure."

From the source itself, he almost said, but stopped as he caught the worried look of sudden concern on her face.

"Then I shouldn't be here," she whispered, hugging her knees tighter. "Since I'm contaminated. That's what Urien calls me. Cursed, and my blood contaminates the pack because of my curse."

"You are not contaminated, and Urien is quick to

judge and condemn. He is not a true leader. An Alpha guards and protects all in his pack."

"Maybe I deserved to be abandoned by them."

The brokenness in her voice twisted his heart. Raphael reached for her, but she inched backward, watching him warily. A heavy sigh fled him. When would she learn to stop evading him? They didn't have much time. He reached out, taking her chin in a firm but gentle grip, forcing her to regard him.

"Emily, we must talk. Now. Not tomorrow, or later. Let's get this settled for once and for all."

His words struck a chord of dread. Emily felt herself want to shrink inside her own skin. That commanding tone brooked obedience. Would he broach the topic she kept wanting to avoid?

Her own death.

Yet his touch was soothing as he slid his thumb over the underside of her jaw. Emily's heart beat faster.

"You've suffered a terrible blow—no, two terrible blows. Finding out you were cursed, which I still wonder if it is true, and being abandoned by your pack."

She blinked, wary of his motivation.

"I'm being straight with you, *chere*." Raphael's mouth thinned to a tight slash before he spoke again. "I don't trust anyone in your pack, especially Bridget and Urien. We need to find out the truth about why you are cursed, if you are cursed, and why destiny has ruled you should die."

When his hand dropped, she felt herself hungering for the contact between them again. Emily felt bereft but inched away, sternly reminding herself of Raphael's true purpose. "Why don't you trust them?"

"I have my reasons," he said darkly. "We'll figure it out on our own. No one else. But you have to trust me, work with me on this. Forget about Raphael the Kallan and Emily the Cursed." He drew closer, and for once she did not back away. His chocolate-brown eyes were shining with determination.

He was her draicaron. He wanted her to forget all she'd been told, all they had been taught to believe, and step away from the traditions that had guided her for twenty-two years.

Risk.

She had little to risk. But could she trust him? She'd walked alone, not trusting her pack, loathing her solitary lifestyle, but adjusting out of necessity. Now Raphael wanted her to bond with him emotionally and go beyond her borders.

The idea terrified her. Dying terrified her more.

She needed assurances. "How can we do this?"

"I don't know how, but we'll find a way, if you will trust me," he told her quietly.

She wriggled her feet, studying them. "I need help," she finally admitted. "I'm really not used to this, being alone and not part of the pack. I just want to belong again, and fit in." She frowned at her bare toes. "Once I used to do everything with my family. Urien and Bridget even took me into town as a treat. I haven't been to town in over a year. I remember the last time I went, I saw a woman with a chain around her ankle. It looked odd, but I liked the jewelry. We're forbidden to wear any because it's of the human world. And her toes, they were so pretty."

"So are yours. You have lovely toes."

His gentle tone lowered her natural defenses. "Hers were painted."

"Paint yours, then."

Surprise flashed through her. "No female in my pack has ever does such a thing. It's artificial, and we are of the earth. If I want to be like them, I have to look like them."

"You can still embrace the earth and paint your toes. Do you want to be like them? Why would you want to fit into a pack that has treated you so badly?" he challenged.

The question caught her off guard. She'd never known anything else. Yet at times she loathed the boring, itchy dress made from natural fibers, wished she could wear her hair differently, wondered what it would feel like to wear a gold chain around her ankle.

Wondered what it would feel like to dance in the meadow, her hair flowing out unbound, and not care who saw and what they thought.

"I suppose I want to be accepted and belong. Doesn't everyone? It's in our blood to run with the pack."

"Not when your pack is nothing more than a herd of sheep. Do you wish to be a sheep?" Raphael turned his dark, intense gaze on her as he swiveled, placing one hand behind him and one on her knee. Heat spread through her at the sizzling contact between them.

"I'm a wolf, not a sheep."

"I meant a metaphorical sheep, someone who doesn't express her individuality and blends in with the crowd. Why can't you express yourself and how you feel, and act as you wish, not as you were expected?"

She studied the tiny gold earring dangling from his left ear. Raphael was such a Draicon. "You certainly stand out from the crowd. Have you always?"

He glanced down at his jeans with an amused smile. "No. It wasn't until I reached fifty that I realized I didn't want to merely run with the pack anymore. I was always trying to be someone I wasn't."

"What?"

His expression shuttered. "Someone I could never be," he said tightly, removing his hand from her knee. He stared out to the rushing water.

Briefly she touched his mind, saw a flickering of images like a movie her father had taken her to see once. Older, sophisticated pureblood French Draicon in New Orleans. A young Raphael, about her age, listening to the same music they enjoyed, dressing carefully to imitate them, combing his short hair exactly like them, wearing shiny loafers with pennies.

Then a flash of Raphael being pushed into the street, one of them took a bucket and dumped it over him…taunting laughter…

The image shut off as quickly. Raphael did not look at her, but his jaw tautened.

Alarm and brief pity surged through her. What had he suffered? The powerful Kallan, treated as an inferior. She'd never considered it. Emily brought her hand forward to touch his arm, offer comfort, remembered, and drew it back. Instinct warned her that his pride would shun such a gesture. Her gentle heart ached for him. How well she knew what it was like to walk alone and have others reject her.

Silence draped between them, broken only by the growl of her empty stomach. Emily blushed.

Raphael studied her. "When did you last hunt? You're constantly hungry because you lack protein."

"I can't shift into wolf," she protested.

"That will change. You will again. One of my duties as your draicaron is to provide for you," he said quietly. "I'll find food for you."

Pleasure rippled through her. He made her feel cherished. She hugged her knees, guarding her feelings.

She must not allow herself to become close to Raphael—or forget who he was.

Emily studied him curiously as he stood, waved a hand, dispensing of his clothing, and shifted into a large gray wolf. Raphael leapt down onto a large, flat boulder in the stream. He studied the racing water, saw a fat rainbow trout swimming against the current. He put his nose in the water and shook his muzzle.

An expletive rang out in their telepathic link. Emily giggled.

"I told you the water is cold."

I can handle it, he told her in their mind link. *I may be warm-blooded, but I am not domesticated.*

Sending her this message, he sprang into the water and seized the trout with his jaws. She heard his inner howl and laughed.

Merde, that water is cold! My nose is about to fall off.

That would truly make you stand out from the crowd, she teased.

Yellow eyes glared at her, then he leapt back onto the rock and bounded up on the bank, the fish in his mouth. He dropped the dead catch at her feet, wagged his tail and cocked his head. *Dinner is served, ma belle.*

Emily burst into another fit of laughter.

What is it?

"I'm sorry, but I don't eat fish," she told him, giggling.

You don't...but you didn't...

"I thought it would be funny to see you brave the cold water."

Raphael shifted back, clothing himself in jeans, black long-sleeved shirt and leather jacket and boots. His dark brown hair was wet. "Funny?" He cocked a finger at her. "Come here. You owe me for that."

She shook her head, laughing still, and sprinted off. He took chase, delighting in the thrill of the hunt, the scent of her invigorating him, arousing him. She was quick, but no match for his tremendous speed and determination. He caught her by the bend of the creek, capturing her in his arms as she shrieked with laughter. Caged by his arms, she wriggled.

"Let me go," she demanded with a smile.

"Never," he said softly, and kissed her.

The electric shock of his warm, wet mouth touching hers sent a jolt shuddering through her. The kiss wasn't as fierce and melding as his first, born of desperation. This was like the soft touch of a butterfly wing. Intrigued, she pressed closer, wanting more. Her mouth became pliant and warm beneath the hard press of his lips. Resistance faded. He smelled like pine forest and clean male, cinnamon spice. Her body felt heavy with wanting as Raphael murmured against her mouth.

"Emily," he breathed.

He deepened the kiss, supped at her mouth, teasing her lips with his tongue. He tasted her as if she were an exquisite banquet, a rare feast. She moaned into his mouth as he lowered her to the cool, soft grass, covering her body with his own. Hard male strength pinned her to the ground, but his mouth was moving over hers. *Open for me,* he murmured into her mind. *Let me inside.*

Her lips instinctively parted, and his tongue slipped inside. He stroked the moist cavern of her mouth, nipped playfully at her lower lip. Emily wriggled beneath him, the empty space between her legs growing moist and throbbing. She wanted to wind her hands around his neck.

Her hands.

She writhed, turning her mouth to one side, and broke the kiss. "Stop it," she said sharply.

Raphael stopped and rolled off. Freed, she sprang up, heat flushing her face. She'd almost touched him. Her stomach twisted into knots.

Hugging herself, she walked away from him, and following the river's course, Raphael accompanied her. As if he sensed her confusion and wanted to put her at ease once more, he talked about the river and the difference between the clear water and the dark waters of the bayou he called home. Gradually she relaxed.

Raphael pointed to the river when she stopped. "Ever go swimming?"

"There are too many rapids."

"Looks nice and cool. In the bayou, we go swimming with the alligators and the snakes." He offered a cocky, charming grin.

She gave a little sigh. "I don't know how to swim. Father never taught me. I think he was overprotective, afraid I'd get into trouble."

He gave her a long, thoughtful look. "Most parents teach their children to swim, so in case they fall in, they can care for themselves until someone rescues them. What about your mother?"

"I never knew my mother. She gave birth to me but left us shortly after."

"Odd," he mused. "I can't imagine a woman leaving her beloved child. It must have been very difficult for her."

Emily felt a small desolation. "He never told me why, just that she couldn't stay with us. He told me that she loved me, but if she did, why would she leave me?"

"Maybe she felt she would not fit in with your pack. Emily, your mother wasn't pack, was she? She was an outsider," he pointed out gently. "All the rest are barren. You are the only youngling, and have been for a long while. Your father had an affair outside the pack."

"You're probably right. Especially if my mother was of mixed blood, and not a purebred, my pack wouldn't welcome her," she mused.

Raphael was silent, staring at the water. She tried to touch his mind but instead found a wall of granite.

Distress filled her. She had probably hurt him with her words. He was of mixed blood.

So upset was she at unintentionally insulting him that she moved closer to the edge, not realizing how close.

"Emily, watch it," Raphael warned.

The words barely fled his mouth when she slipped on a loose rock and lost her footing. A scream tore from her throat as she tumbled down the bank, straight into the roiling river.

Chapter 5

Raphael waved his hand, dispensing his clothing, and shifted. He plunged into the fast-moving current as wolf, swimming with the current. In his human form, he was a strong swimmer, but he couldn't risk the shock of the cold water slowing him for one minute.

Emily was swept downstream, and he had to reach her before she drowned.

Raphael lowered all his mental barriers, called out to her using their mind link. *Emily, where are you?*

A terrified scream rang in his head. He swam faster, paddling with the current, and saw her red head bobbing up and down. Still alive, still managing the wicked torrent. He allowed himself a flash of relief when he saw she wasn't fighting the current but letting herself drift with it. Still, she could not swim.

Raphael reached out with his mind as he treaded water in her direction.

Good girl. Keep letting the current take you, keep your head above water. Use your arms and legs and piston them, like you're making circles.

Suddenly they rounded a curve and came to a small raging waterfall. Raphael's heart stopped as he saw her head bob and then vanish beneath the water.

He swam to her faster, feeling her screams inside his head. Damn it, where was she, how long was she down?

Emily, put your hands over your head. Keep it from getting hit.

He finally reached her and dove beneath the lacy white froth. Paddling toward her, using all his strength, his front paws touched solid flesh. Emily. Raphael shifted instantly, his arms lacing about her midsection. He pulled her free.

They surfaced, Emily limp in his arms. Not breathing. Terror stabbed him. She'd been down at least three to four minutes. Enough time for brain damage.

With one arm hooked about her waist, he used his other in long, powerful strokes to steer them toward a calmer pool near the shore. He dragged her halfway out of the water, and as he start chest compressions, she choked and coughed up water. Her breathing hitched, but her eyes remained closed.

Raphael rubbed her chest, her arms, trying to warm her. "Em, wake up, little one, wake. Em, *chere,* talk to me."

She coughed, opened her eyes, and began shivering. Relief flooded him, made his limbs weaken. "Say something, *chere.*"

Her blue lips moved. "What is *chere?*" she croaked.

Raphael sat back on his haunches and laughed weakly. He cupped her face in his hands. "It's an endearment in Cajun French, meaning sweetheart."

He went to grab her hands, chafe them into warmth, but she jerked away.

"N-no, don't touch me, y-you'll get hurt."

He couldn't, but he wasn't about to argue, so instead he started to drag her entirely out of the water.

Suddenly she screamed and her body jerked.

"Something's got hold of my foot," she cried out. "Ow, it hurts, Raphael, it hurts."

The calm pool suddenly boiled and frothed, as if millions of fish appeared. Blood began streaking through the crystal-clear pool. Emily's blood.

Raphael pulled hard, yanking her free of the water, up onto shore. He stared in horror at her bare right foot.

Dozens of tiny bites bled, her flesh looking shredded. He uttered a curse and whipped his head from the water to her foot. Knowing she needed healing, knowing whatever was in the water must be killed.

He was the Destroyer, a killer.

He could not use his blood. It was forbidden. Yet as the thought surged through him, the bites vanished, replaced by smooth, pale flesh.

He turned his gaze to the water. Shock slammed into him. The reddened water, turned crimson by Emily's blood, was filled with dead fish.

After covering Emily with his jacket, he gave her a quick kiss.

"Warm yourself. I'm going in."

As she made a feeble protest, he dove into the deep pool. The fish, all Morph clones, vanished into clouds of gray ash. But he spotted the original, his senses detecting it as if had laid a scent trail. Raphael dove deeper, and his hands closed around it. Sharp teeth weakly closed around his fingers. He kicked for the surface.

Fish in hand, he emerged. He treaded water and studied the mouth gaping open and closed, showing rows of pointed teeth.

Piranha. They did not live in cold water, but the cold had not killed this one.

Even as he studied it, the fish died.

With a muttered curse he flung the fish into the air, directed a thought of pure energy. The piranha incinerated instantly and exploded into ash.

How had these Morphs bypassed the safeguards on the Burke land? Emily killed with her hands. Everything she touched died. Yet these fish died from ingesting her blood as if it were too potent for them. As if it were too powerful for evil.

He swam back to Emily lying on the shore. Very gently he cradled her in his arms. "Let's get you home, and warm."

Despite the wet clothing, she no longer shivered. Raphael cast a backward glance at the dead fish.

Why had they died?

Much later that night. Emily stood at the foot of a sturdy, aged oak tree. Above her head, a cluster of berries hung temptingly out of reach. She'd have to climb to reach the mistletoe plant.

Raphael had been solicitous and caring, lighting a fire in her fireplace and covering her with a warm blanket. After a while, she'd asked to be alone. His tenderness only made her miserable, knowing it would not last.

The incident with the fish had bothered her. Clearly they were Morphs, but why had they died? Raphael had questioned her, but she evaded him. She couldn't tell him about the gift of her blood giving life. If he knew about her powers, as her pack had, would he also see her as an abomination? She shuddered, remembering what happened to her grandfather.

What Urien had done afterward.

Raphael must not know more of her secrets. Distance between them was best. How could she allow herself to grow close to him? He was too different, too much a proud figure who stood out from the pack. A Draicon who rode a metal monster, wore hide of the cow and went without a pack.

Even though her own pack had rejected her, she longed to belong. For too long she'd been alone. Family was all she knew. Even her family was better than being alone.

After drying off, and making a small meal of leftover scraps, she'd tried to read more of the texts, but the mixture had sat out too long. She needed fresh berries, and her emotions were far too strong to decipher the words.

Translating the entire prophecy would give her answers.

With tremendous reluctance, she removed her gloves to gain better purchase on the tree. In her bare feet, she began to make her way up the tree. Bark scraped her arms, but she did not slow down. When she reached the limb holding the nearly ripe berries, she inched farther out.

Harvesting the berries was a delicate business. It had

to be done by moonlight and the sprig cut with a golden knife, her hands purified by saying the sacred words, or the berries would become contaminated.

This was the last sprig on the tree. If she lost these, she'd have to look off the property for others.

Wrapping her legs around the limb, she lay lengthwise, her arms free. In her dress pocket was a small gold knife used for ceremonies. The berries must be cut by her bare hands. She closed her eyes, stretched out her hands and uttered a prayer to the goddess Aibelle and then reached for the knife. So close, so very close...

"What the hell are you doing up there?"

The deep male voice startled her. Emily yelped and lost her precarious grip. Raphael's alarmed shout filled the air with her scream as the dagger slipped from her hands. Her arms flailed instinctively, and she fell. Air rushed by as she pinwheeled her arms, trying desperately to slow her descent.

Two strong arms caught her as if she weighed no more than the berries. Emily gasped as Raphael held her. Silver moonlight dappled his face, accenting his wry expression.

"I came out for a walk in the moonlight. I didn't expect to catch a falling star."

His tone was gentle, teasing. Emily's heart pounded harder in a different way as she stared at him, her arms dangling loosely. Dark bristles shadowed his square jaw, and his smile was reassuring. Then his expression shifted, turned more intense.

"What does one do with a gift fallen from the night sky?" he mused.

She felt odd, yearning, her body sweetly tense as the blood surged in her veins. His grip on her was secure, and she felt no fear, only sudden desire.

He gave her no further opportunity to contemplate as he lowered his mouth to hers. Emily's lips parted under the leisurely pressure of his. She felt his tongue slip past, seek hers. Emboldened, she touched his and began a delicate dance.

Very gently he lowered her to the damp grass, his arms secure around her. Raphael half covered her, never breaking the kiss, his mouth sipping at hers.

The aching between her legs intensified. She wasn't experienced, didn't know what she wanted, only that her skin felt feverish, her body felt pleasure and she wanted more. More of him, more of his delicious taste. Emily nipped his lower lip, then sucked on his tongue.

A low growl rippled from his chest as he tightened his grip and deepened the kiss. Emily sighed into his mouth. She raised her hands, eager to touch him, wind her hands around the strong muscles of his neck…

Her hands.

She would hurt him.

A shriek sounded into his mouth as she writhed and struggled to be free, realizing the danger of their embrace. Raphael tore his mouth from hers with a surprised look. He rolled off her as she bounded to her feet, rubbing her hands, her limbs weak and quivering.

"Stay away from me," she warned, holding out her bare hands.

"All right, easy now," he said softly. "But don't be afraid, Em. I won't hurt you."

It's you who will get hurt, came the fleeting thought.

She shoved a quivering hand through her long hair and glanced upward.

"Why were you in the tree?" He asked the question as calmly as if they hadn't been involved a minute ago.

Emily inhaled a deep breath. Raphael had a tendency to make her forget all sense, sweep away the present and all its concerns as if the world didn't exist.

Her world, her very dangerous, dark world. She grabbled for her gloves, donned them swiftly.

"I had to cut the mistletoe to translate the ancient texts, and it has to be done by moonlight, because the light during the day—"

"Is too intense." Raphael nodded. His gaze fell downward at the gold knife she had dropped. "And it must be done with a solid gold knife."

Surprised, she studied him, the formerly relaxed stance now taut with alertness. He craned his neck and stared upward. "I can't have you falling out of the tree again."

Dumbfounded, she watched him climb upward, as agile as if he'd been born to it. Emily forgot to breathe as he reached the limb and shimmied out. Raphael waved his hand and the Sacred Scian appeared in his palm.

Sense returned. He would cut the berries, but he didn't know the sacred words. Everything must be perfect, and Raphael in his good intentions…

Would ruin everything.

"Stop it, stop it, don't touch them," she cried out, running to the tree trunk.

"Don't worry, I've got it under control."

Using his left hand to cling to the limb, he sawed at the sprig of mistletoe with his left, using the golden dagger.

"No, no, wait, no, you'll ruin it!"

But he had already cut the leafy bough of berries. Raphael replaced his dagger and wrapped both hands around the limb, his body dangling fifteen feet in the air.

"Get back," he ordered.

She staggered back, her heart in her throat, misery choking her as he dropped and landed on his feet as if jumping off a small rock. Raphael made a formal little bow and presented the sprig to her with a flourish. "Your berries."

She did not take them, but stepped back, her stomach knotted. "It's too late. You ruined them. You weren't supposed to do it. You're an outsider who doesn't know the tradition. I told you not to do it, and now there's no more left."

His expression shifted to a guarded look. "Excuse me for contaminating your damn berries and worrying about you breaking your neck."

He strode off, hands jammed into the pockets of his jeans, his shoulders rigid as river rock. Emily stooped over and picked up the mistletoe. A lone tear trickled down her cheek.

She ignored it as she clutched the berries and walked back to her cabin. Inside, she tried to make sense of the texts, but her vision was far too blurred. She gave up.

In less than three weeks, she would die at the hand of her mate.

Chapter 6

Dawn broke with the soft chirp of birds outside her window. Emily sat up, rubbing her eyes. Cool air drifting through her open window brushed against her cheeks.

Winter was fast approaching. The thought was a rough jolt to her sleepy senses. There was another tree with mistletoe on a neighboring, abandoned farm. Perhaps the berries had ripened there. Fresh hope filled her. It would be worth the risk of leaving the pack's property.

A familiar, sensual scent filled her nostrils. Emily slipped out of bed, drew on her robe and belted it around her. In the living room by the river rock fireplace, Raphael sat in one of her comfortable chairs. In a long-sleeved blue shirt and faded jeans, he looked alert and watchful.

Long, dark hair curled down to his shoulders. He said nothing but regarded her with his steady gaze. The tiny gold earring swung from his left ear.

"What are you doing here?" she asked.

"Watching over you. With Morphs invading your territory, I'm not leaving you alone."

The thought that he guarded her while she slept warmed her even as it made her uneasy. With him this close, he'd be hard to evade. Emily clutched the folds of her robe to her throat as she studied his impartial expression. "Would you like some coffee?"

He nodded and she went to the adjoining kitchen. As she measured out the grounds, she felt him behind her. Silent. Even with his large size, he walked with stealth like his wolf.

She hadn't shifted in so long, she'd nearly forgotten what it was like to be wolf and run with the moon.

Emily poured the water and switched on the automatic coffeemaker. She turned, nearly colliding with him. Raphael was inspecting her kitchen.

"Got anything for breakfast?"

"I'm fresh out of game, so you have a choice of fresh fruit or fresh fruit."

She hadn't meant to sound so bitter and sarcastic. Raphael cocked his head. "You have fresh fruit? And you haven't been off the property in how long?"

"I grow my own."

His chiseled jaw dropped. "In autumn?" Raphael paced to the living room and opened the screen door. Emily felt a dim amusement.

"The garden is hidden behind a rock wall, to keep out the animals," she called out.

When he returned, he gave her a long, thoughtful look. "Melons, vegetables, pears, peaches, even lemons, and this climate isn't suited for growing citrus. How, Emily?"

She shrugged. "I've always had an affinity for growing things. It's natural for me."

"But not for most Draicon." He leaned against the wall, folding his arms across his broad chest. Muscles in his biceps bulged. Emily swallowed hard, remembering the feel of his powerful body atop hers, the tensile strength in him, the odd friction caused by the bulge at his crotch. The odd throbbing began again between her legs. She turned her back on him, hunted through a cabinet.

"I also have toaster pastries."

"What kind?"

Emily opened a cabinet door and fished out a box. Raphael read the label, quirking a dark brow. "Brown sugar. You have a sweet tooth."

He pulled two pastries from the foil wrapping and placed them into the toaster. While he waited, he rummaged through her refrigerator. Emily leaned against the wall, watching in bemusement.

"Are you looking for something in particular?"

He closed the door. "No fresh meat, no frozen, either. What the hell have you been surviving on these past few months? Certainly not melons and toaster pastries."

"I get along fine," she shot back. "Is it your job to criticize my choice of cuisine? What are you, a wolf epicure?"

"It's my job to ensure you're eating right."

"So I'll be nice and healthy when you execute me?"

The toaster popped up the pastries. Raphael took them and hunted through her cabinet. He removed two china plates and placed a pastry on each one. She fetched two coffee cups and filled them from the coffeemaker.

He carried the plates to the table and put one before each seat. He pulled out a chair for her, waiting for her to sit as she set down the mugs.

Emily sat, staring at the pastry. She disliked these, which was one reason why they still sat in her cabinet. But she broke off a piece and forced herself to slowly chew.

For such a large male, he ate slowly in small bites. When he finished, he wiped his mouth with a paper napkin and sipped his coffee.

"What do you eat, Em?"

She liked the informal nickname. "Whatever I can. Once a week, Urien sends someone to put frozen meat into the storehouse big freezer. It's in the shed across the drive, where they store winter equipment. I suppose Urien still feels the need to provide for me, but he doesn't want to risk coming into direct contact and being contaminated. I checked a couple of days ago, but he forgot to stock the freezer."

"So you've subsisted on whatever you had. He's neglecting his duty to you. He should be caring for you, as a leader cares for all in his pack." Disapproval rang in his deep voice.

No one had cared for her, not in months. She had functioned fine on her own. Better than to suffer the disdain and averted gazes of what once was her family.

A lump clogged her throat. She swallowed a small sip of coffee past it, keeping her thoughts guarded. "Do you come from a large family?"

"Very large. We all take care of each other and have from the time we were *jeune,* young." Raphael studied his empty plate. "I was brought up in a large house in the bayou, with four brothers. I was the youngest, until we adopted Damian. He's only eighty, twenty-five years younger than me."

"Adopted? You took in a Draicon not of your own blood?"

His gaze was even. "When he was barely changed, his family was killed in a Morph attack, and we found him hiding in the woods. Damian is a pureblood, of French descent."

"But you're mixed blood. Did he have trouble adjusting?"

Raphael regarded her with his intense dark eyes. "No, he was quite happy to lower his standards and live among the lower class of Draicon."

Emily sensed she'd insulted him. She tilted her head at him and softened her gaze. "I didn't mean it in a bad way. I've never met anyone like you. What is your family like?"

"My people have an honored, proud lineage. We're survivors who have fought off all Morph attacks and lost none of our pack to the dark side."

Curiosity stole over her. Her pack embraced things of the earth and shunned many things that stole away their attention from it. They used electricity and other utilities grudgingly, and Urien had a telephone installed after her father had brought her home as a baby. They clung to traditions many Draicon ignored.

And they had never been attacked by Morphs, not in years. *Maybe we haven't been truly tested,* she thought in a flash of insight.

"What about your other brothers? Are they like you, warriors? Do you like the same things?"

A reluctant smile touched his mouth. "Damian's

closest to me, but he's seldom around. Gabe and I like playing electronic games. I usually beat him."

At her tiny frown, he explained. Emily shook her head. "Games where you play warriors on a computer? I saw a computer when my father took me to the library. Father told me that I should know everything of the human world as well as of the Draicon, so I would better appreciate the gifts I'd been given." She stretched out her hands and felt the familiar stab of sorrow. "Except I don't call this a gift."

"Maybe there is a purpose for it," he suggested.

"Just as there is a purpose in you being our Kallan, being sent to execute Draicon who deserve such punishment?" she challenged. "What if you decided to go against your duty?"

Stone-cold eyes met hers. "Then my brother Gabriel would die instead. The contract I signed with Urien stipulates it."

He pushed back his chair, standing to his full height over six feet. He seemed to suck up all the space in her tiny kitchen. "If you're finished eating, I suggest we proceed with your *trasna* lessons."

Panic welled up inside her. "I have to shower and get dressed."

"Meet me outside on the path when you're done."

"I don't want, or need, any lessons."

He sighed. "Emily, I will discharge my duty to you. It doesn't mean I'm giving up hope that your life will be spared."

"Then don't waste my time with lessons about dying when I need to find a way to prevent my death."

He made a low sound in his throat. "Then let me help you."

"You can't help me. Look what happened last night. That was the last sprig of mistletoe."

Raphael looked away, his jaw tensing. "We'll find another way. But first, lessons, and tomorrow, I'll take you to town to a nice restaurant. I can sense the hunger in you."

This Draicon mate of hers perplexed her and surprised her. She remembered the last time she'd gone into town. Some women, young and pretty, had pointed at her and snickered. Emily hated it. She stared down at her lap and the shapeless dress.

For once she wished she looked pretty.

"I don't like going into town."

He gave her a long, thoughtful look. "You will with me. You'll have fun."

"But won't people stare at us?"

His jaw went taut. "I never cared much for the opinions of others. Let them stare. We need to start on your lessons, and most find it difficult to concentrate when hungry. You're starved."

But not so much for food, she thought sadly as he turned and left the room. The back door slammed behind him.

The sounds of the shower made Raphael clench his jaw as he stocked Emily's refrigerator with the meat from his own. He closed the door, imagining her beneath the spray, her luminous face upturned to the water. Droplets glistening on her naked, lush body, beading on taut nipples, cascading with a river of soap bubbles down to her navel. Desire clenched him in an iron fist.

Instinct screamed for him to strip, enter the bathroom and step into the shower with her. Draw his arms around her waist and pull her soft body against his hardness. Palm her breasts and rub his thumbs gently over the hardening nipples, then slide the soap down her midsection, down to the fiery thatch of curls, cleansing her, arousing and preparing her for his entry.

Instead, he headed for her porch, sitting on her porch rocker as he listened to soothing Cajun tunes on his iPod. Raphael closed his eyes. When he traveled, he always brought his culture with him to avoid homesickness. The music kept him close to his roots, no matter how difficult the assignment.

This assignment proved the most difficult of all. Why wouldn't Emily work with him?

He scented her even before she stepped out onto the porch. "What is that thing?"

Raphael opened his eyes and saw her pointing at his iPod. "My iPod. It stores and plays music."

"In that tiny box?" She sounded incredulous, curiosity flared on her lovely face. "May I?"

Raphael slipped the wireless headphones over her head. The brief contact was sizzling and heat flared between them. He watched, transfixed by the charming smile stealing over her face.

"It's so different," she marveled. "Very lively and upbeat. And the language—what is it?"

"Cajun French." He leaned against the porch rail, guarding his thoughts, waiting for her to pass judgment. But she seemed absorbed in the music, even tapping her bare left foot a little.

"It's your pack's language. It sounds as musical as the songs."

His guard slipped down slightly. "It's not pure as the

French Damian was taught, but it has its own slang and words. Some of the words are a mixture, and some stand on their own."

She removed the headphones and put them aside. "Would you teach me? I'd like to learn."

Surprised, he considered her. Her rosebud mouth was lush, begging to be kissed. His gaze traveled down the length of the shapeless dress. Raphael envisioned her naked on his bed, pale flesh gleaming, the red curls between her legs moist with arousal. Her slim legs draped about his hips as he plunged into her sweet feminine flesh over and over. *"Tu veux aller au coucher avec moi à soir?"*

Her sweet smile heated his blood. "That sounds lovely."

Raphael drew in a ragged breath. Yes, he would like her in his bed tonight. But he had to take it slow. "Later. Let's start with your other lessons."

As they sat cross-legged on the soft grass outside her cottage, Emily appeared distracted. Raphael realized the challenge facing him. She hadn't shifted into a wolf in more than a year. She feared contact with humans. She had lived isolated on the farmhouse, shunned by her pack and surviving on her own for a year.

How could he teach Emily to prepare for death when he was too interested in teaching her how to live? His own emotions were in turmoil. How could he be emotionless and close to her? The allure of her filled his body with hot longing. He was experiencing all the natural desires a male Draicon felt upon finding his mate.

Most draicarons didn't also face killing their mates.

Setting his hands on his knees, he breathed deep. "Part of your preparation is attuning yourself to the deeper senses and separating yourself from this world."

"I don't want to separate myself from this earth. It's part of me."

"Emily, work with me," he insisted. "You're not accomplishing anything this way."

Her large green eyes studied him. "You're the Kallan, yet you are of this world with your machines that play music, and your contemporary ways. How can you teach me about the spiritual plane, the Other Realm, when you know nothing about the earth?"

He spread out his hands. "My people know equally of the earth and its secrets, only we live in a different environment. I know every inch of my world, my bayou. It's my life."

How could he break through to her? Raphael jammed a hand through his long, dark hair. Sudden insight filled him. He went to the gnarled trunk of a maple tree that had stubbornly refused to turn colors and beckoned to her. As she joined him, he touched the bark.

"Watch. If I were not in tune with the earth, would I have the power to do this?"

Her eyes widened as he blew gently on the bark and iridescent sparks traveled up the mighty trunk to the limbs. The green leaves changed to rich crimson. A small gasp fled Emily.

One leaf gently fluttered to the ground. He picked it up, cradled it in his palm. "The cycle of life in the earth exists for a reason. The tree needs her rest in the winter, to regain the energy in spring and renew herself."

Raphael touched the leaf with a single finger, directing a blast of energy at it. It crumbled into dust in his hand. He blew at the dust, sending it scattering into the wind.

"The decaying leaves feed the earth and provide a

rich compost," he added, watching her face. "It's necessary to life."

"But life is not always boring and predictable. What if one tree resisted change?" She touched the bark. "I hate saying goodbye and was happy to see it remain green and filled with life. I always loved spring." Her voice dropped. "I hate death."

His heart turned over at the quiet despair in her voice. "Life is a journey, and death is only part of the journey. As Draicon, we were never meant to remain here, but came here to learn of the earth and its world, Emily."

"My journey is ending. I don't want it to end." She flung her arms out. "I feel as if I have more to give, more to live for than being a sacrifice for my people. I want to celebrate each moment, not look at it as if I were the tree, resigned to the approaching winter, the darkness and the icy cold."

Raphael wanted to seize her gloved hands, pull her to him. He knew he must tread cautiously this first time she was so open. "We both can find a way, Em. I'm on your side. I am your draicaron." He went to her, drawn by her delicate beauty, the rose-gold of her hair and the translucence of her fine skin.

"I want to help you, but you must stop running from me. Work with me. Trust me," he said softly. "I want to help you find the spring again, and stay there."

"Even if you are the Kallan? The dark winter?" Her voice was sad.

"Not always. Let me be your spring."

Her breathing deepened as she touched her hair. "What about summer? With all its heat, the burning sun bringing life to the earth, making it grow and flourish.

The hot, hot summer. Is there heat inside you enough to chase away the dark winter and warm me?"

His breath caught at the husky teasing in her melodious voice.

"Yes," he murmured. "I can warm you. Enough to chase away all the coldness and keep you warm in my arms. Come here, and let me show you."

The deep command in his voice compelled her to turn. Emily started toward him in a sultry walk she'd never before displayed. The walk of a female enticing her mate.

Raphael eyed her with hunger, thinking about lying with her as his body demanded. Pinning her down with his weight, making her feel the same passion he did and coaxing a sigh of surrender from her lovely throat. He felt his blood heat as his gaze caressed the slender column of her throat. He would nuzzle her with tiny kisses, and then nip her, marking her as his own so no other male Draicon would dare draw near her and would know she was his.

Gazing upward, he caught her looking at him. Her rosy lips were parted, a delicate flush tinted her face. Her pupils widened. He caught the musky scent of her arousal.

Raphael stepped closer, his breathing hard and fast. His cock hardened as he studied the way her gaze locked with his, the intense yearning of her expression.

She shuffled forward, and then back, a shy dance. He knew this dance of the female, her natural caution warring with intense passion. Shyness with eager anticipation.

He advanced, his body tensing with aggressive need to dominate and claim. Raphael forced himself to move slowly. Must not scare her. All else was forgotten, but this driving sexual need for her. Emily did not retreat. She remained motionless, her hands in their ugly mustard-yellow casing of gloves now shoved behind her back.

He drew close enough to see a slight sprinkling of ginger freckles on her delicate, upturned nose. Close enough to count the light gold lashes feathering her large eyes, see the swirls of green in the irises shift to blue and then deep violet.

Raphael blinked. *Her eyes changed color?*

And then she parted her lips and lifted her face to him, like a daisy eager for the sun's caressing rays, and he forgot about everything but fusing his mouth to hers.

His hand gently caressed her soft cheek. Raphael cupped her face and kissed her, feeling the electric shock between them as their lips touched. Emily sighed into his mouth and closed her eyes. He did as well, tasting her, his blood roaring through his veins, his body humming like a live current. She was of the earth and nature, pure as a crystal stream, and he ached to dive into her, plunder her sweet, innocent depths with his hardened body, let her know a male's driving passion while awakening her own.

When she did not pull away, he deepened the kiss, coaxing a response with increasing plunges of his tongue, teaching her by advancing and retreating, as if they dueled. Emily followed his lead, the rapid sounds of her breaths and the small sighs of pleasure urging him to take it to the next level.

He ran a hand down her side, ignoring the coarse dress, feeling for the lush body trapped by ugly brown fabric. Her waist was tiny, her hips flared. Raphael's heart pounded harder as he traced a line back to her breasts.

He cupped one in his hand, gently, so as not to alarm

her. She made a small, startled sound, and he soothed her by murmuring into her mouth. Beneath the tender caress of his palm, her breast was full, heavy as he'd imagined. Raphael ran a thumb over the cresting peak and she moaned into his mouth. The scent of her slammed into him like a lightning bolt.

He could take her. She was growing ready and he was more than ready.

Thoughts drifted into his head from her. He felt like a vibrating tuning fork, ready to receive any of what she wanted to send. Raphael opened all his senses to her, excluding everything else. Sensations flooded his mind from Emily. The sharp, painful arousal and aching need, the confusion and anticipation threaded with a tiny fear of the unknown.

Will you be gentle with me, as you promised?

Yes, he murmured back telepathically. *Oh, yes, chere.*

His thumb began making small circles over her pearling nipple while he leisurely flicked his tongue into her mouth. Emily whimpered and pressed her body against him. Her hips naturally came into contact with his as she parted her legs and nestled against him, as if trying to seek relief for the sharp, flowering ache. Inwardly he smiled, knowing what she wanted.

He was quite adept at providing it. When he skimmed down her body, resting a palm on her belly, she quivered. Raphael brought his hand close to the juncture between her parted thighs. When he started to delve between them, she jerked away with a cry.

Her wide violet gaze flashed confusion. He read her shyness, hesitation, the bloom of pleasure twining with shock at his daring intimacy.

Emily was a true innocent, he thought ruefully. He had to show her he'd bring her pleasure, but perhaps this was too much.

You don't have enough time to woo her as you'd like.

Raphael made a soothing noise, sought her mouth again as he cupped her cheek. She resumed kissing him as he kept his hands on her face. She relaxed into the kiss and opened to him once more.

This time, he thrust into her thoughts. Raphael sent her images, slow, gentle strokes between her legs, relieving the intensifying ache there, parting her feminine softness with his fingers and sliding between her growing wetness. The scent of her arousal intensified and she moaned into his mouth, but he did not break the kiss. His cock grew painfully hard, but he persisted.

Her pleasure, not his.

In her mind, he touched her where his hands did not. He stroked back and forth, culling moisture from her body. She was wet for him, dripping, but it was not enough. Not yet. He touched the center of her he knew would bring the most pleasure, whispering soft encouragement not to fear him, to relax and let go. Raphael felt her body grow taut as an unwavering oak as the sweet tension built and built….

In her mind, he slipped one long finger deep inside her channel and flicked a thumb over her pearling center. "Em, now," he commanded.

She screamed into his mouth and broke contact, her head falling back on her neck like a drooping flower. Her petite body trembled with the force of her orgasm.

Her first, he thought proudly.

When she opened her eyes with a dazed look of

languid pleasure, he saw a reflection of the male triumph in his own eyes. Raphael chuckled and gently kissed her cheek.

"Did you enjoy it, *chere?*" he whispered into her ear. "I can do much, much more. Let me touch you. My hands can bring you much pleasure."

Too late. *Hands.* Dazed pleasure fled her eyes, replaced with grieving awareness. Emily yanked away from him, brought her hands up as if to keep him at arm's length.

"I can't touch you," she said brokenly. "Never. How can I ever be a mate to you when I cannot touch you to bring you pleasure in return?"

The anguish in her voice echoed the same in his heart as she separated from him and walked toward her cabin.

Chapter 7

The next day, Emily stood before her full-length mirror. Dismay filled her as she touched the glass, studying the ankle-length dun dress. Buttoned to the throat, the shapeless garment covered nearly every part of her body.

It was also as ugly as burlap.

She never thought she could be attractive to a male, and yet Raphael was clearly attracted to her. It was more than simply chemistry, but a connection on a deeper, more intimate level.

Her cheeks had been flushed with heat, her body had felt a shock of pleasure when he'd done those things to her. Remembering his long, slow strokes between her legs filled her with sudden warmth and yearning.

Her eyes turned violet again.

Touching the glass, she marveled. They had never

turned that color before. No one had ever made her feel the way Raphael had.

She longed to touch him.

She could not.

Emily tugged at the dress, fervently wishing she could discard traditional dress for something exciting. Clothing that made her feel pretty for him. Maybe those jeans, as he called them. The denim. Or even trousers made from leather.

Remembering how the leather trousers had molded to his powerful limbs and the firm curves of his muscled bottom, her cheeks flushed further. It was wrong, this attraction she felt. She couldn't allow herself to experience the natural desire all draicaras felt for their mates. Falling for him would distract her from the important task ahead—saving her life.

He said he wanted to help. But she didn't dare trust him. She was all alone in this.

He was so different, daring and walked his own path. Not part of a pack.

Emily couldn't see how their worlds could mesh, even if circumstances were different. Raphael knew nothing of the old traditions, seemed to disdain them. She was too mired in the ancient ways.

Yet, maybe she could at least change her dress. Adorn her slim ankle with a thin gold bracelet.

She swirled around, trying to imagine herself in a pretty dress with tiny sprigs of violets.

Outside, she heard the roar of the beast named Harley. Emily flushed again and ran down the steps, her heart pounding with excitement. Harley was purring as Raphael sat on the wide seat, his long legs encased in leather. Her admiring gaze swept over his muscled thighs.

He swung a leg over the saddle and stood. "Ready?"

Breath caught in her throat. He was so handsome and striking, his eyes as dark as the black night, the wide, mobile mouth set with determination. Black leather gloves covered his hands. Dressed in his black leather pants, black T-shirt and jacket, he looked imposing. Dark. Powerful. A Draicon impervious to all, the most dangerous of all their race.

She grabbed a fistful of skirt, feeling awkward and ugly in comparison. How could she accompany him, in all his dark beauty, into public? They stared—the humans always stared when she went into town. Sometimes they laughed.

"We can take one of the pack's trucks. They would allow you to borrow it, because you are the Kallan," she offered.

He turned a key and Harley stopped growling. "My bike will do us fine. It's safe and you can ride behind me. But that dress has to go. Got any slacks?"

Misery coiled in her stomach. The demarcation between her world of ancient tradition and his was an unbreachable chasm. He easily slipped between the Draicon world and the human world. She stood out like a weed among a field of beautiful flowers.

"I've changed my mind. You go. I'll stay here. I don't want to go shopping for new clothing," she mumbled.

She headed for the refuge of her trees. In his deep voice, Raphael called for her to stop.

"I'm tired of you running from me, Em."

She ignored the warning. He was powerful, but she was fast.

Something snagged her bare ankle, snaked around it, stopping her short. Bemused, she glanced down. Her eyes widened.

One of the vines wrapped around the oak had slithered down the trunk and coiled around her ankle like a playful cat. It held her fast.

She whirled and saw Raphael regarding her in silence. It was him doing this. She quivered in the face of so much power to control things of the earth.

Listen to me, Em. You're not running anymore. You can't escape this. Us. What's happening. Why won't you let me help you?

She gave her foot a firm tug, but another vine wrapped around her other ankle. Two more snaked out and caught fast her hands. Like gently reeling in a caught fish, they tugged her backward, until she was held fast against the tree trunk, her arms and legs imprisoned.

Inwardly she marveled. What power this Kallan had. Such dark power that she'd never before seen.

He didn't know she could easily loosen the vines, spring free and dash away. Yet the intense look on his face as he walked toward her kept her captive.

Bracing his arms on either side of her, he leaned forward until his warm breath feathered over her cheeks. His dark gaze was unfathomable.

"Yes, I have more power than you can imagine. I'm not like the other Kallans. I'm darker, but I still can influence things of the earth. So for once you will stay put and listen to what I have to say. I know you want to go shopping, so that's what we're doing. But you have to start opening up to me. Because if you don't, your life will remain tied up like you are now. Stop eluding me as if I'm the enemy."

He stroked a finger over her cheek, making her shiver with yearning. "I want to help you, protect you, provide for you."

His mouth settled gently over hers. Her eyes fluttered closed.

"Now you don't have to fear touching me, little one," he whispered into her mouth. "Let me touch you instead."

Emily felt his tongue sweep over her lips and opened to him, eager for more of his delicious kisses. He cupped her face as she tasted him, and her body ached sharply. His muscled body was firm against hers. Raphael shifted his weight, letting her feel the hardness between his legs. Intensity spiked as he cupped her breast, stroking her hardening nipple. She writhed, held fast by the vines, panting for more as he stepped back.

The burning intensity in his eyes seared her. His gaze dropped to the ugly dress. "This sackcloth has got to go," he muttered.

Fabric parted beneath his quick, nimble fingers as he unfastened the buttons. The dress gaped open. Erotic pleasure seized her as the cool air washed over her exposed, naked skin. Raphael studied the heaving covering of her sturdy underwire bra, a question in his eyes. Emily answered it telepathically. *Take it off.*

He unhooked the front fastening and slowly slid off the cups. He cupped her breasts and stroked his thumbs over her nipples. She felt them ache and harden.

He bent his head and took one into his mouth, tasting her. The wet heat of his mouth felt electric as he swirled his tongue over her nipple, then suckled gently. Emily whimpered and thrust her hips forward, not knowing what she wanted, the burning tension building between her legs once more. Raphael released her and gently placed his hand over her pumping midsection.

"Easy," he soothed. "Later, *chere.*"

He stepped back, waved his hands and the vines released her. Emily fastened together her dress, gulped down a breath, gratified to see him breathing as heavily as she was.

He hadn't been unaffected. After a minute he seemed to get himself under control. Raphael studied her clothing. "If you don't have anything else, you can wear one of my shirts."

Emily gave him a sultry look. "I like the way you convince me to change my clothing, but I think you'd better not do this in a dressing room."

He threw his head back. His deep, rich laughter caused a funny flutter in her stomach.

Minutes later, her breathing under control, her feelings awash in confusion, she met him outside, dressed in the baggy trousers her aunt Helen sometimes wore to garden. They were patched and frayed but all she had. The shirt Raphael gave her was huge, but it felt warm and comforting. It smelled deliciously of him—his male scent and spices. She kept stroking the gray cotton, loving the feel of it.

She felt warm for the first time in days, encased by his comforting scent. Warmth fled when she stood before his motorcycle, staring uneasily at Harley.

Raphael gave her an appreciative smile. "I like you in my shirt. It's as if you're wrapped in me."

She hung back. All the familiar in her world was behind her. The trees, grass, the earth. Raphael's riding machine was foreign, a large, quivering beast that belched noise and intruded on the serenity of pack lands.

A rill of fear rippled through her. If she rode with him and took this risk, it meant leaving her world behind and trusting herself to this dark stranger who knew nothing of it.

"Em?" Raphael held out his hand. "I promise, I'll take good care of you and I won't let you go."

"I don't know. I've never done this." She walked around Harley, studying the shiny metal, the numerous gadgets. "How does it work?"

Approval radiated from him. He pointed out the midsection. "Twin B engine, makes the ride smooth and even as the bayou on a humid day. No vibrations." He flicked his fingers at the front. "Windshield, headlights. I used to have a smaller bike, without a windshield, but got tired of eating bugs on the highway when I had to travel across country."

Raphael bent over, leather stretching smoothly over his taut bottom, and patted the box on the bike's side. "Saddlebags, with chrome studs, where I store my gear. Good for all the long-distance trips I make."

Emily hitched in a breath. "I like the view," she murmured, staring at his behind.

He squatted and flipped down a rubber-coated piece of metal. "These are for whoever rides with me. Footpads so you can rest your feet. Nicer than pegs. The ladies appreciate the extra comfort."

She rested a hand on the leather seat, a little stab of emotion arrowing through her as she thought of women in back of him, their hands clinging to him. "Have you ridden with many women?"

He gave her a burning look. "Yes, in the past," he replied evenly. "But I'd rather have you, only you, from now on."

A warm tingling filled her. She sensed a deeper intent behind his words but didn't question it. Raphael held out his hand. "C'mon, *chere.*"

Taking a step toward him was a step out in trust. She took a deep breath. What did she have to lose? She'd never taken risks before. It was about time to see what the rest of the world had to offer.

Emily placed her gloved hand in his. A smile of pleasure touched his mouth, and he helped her onto the bike. She put on the helmet he gave her, the hard shell feeling as if she'd stuck her head into a small cave. He chuckled and adjusted it so it didn't swim over her smaller head, flipped down the face shield. Raphael settled in front of her, his broad back a solid wall of muscle covered in black leather.

"Put your arms around me and just hold on. You can lean against the backrest if you like."

Emily's heart raced.

"It's okay, Em. I'm immortal. Your touch can't hurt me. Even without your gloves."

Slowly she slid her arms around his lean waist and leaned into him. A smell of leather and his delicious, spicy scent flooded her senses. Pleasure filled her, as she snuggled closer, opening her thighs to couch his. He tensed, muttered something in his native Cajun and turned the key. The monster roared to life as she settled her feet on the footpads.

Raphael turned. He cupped her chin with one gloved hand.

"Remember, I'll take care of you. If you get scared or need something, just tap me on the shoulder."

Why? All I need to do is talk to you like this. She mentally reached out to him. Another smile touched his mouth.

Excellent.

Arm muscles tensed as she clung to him. Emily squeezed her eyes shut as he roared down the drive. When they reached the main road, she opened her eyes. The wide leather seat beneath her was comfortable as promised. Wind gushed past her in a rush. Fresh air, the dank scent of leaves and freshly mowed fields filled her nostrils. The feeling was exhilarating and liberating, but as he bent over the bike and turned right, alarm filled her.

This isn't the right way to town. Where are we going? How long will it take to arrive? What will we do when we get there?

Shh, he crooned into her mind. *So many questions. Just relax and let go, enjoy the journey.*

But what if we run into trouble? It's dangerous here in the human world. Anything can happen.

Little one, let yourself live for the moment. It's part of life's adventure, to forge ahead without a plan. Just close your eyes and feel.

Emotion clogged her throat. She felt too stiff and fearful of the unknown. But she closed her eyes and tried. Emily listened to the gush of wind racing past, smelled the fresh scent of water nearby. She tried to relax and imagined they were without boundaries or restrictions.

His broad back felt like a sold, sheltering wall. Wariness faded. Raphael was her draicaron, and she had no choice on this trip but to trust him. He controlled the growling beast they rode, he was in charge.

Slowly, she released her fears as if they were dandelions floating in the wind. A new awareness replaced the fear. *I'm free. It feels like flying,* she marveled.

That's why I love bikes. Nothing else will do. I relish my freedom, to be able to go anywhere I wish.

Emily tentatively released her grip on him. Confidence filled her as she spread her arms wide, like eagle's wings. Laughter spilled from her.

I'm flying!

She heard his laughter echo in her mind. *Want to go faster?*

Oh, yes.

Hold on to me, then.

She squeezed him tight. Wind whipped past them. Pleasure filled her. Riding like this, nothing but open space before them, she understood why Raphael chose this way to travel. When another motorcycle passed them in the opposite direction, Raphael dropped down his hand in greeting. The other biker did the same.

After a while, they reached the town. He guided them into a shopping center parking lot, found a space and stopped the bike and kicked down the metal stand.

Swinging off the saddle, he held out his hand. Emily hopped off, pulled free from the helmet. Her gaze widened at the humans milling about, chattering as they went in and out of the shopping mall.

It was silly to be afraid of them. Three pretty, young girls drew closer. They were dressed in short skirts that kicked above the knee and shirts that clung to their breasts and midsections. Their faces brightened as they gazed at Raphael.

Something twisted in Emily's guts.

The girls looked at her with doubt. They pointedly stared at her baggy shirt, the faded, patched trousers, and laughed. The tallest, a blonde, said something in a haughty tone.

Emily tapped Raphael on the shoulder. *What is a fugly trailer trash?*

A scowl flashed over his face as he glanced at the trio. Raphael slid an arm about her waist. *Never mind what they said. You're beautiful as you are.*

I wish I could wear their clothing. I'm tired of feeling different.

His dark gaze grew thoughtful, but he merely spoke into her mind, *Come with me. I'll fulfill your wish.* Deliberately, he turned his back on the goggling girls, cupped Emily's face and kissed her. It was a whisper-soft brush of his mouth, but she trembled at the sizzling contact between them. Raphael gave her a smile filled with sensual promise, then clasped her gloved hand.

I don't know their language. I can't communicate in this world.

I'll teach you, chere. Inside, while we're shopping.

Emily studied the girls with a sad look. *They want you. They're trying to get you to notice them.*

He squeezed her hand. *Who? All I see is you. You're the only one for me.*

A small smile curved her mouth. She glanced at the blonde, who pouted at Raphael, one hand on her hip. *I don't know why the tallest one is interested in you. She is carrying a child.*

His eyebrows shot up as he glanced at the girl. *Seriously? She's not showing. How can you tell?*

Emily shrugged. *Her scent. I can detect females who are bearing new life.*

"Interesting," he murmured aloud, sliding a hand around her nape. Raphael stroked her skin, sending a shiver of pleasure down her spine. "You, Emily Burke, fascinate me. Let's go shopping."

For the first time in weeks, she felt uplifted. Emily went with him, sweeping past the staring girls.

Emily emerged from the dressing room and pivoted.

Raphael couldn't think. Breathe. Damn she had been lovely before, with an ethereal, fairylike quality, but this clothing turned her into a sexy siren. The jeans, her choice, hugged every inch of her limbs, molded to her rounded bottom, accenting her curves. The white scoop-necked shirt was equally revealing, clinging to her generous breasts and revealing what had been previously hidden.

She was gorgeous. A hot number, as Gabe would say.

He couldn't think of Gabe now, the fact his brother put his life at risk for this transition. Male instincts roared to the surface. He wanted to take Emily by her gloved hands back to the dressing room, tug the new jeans past her hips, spread her legs wide and thrust deep inside her.

Take her standing up against the wall, watching her pretty face flush with arousal. Feel her wet heat surround his surging cock, hear her tiny cries of excitement echo in his ears as he made her climax.

She was a virgin, he sternly reminded himself. Her

first time shouldn't be rough and impassioned. He would take extra care with her and be gentle and slowly teach her to respond to her natural desires.

Raphael complimented her look, admiring the flare of color tinting her cheeks as she murmured thanks. He fingered a stray curl escaping the tight knot of her hair and frowned at the rich golden red mass she kept bound. "What about your hair?"

"It's fine as it is."

A note of defensiveness hovered in the words. Later. Not here in public, but the first time their bodies were joined, he would see her hair released in a waterfall of curls spread on his pillow. For his eyes, and his alone.

Heat flooded his body at the thought of her drowsing in the lassitude of sexual satisfaction.

Oh, yes, chere. You will. With a little mental push, he sent her the image.

Emily's eyes widened and darkened. He chuckled and ordered the sales clerk to assist her in cutting off the tags so she could wear the purchases. He gathered up the two dresses Emily wanted as well.

Outside, Emily shivered, so Raphael shrugged out of his leather jacket and draped it over her shoulders. She thanked him as she slipped into the coat, the sleeves draping past her gloved hands. She looked adorable. He wanted to keep her warm in other ways, entering her in the dark night, covering her body with his so she'd never shiver again with anything but pleasure.

She nibbled on her luscious lower lip as they walked back to his Harley. "So, you prefer these trousers, the jeans? Why did you wear the leather pants when you first arrived?"

"To show off my package." He winked at her.

"What is a package?"

"Something I'll teach you about later," Raphael murmured, his blood heating anew.

Reining in his control, he helped her back on the Harley. They rode through town, toward a restaurant he liked. After parking in a hard-to-find empty space, he escorted her toward an Alpine-shaped building.

"You'll like this place. It has great steak. Cooked just like we want. Raw."

He was charmed at the shy smile she gave him.

Several motorcycles were parked outside the restaurant. Raphael went still, recognizing the scent. Draicon. Outside the Burke pack, he hadn't seen another since his arrival. These were bikers, and he felt instant camaraderie. Male possessiveness swept over him as he glanced at Emily.

"Stick close to me," he said quietly, holding her elbow.

Sitting at the bar inside, five tough-looking males wearing leather nursed longneck bottles of beer. They whirled about on their stools as he and Emily entered. The males slid off, swaggered forward. One eyed Emily with a little more than polite interest, his gaze centering on her breasts.

Raphael uttered a warning growl deep in his throat and tightened his grip on his mate. The male biker edged back and looked elsewhere.

The shortest of the five, a burly Draicon whose head was covered in a blue bandana, stepped forward. "Haven't seen our kind about in a long while. Only human bikers." He grinned, showing even white teeth. "How's it going, dude?"

Returning the other's knuckle salute, Raphael relaxed, feeling a pull of kinship.

"Kevin, Upstate New York. You are?" the leader asked.

He introduced Emily by first name only and gave his full name. The other males stepped back, staring at his white lock of hair, then him, then dropping their gazes, their stances suddenly respectful. He felt the previous friendliness flee, replaced by thick unease. They knew who he was. Suddenly he felt very old and weary.

It was always like this. Always on the road alone, others fearing him too much to let down their guard. How did you make friends with the one Draicon who could kill you without consequence?

Kevin spoke in a lowered tone. "You're the Kallan. Why are you here?"

"What are *you* doing here?" Raphael challenged.

The leader glanced at his companions. "Passing through, touring the park, that's all. This area has bad vibes for us. We've heard stories about what happens to Draicon who like to remain."

He felt Emily go still. "And?"

"They don't last long enough to write home about it." Kevin gave Emily the barest glance. "There's been rumors about Morphs. Hard to tell with all the wildlife, and the Morphs learned to cloak their scent, too. I'd hold tight to your female."

"I plan on it." Raphael swept them all with a searching look. "Have you seen anything?"

"Bear on a hiking path where we camped," spoke up the Draicon who had eyed Emily. "Just a bear, though. He showed us his teeth and we showed him ours. Ours were bigger."

The five chuckled and then fell silent, as if laughing before the Kallan broke unwritten protocol. Raphael inwardly sighed. Curiosity radiated from Emily, who stared at Kevin. "You like wearing leather pants. Is it to show off your package, too?"

He bristled as Kevin smiled at her. Testosterone filled the air as a challenging growl rumbled low in Raphael's throat. He'd never seen males back off so quickly.

Kevin nodded to Raphael. "Be careful of your female, Kallan. Around these parts, things aren't as they seem."

They returned to their beers, Raphael gazing thoughtfully after them. Reports of Morphs and vanishing Draicon. Suspicion flooded him. Morphs only inhabited territory where they could find likely food sources. Killing humans provided some energy, but the most powerful energy came from killing a Draicon and absorbing the energy of their dying terror.

He put the thought aside to examine later.

Upstairs, the restaurant boasted a hardwood floor, floor-to-ceiling paned windows and green painted walls. Staring upward at the hand-carved wood beams on the sloped ceiling, Emily bumped into an elderly woman. The woman glared, despite the apology Emily offered. Raphael protectively stepped between them, guiding her to a far corner booth, ignoring the woman's loud remarks about "criminal biker types who shouldn't be allowed inside decent places with decent folk."

"I didn't realize I was a criminal element," Emily whispered.

"The way you look makes me want to do something very illegal, right here and now." At her bewildered look, he added, "Starting with that lovely mouth of yours."

Her smile lifted his spirits.

The ponytailed waiter came over with a laconic stride. "Take your drink order?"

"Microbrewed beer?"

The waiter rattled off a selection. Raphael ordered two mugs. "We're thirsty," he said mildly, his words putting a hurry to the kid's steps.

"Sweet," Raphael murmured, gazing at Emily as she looked around with interest. At her inquiring look, he added, "You."

Emily blushed. His body stirred as he imagined the rosy flush tinting her entire body as she lay naked beneath him, the sultry look in her eyes turning them to...

He leaned forward, fascinated. "Your eyes are changing color just like before. They were green, now they're violet. No, more like amethyst."

She touched the corner of one eye with a gloved finger. "Yes, they do that."

Interesting. No Draicon he knew ever shifted eye color. Only one being he'd ever met could do that, and she was not Draicon. The thought slammed Raphael like a sledgehammer. He studied Emily carefully.

Impossible.

The waiter returned with their drinks. Raphael lifted his mug, drank deeply as she sipped, her eyes widening in apparent surprise.

"It's good," she said, drinking more.

"I'm trying to get you tipsy so I can take advantage of you and have my wicked way with you," he murmured, winking at her.

"Then I'd better drink more and faster," she shot back, smiling.

He laughed, delighted with her spirit. The pretty flush on her cheeks contrasted with her translucent skin. Raphael reluctantly studied the menu instead of Emily as the waiter returned.

"I'll have the filet mignon, very rare, with fries." He snapped the menu shut.

She smiled at the waiter. "I'll have the sirloin, medium rare, and potato salad."

As the waiter left, Emily glanced around curiously. "I only ate out in public a few times with my father," she explained. "Urien disapproves of mingling with humans."

"Well, it's about time you started breaking some rules." He leaned back, one arm draped over the booth's edge. "Why do you keep following a pack who has shunned you?"

Emily toyed with the paper napkin in her lap. "I suppose because I know nothing else. It feels comfortable."

"Did that dress you wore feel comfortable?"

She looked surprised. "Not really."

"Then, like the dress, you should discard the rules. If they don't fit you, stop being a slave to them."

"I'm not a slave to them." She narrowed her eyes.

"If you're not, why not let down your hair," he challenged.

She stared down at her lap.

"Besides, you've already broken at least one rule. Doesn't your pack forbid eating anything but natural food? I wouldn't call a toaster pastry natural food."

A half smile touched her full mouth. "That was Helen. She encouraged me to buy them. I wanted them because they looked sweet, and I adore sweetness."

He removed his arm and leaned closer. "So do I. There is something to be said for sweetness."

He could show her exactly how sweet. Raphael half closed his eyes and reached out to her. He sent her an image of exactly what he wanted to do to her. A furious flush tinted her cheeks as her lips parted. Raphael was charmed as she glanced shyly away, toying with a stray tendril of her hair.

He felt pressed to push her harder and faster than he'd like because they had little time.

Emily's gaze met his, the spark of arousal flaring in her amethyst eyes. "You never follow the pack, do you? You're very unconventional."

"I can't follow the pack," he said quietly.

How could he explain to her that his life was filled with power, but with power came loneliness? Others distanced themselves from him. Even his family, those he was closest to, regarded him with awe. He knew his father, the Alpha, had been relieved when he struck off on his own. It was one type of power play to discipline his brothers into obedience necessary for the pack.

But how did you force a Draicon who could take your life, without consequence, into submission?

"You're a loner," she said suddenly.

Raphael nodded.

"I guess I am, too. But I don't want to be."

Amethyst faded from her eyes, replaced by gray, as if the irises were dark storm clouds filled with rain-drops. Sorrow tinged her voice and his heart turned over. He knew the kind of loneliness that came from being different, having a power no one else understood and everyone feared.

"You're not alone," he pointed out. "I'm here with you."

The tremulous smile she gave him was like watching the sunrise steal over the bayou, filling the dark world with radiant light. Her eyes became green again, and he felt lost in their depths and the brilliance of her smile.

Her smile faded. "Do you think that's why Aibelle cursed me with the death touch, because you and I are mates? And now I am like you, someone who kills?"

Raphael felt as if someone sliced his heart with a hot knife. He physically ached. The waiter returned with their plates of food. He motioned toward her meal. "Eat. You need the protein," he curtly ordered.

"It isn't easy, what you do, Raphael. You must possess great strength."

Her soft voice eased the tremendous ache in his chest. As she dug into her steak with enthusiasm, eating fast but with dainty bites, he picked up his steak knife. "I don't enjoy it."

"But those you help cross who are elders, and ready, they are thankful. I've read the ancient texts. I know the importance of the Kallan. You're so different from them."

"Because I'm not a pureblood," he mocked.

Emily looked surprised. "No, you're not. I know what Urien has said in the past about Draicon he considers inferior. I heard him say, long ago, that you were not qualified because of your heritage."

The piece of steak lodged in his dry throat. He swallowed hard. "And you believe everything he says."

"No, I don't." She drained her beer and he stared in surprise. "If I did, I wouldn't be desperate to find what the texts say. I'd gladly accept his word instead, and go to my death willingly."

Emily thumped the mug down on the table.

"You're a fighter. You wouldn't," he insisted.

A small smile touched her lips. "I wouldn't."

She hiccupped, and he smothered a grin. She was tipsy, and emboldened. He liked her this way. Hell, he'd like her any way.

"Besides, Urien complained about your manner of dress, and now that I see you, I like it. But I would not like seeing the other, elderly Kallans in the leather trousers." Emily leaned forward.

"Because they were more suited to their robes and their learning?"

"No, because their butts weren't as nice and tight as yours."

Heat spread from the base of his neck to his cheeks. Emily laughed. *Merde,* was he blushing? He hadn't in years, not since that last time in Reno when a buxom, drunk brunette with the gleam in her eyes had grabbed his crotch in the casino lobby and commented...

Emily leaned forward with interest. "She said it was as big as a stallion's?"

Raphael felt his face heat further, and Emily burst into laughter. He laughed, too, glad to see the sparkle return to her eyes, and see her dig into the steak.

He'd barely cut into his steak when the darkness caught his attention.

It began as a gray smoke, filtering through the air and cutting the chatter of the diners as if slicing through their vocal chords. Only he could see it. Only he watched it thicken and turn to onyx.

Only he knew what it was, and suddenly he was no longer hungry. Raphael set down his fork, a lump gathering in his throat. He hated this, but it was part of the gift of being Kallan.

Part of his own lonely curse.

Emily stopped eating and watched him. "Raphael, what's wrong? Your eyes—you look so unbearably sad."

The gentleness of her soft voice chased away a little of the chill settling deep into his bones. He took a deep breath, wishing he could evade her answer.

She deserved the truth about what he was, who he was and what he could see.

"Someone's going to die," he said quietly. "I sense it. Here. Now."

He'd barely spoken when it happened.

The blue-haired woman who had berated Emily began gasping, then fell out of her seat onto the floor. Emily stared as other diners bolted out of their seats and raced to the woman's side. Dread churned in Raphael's stomach. He was forbidden to use his blood to aid both Draicon and human. The elderly woman faced the inevitable. Her heart had given up, and it was simply her time to go.

The darkness rose inside him, smothering him with weary knowledge. He felt death grasp the woman.

He could do nothing.

Emily looked up at him with a pleading look. His chest tightened as she whispered into his mind. *Help her, please, Raphael.*

"I can't," he told her thickly.

Emily slid out of the booth and pushed through the crowd to the woman. She knelt gracefully at the woman's side. Raphael snapped at the milling crowd to get back. They obeyed the steely command in his voice.

Alarm filled him as his draicara picked up the victim's pale hand in her gloved one.

Emily wanted to save a life that could not be saved.

He had to shield her from view. The bolt of energy directed at an empty table started a small fire under his control, but it caused enough of a distraction to take away people's attention from what Emily was doing.

What she was doing made him stagger back in shock.

Her focus unabated, she tugged off her gloves, grabbed the woman's steak knife and cut her hand. Emily held her bleeding palm over the woman's parted, blue lips and dripped four drops of blood into her mouth.

As the cut on Emily's hand healed, the woman began to cough and then gulped in several breaths. Emily pulled back on her glove, avoiding his gaze. She gently murmured comforting words to the woman.

Raphael lowered the blaze to a flame easily put out by the manager, who came bearing a small extinguisher. He helped the woman sit as his intense gaze pierced Emily's.

"Thank you, young lady," she said, looking up at Emily. "I don't know what to say. When I saw you earlier, I thought you were one of those criminal bikers who terrorize people, and here you are, saving me," the woman said, sounding contrite and confused.

"If someone dresses a little different, it doesn't mean we're bad. It was just a little scare, ma'am, and you can thank my girlfriend for knowing CPR," he murmured, using a deep, hypnotic tone to convince the woman that was exactly what Emily had done to her. "You'd better think about getting yourself checked over."

The woman started to thank him as well. She hiccupped. Her careworn face flashed surprise. "Oh, my. I feel…odd. Rather like I'm inebriated."

Emily hiccupped as well and looked abashed.

Oh, hell, he'd better make a hasty exit. Raphael stood, taking Emily firmly by the elbow. He threw several large bills on their table, more than enough for the bill and the tip, and escorted her downstairs and outside.

Not until they'd reached his bike did he stop. His draicara kept hiccupping, until he told her to hold her breath. When she did and finally stopped hiccupping, he gripped her shoulders lightly.

"Emily, how did you restore life to that woman?" he questioned in a low voice.

Color tinted her cheeks. She hastily avoided his gaze. Raphael reached over, cupped her chin, forcing it up. "Emily, answer me."

"I can't stand seeing anything suffer, an animal, or a person or even a cranky old woman," she said in a low voice. "I had to save her. Because she wasn't dead yet. And I knew I could."

He grasped both of her wrists gently, turned them over so her hands were palms up. "Your blood gives life."

"Four drops of my blood." Her full lower lip wobbled tremulously. "I was granted the gift of life with my first change into wolf. I can restore life with four drops of my blood, representing the four seasons. But when I turned twenty-one, Aibelle cursed me with the death touch. It was during a dream, when the goddess came to me and said the power of life and death rested within me. My hands now kill as well."

"Why didn't you tell me?"

He heard her audible swallow. "I was afraid you'd be

like my people, and judge me as being proud, seeing this as another reason I shouldn't live."

"Hey," he said softly. "I am not like them. I always investigate the facts. Did the goddess say why you were given the death touch?"

She wrinkled her brow as her gaze grew distant. "I couldn't remember. But my aunt Bridget said I was cursed because of my pride and haughtiness." Her voice dropped to a bare whisper. "It was after my first change into wolf that the pack started to avoid me, because I was different."

It made no sense. Emily was no more proud and haughty than he was a sheep.

He longed to clasp her hands to comfort her, but instead he softened his expression. "Why did Bridget say you were vain?"

She studied her gloved hands. "I don't know. I never abused the gift given to me. I tried doing the right thing, helping instead of hurting. I don't know what I did wrong. I've tried translating the ancient texts to see if she was right, and I can't."

She bit her quivering lip. Raphael's hackles rose. All his suspicions flooded to the surface. "So all you have to go on is the opinion of your aunt."

"She wouldn't lie to me. She was like my mother."

Mothers could turn on their young. His thoughts raced around like a dog chasing its tail. What if the pack wanted to get rid of Emily, and this provided a perfect excuse? Get him to do the deed, and they would be rid of a perceived threat.

With such a tremendous gift to restore life, the pack might not value her ability but fear it. Packs sometimes turned on one of their own who didn't conform, and a Draicon who displayed powers beyond their own could prove dangerous. Upset the balance.

He flashed back to when his own father told him to go live on his own. He was family, and would always be welcome, but he could no longer permanently live among them. It would prove too dangerous.

What if the Burkes tried the same with Emily, only they wanted her executed?

"Emily, did you ever use your gift of life to bring back one of our race?" he asked slowly.

Guilt shadowed her face. "Once. It was shortly after I turned fifteen. Usually the pack didn't let me go on a hunt because I had a tendency to be softhearted, but I pleaded, and Father insisted, so Urien allowed me. He told me to stay at the rear. We brought down a deer. Michael, my grandfather, he was elderly and not as quick. The buck gouged him in the belly. He was weak and lacked the energy to heal. Tradition forbids us from using modern medical intervention. If one of us gets injured and doesn't heal, we are supposed to let death claim us, as would be done in the wild. We thought we'd lose him, but I stole into his room and gave him my blood."

At his stare, she looked defensive. "He was in so much pain. I couldn't bear it, and Urien forbid us from giving him something that wasn't of the earth to ease his suffering. I only wanted to help. He kept screaming and moaning."

"He lived?"

"For a while. But after, Father told me Grandfather died a few days later." She raised her troubled gaze to his. "I always wondered, I think—Urien may have killed him because he wasn't supposed to live."

Alarm filled him. Emily battled her own wolf nature to hunt and kill. Now he knew why she felt reluctant to shift.

He also knew why her pack would view her as a threat. She was a rule breaker after all, and she constituted a dangerous threat to a pack firmly embedded in tradition.

Worry shadowed her face. Raphael tossed her the helmet. "Put this on. We need to get back. Now. There's something you must show me."

"It sounds important."

"It is," he said grimly. "It very well could be the reason why your pack thinks you should die."

Chapter 8

They stood before the maple tree Raphael had turned crimson. Emily held the kitchen knife in one gloveless hand. Her fingers were delicate and long, he noticed absently. Raphael rubbed his chin.

"Em, do it."

With a tiny sigh, she sliced her palm, approached the maple and dripped four drops of blood on the bark. As the laceration healed, they watched the leaves turn green.

He marveled at her ability, even while it raised a flood of questions. Questions he'd ask later. If Emily were cursed, why did she have such a rare gift? "That's how you grow the garden. Your blood brings life to all things dying."

"And you will end it," she said softly.

"Not if I can help it," he said grimly. He ran a hand

over the tree's trunk. "Death is a part of life, and Urien may resent this, and you. He could perceive it as a threat."

Her lovely mouth twisted with sudden pain as she jammed her glove back on. "Do you think my people hate me because of it?"·

Raphael hedged, not wanting to upset her, but knowing she deserved the truth. "I suspect so. The gift you have could be seen as an abomination by your pack."

"All I know is it made me stand out from them. I didn't want it. I remember how it used to be growing up. And then I had my first change into wolf, received the gift of blood healing and everything was different." Emily stared into the distance. "I started to want to heal injured animals, instead of pounce on them as meals."

Raphael's jaw tensed. "Most packs don't embrace different. They'd see it as an intrusion, a potential threat. Which is why I need to see the ancient prophecies to confirm what Urien and Bridget tell me. I need to make sure they're not contriving all this to get rid of you."

Confusion swirled in her green eyes. He attempted to explain. "Your pack is traditional. The gift you possess is unusual. And, as Draicon, our wolf selves hunt and kill prey. We don't heal animals. Tell me why you haven't shifted in a year? Is it because you don't want to kill?"

Emily bowed her head and he felt her inner sorrow. "Do you know what it's like to be outcast, be different after everyone has loved you for so long? I remember the picnics we used to take, the explorations into the forest to gather herbs. Urien used to read our pack's history to me each night, and Bridget would teach me how to cook with herbs. Then I became an oddity. I just wanted to belong and be like the rest of my pack. I thought if I never shifted, they would see I don't want to kill, either as wolf or with my touch. Urien, the others, they said my touch always kills and I'm the very nature of a beast, without thought, only base instinct. So I thought if I never changed…"

Her voice drifted off. Compassion surged through him. He wanted to draw her into his arms, comfort and protect her. As he took a step forward, she backed away.

Raphael withdrew. "You thought if you didn't shape-shift, it would prove you didn't want to kill."

At her nod, he rubbed his chin and sighed. "*Chere,* it proves nothing. Your pack still shuns you and all you've done is fight your own longings. It's your, our nature, to be wolf. You cannot fight it."

She lifted her gaze and he saw the fight in her eyes, the stubborn strength he relished. "I can."

He held out his hand. "Then come with me and just run with the night. Let me teach you what it's like to be wolf once more. Shift with me."

Holding her hands before her, she studied the thick gloves.

Hoping to coax her, he slowly shucked off his clothing. Emily's gaze widened with frank female appreciation as she studied his naked body. Raphael smiled, feeling the connection between them.

But her expression shifted into anxiety, so he swallowed a sigh.

"Come, Emily. I won't lead you to harm. I'll watch over you. Run with me."

She hung back. "No. I don't feel like it." Emily turned away. "I'd rather be alone. Please. Just go away.

You can't understand, not you, not what you are. Who you are. I just can't do this."

Frustration filled him. She still distrusted, thought he could not help her. How the hell could he get her to open to him?

The door slammed as Emily returned to the cottage, the sound echoing through the still woods. Raphael growled. As Kallan, he was required to be level, calm and emotionless.

He'd never felt any of those since meeting Emily. She vexed and frustrated him. Drew him closer and then darted away like a hummingbird. Stirred him to sexual longings he'd never before experienced.

Running as wolf would release some of his pent-up frustration.

He eyed her cabin as she turned on the lights. Raphael paced around the exterior, lifting his hands and softly chanting. Iridescent sparks filled the air as the magick shield draped over the perimeter.

Assured she was safe now from Morphs, he needed to replenish his energy. Hunting would suffice. He began to pace, and then to run, shifting even as he loped forward, his body bulging and changing, fur replacing skin, fangs erupting in his mouth. Wolf replaced man, eager for the hunt, to sniff out fresh prey and howl with pleasure at freedom.

Raphael ran to the property's edge and hesitated. He glanced backward at the lights shining from the farmhouse. The air was so still he could hear the insects dancing in the breeze.

He needed no boundaries.

He wondered why Morphs had invaded their property, broken through their shield. The Burkes were the purest blood, and had the strongest magick, so he was told. The shields should have held.

Forging ahead, he crossed the road to investigate the nearby forest.

The woods here were thick with oak and maple trees, and he scented rabbit, squirrel and raccoon. Yet these woods held a slight menace, laced with a darker scent, and the air was thicker.

Following the trail of a rabbit, he paced deeper into the woods. They were like the dark woods in fairy tales he'd read. He rounded a corner, half expecting the witch's cottage from Hansel and Gretel to appear.

But in the tiny clearing wasn't a witch. It was something worse.

A pack of about twenty wolves stood silently, watching him. Salvia dripped from their fangs as they snarled at him. As they blinked at him, yellow eyes turned soulless black. He instantly picked up their scent. Rotting garbage, decay.

Death. Morphs.

His hackles rose as he tensed and prepared to fight. Thoughts raced through his mind like light images. With this much of the enemy so close to their lands, why hadn't Urien sent the males to dispatch the enemy? Had their pack become so weakened and listless that they lacked the spine to protect the females?

Raphael knew he had to take them down now, before more breached the Burke lands and threatened Emily.

Slowly, he advanced toward the Morphs, assessing their strengths and weaknesses. There were only two. The others were clones, their scents weakened, unlike the originals. In human form, they had learned to disguise their scents, but not in wolf form.

They rushed him all at once. He thrilled at the challenge, his blood quickening as he took them on. Fangs and heavy muscles went to play as he fought, killed. He took them down and watched them die.

Almost all of them.

Raphael backed away, shaking his muzzle. Something was wrong, yet all his senses showed nothing. The enemy was dead.

He trotted out of the woods, glad the danger to Emily had been reduced, dismayed at the hunger still gnawing at him. As he picked up the scent of another rabbit, Raphael felt a sharp pinch in his hindquarters. He turned, nipping at the offender. Nothing but a bramble pricking him.

The rabbit bounded into view and he forgot all else. Hunger and instinct drove him as he gave chase. Yet he felt a curious draining feeling, and his normally rapid speed slowed.

The rabbit disappeared into the undergrowth.

Something was very wrong. Raphael stopped, alarmed at the intense itching in his hindquarters. He shifted back and stood. Damn it.

Not all the Morphs had died.

Even as he found it, on the back of his left thigh, it grew from the size of a quarter to a half dollar.

The tick/Morph began to grow as it bulged with his own blood. Draining him. Raphael cursed. If he didn't get the whole thing, it could regenerate and keep feeding.

Alarm filled him as the tick expanded to the size of a baseball. Feasting on him, his immortal blood. The dizziness began. He staggered and leaned against an oak tree for support.

Grimly he set his jaw and concentrated, directing pure energy at his right hand and then at the intruder.

It exploded in a spurt of his own blood.

He inspected the wound. The tick was dead, but the bite it left still streamed blood. He clenched his teeth and, using his energy, cauterized the wound. The burn made him want to howl.

Raphael directed more energy at incinerating his blood droplets into ash. Then he waved a hand, clothing himself once more.

Never had he been this weakened, this drained. His mind distracted by Emily, he'd forgotten to check for hitchhikers. What the hell was wrong with him that he'd forgotten the basics?

Limping heavily, he headed for his cabin. Hunger gnawed at him. He needed energy, fast. A thick steak.

As he passed by Emily's cabin, he spotted her sitting on the front porch in a rocker. She leaned forward, studying him.

"You look like you're hurt. What happened?" she said anxiously.

He waved a careless hand. "Nothing."

"Doesn't look like nothing." A tiny frown dented her forehead. "I thought the Kallan was impervious to injury, and your healing abilities are far superior than other Draicon's. The other pureblood Kallans were."

She thought his impure blood was his weakness. Anger surged through him. Raphael leveled a look at her.

"I told you, I'm not like other Kallans."

As he dragged himself back to his cottage, switched

on the lights and then headed for a fresh steak in the fridge, he wondered if she were right.

There seemed no way their two worlds could mesh. Not when his bloodlines stood in the way of their ever bonding as mates. Emily could not fit into his lifestyle. A hollow feeling settled on his chest at the thought of her even trying. His darkness contrasted sharply to her lightness. If they ever did bond, he would blot out everything good and innocent about her. In the mating lock, when bonded mates exchanged emotions and powers, would she absorb his dangerous powers and become as jaded and cynical?

She didn't want to be different.

With him, she'd have no choice.

Raphael hunted through the refrigerator and realized he'd have to defrost his supplies, since he'd given all the fresh meat to Emily. He removed a package of hamburger to thaw, then collapsed onto the nearest chair. Not good enough for her. No matter what he did, how powerful he was, his mixed blood meant he could never become equal to her.

His duty was clear. The future was murky. He didn't want to do it, but he had to find out.

Emily's destiny. Her death. He could foresee it, if he wanted.

The soft rap at the door made him tense. Summoning the strength, he limped over, opening it, knowing who stood outside. Raphael leaned against the jamb. "What is it, Emily?"

She thrust a covered platter at him. "I thought, since you were nice enough to stock my fridge, you'd need this."

The steak beneath the cover made him salivate. Balancing it on one palm, he opened the door. She went to his kitchen, looking pretty and delicate in the new floral dress she'd purchased.

"Why are you doing this?" he asked.

Gold-tipped lashes hid the expression in her eyes as she studied his feet. "Because you need me."

Raphael caught her gloved hand in his. "Sit with me," he said quietly. "I hate dining alone."

Her mouth tilted upward in a soft smile, and he was touched by the sweetness of both her gesture and her expression. He put the hamburger into the fridge and watched her bustling around the room and preparing the meal. No one ever questioned his needs before. No one since his parents had cared for him or dared to confront him. He was expected to be everything and have no need of anyone.

Needing her made him feel oddly vulnerable, yet deep inside, he hungered for her companionship, the sweetness of her femininity. She was one of the very few who dared to treat him normally. To tease him, mock him, and knew he liked it, liked the informality between them.

Damn, he needed her, and he didn't like needing anything, or anyone.

The steak was thick as a tire wheel, rare, sprinkled with green flakes and smelled delicious. He inhaled the fragrance and cocked an eyebrow at her. Emily set his plate on the table.

"Rosemary, sage and other herbs for balance," she told him.

Mischief danced in her green eyes, and they lightened to teal as she stood on one foot, extending her leg like a ballerina's. "See? Balance."

Charmed, he took her slim ankle in one hand, examining it, feeling a mischief of his own. His eyes widened at the glint of thin gold draped about her ankle. He picked it up with a question in his eyes.

Emily lifted her chin. "I bought it when you weren't looking. I like how it looks."

"So do I."

Raphael pushed up the hem of her dress, exposing the curve of one calf. He slid another hand over her skin, delighting in her sharp intake of breath and the scent of her arousal, then he stopped.

"Your legs are hairless, smooth," he noted, frowning. "I thought your pack embraced everything natural."

Pink tinted her cheeks. "We are. They are. Unlike them, I, ah, don't have any."

"Body hair?" he asked frankly.

Emily flushed further. "I'm not like other Draicon females," she muttered, yanking her foot free. "Father told me so. I'm only fertile in the spring and I never developed any hair like they do."

Surprised, he studied her, then sensed her embarrassment of being different. Raphael cupped her cheek. "Hey, *chere*," he murmured. "You're beautiful, and nothing would change my opinion of that."

Her smile was like the sunrise. "You're beautiful as well," she said, then pulled away with a teasing glint in her eyes. "For a big, hairy male."

Raphael laughed as she danced away.

As they ate, Emily filled the silence by talking about poetry she enjoyed. They began a hearty discussion about books. He enjoyed rattling her cage, watching her eyes spark with fire and passion as she disagreed with him, and equally enjoyed watching her sigh with pleasure when she talked about her favorite poets.

Pushing back from the table, he felt stronger physically. Then he remembered.

The steak soured in his stomach. He had to do it, for her sake. If there was a way he could see saving her, he must.

"Emily, come here."

At the deep timbre of his voice, she approached. He released a breath. "I have to see something. Don't be afraid. Let me look into your eyes."

"Why?"

"I need to see what the future holds for you. It will tell me what your destiny is."

She hung back, her hands clenched at her sides. For a moment he thought she'd not trust him but would turn and walk away. When she stepped forward, he felt a surge of relief even as he dreaded what he must do.

So many times he'd done this with others. Never someone this close. Never someone who mattered this much.

He closed his eyes briefly, summoning all his strength. Opening them, he very gently cupped her cheek with his left hand. With his right thumb and forefinger, he opened wide her right eye.

Staring deeply into it, he sought the information only he as Kallan could find.

To foresee her future.

Her death.

But as her green irises shifted to storm-cloud gray, he did not see Emily's demise. Instead, he saw raindrops.

Crystalline droplets of water falling from the sky, as

if it wept. More and more cascading down in a torrent, striking the ground like hard bullets. A shapeless form hovered in the background. He strained to identify it.

The form shimmered, took on a body. A naked man, shoulder-length black hair plastered to his head like a helmet, his muscled shoulders heaving as if he sobbed.

The man cried louder, and the rain fell harder. Raphael's heart twisted at the man's wrenching grief, as if he'd lost his soul. His heart.

His life.

A scream echoed as he lifted his head, crying out to the sky. Raphael's heart stopped. He dropped his hand, and stepped back, a horrified cry lodged in his throat.

He had not seen Emily's future nor foreseen her death.

Instead he'd seen himself, crying over what he must do, the dictate that he could not ignore.

The prophecy was clear as the raindrops. In the depths of her eyes, he sobbed, reacting to the order he'd been given from one who could not be questioned. No way out, no escape from the horror of his future.

Raphael shuddered.

Chapter 9

Raphael had escorted her formally back to her cabin, his handsome face taut. He said nothing about what he'd seen in her eyes. No words were needed. The grim expression told her enough.

After he politely bid her good-night, and made no attempt to kiss her, she watched him leave. He obviously would not watch over her tonight.

His broad shoulders were set as solid as granite. Here in the privacy of her little home, she allowed herself the luxury of grief. She was well and truly alone.

She hated it. Hated being apart from all others, and condemned because of it. Raphael was set apart just as she was. Yet he had not known the isolation she had, the fear of always being driven off.

Little she could do about it now. With a philosophical shrug, Emily climbed between the clean, white sheets and fell into an exhausted slumber.

The nightmares soon began. Sharp, jagged, tainted with stains of old blood and blackness. She raced through her beloved woods. Prey. Naked, alone, she ran, stones cutting her feet. Cold air slapped against her flesh. Her breath came in harsh pants. They chased her, hot and eager for her blood, their claws reaching out for her, so close she could feel the talons hovering near. There, in the distance, a figure, tall and strong, waiting for her. Her mate, who would save her. Emily cried out, reaching for him with frantic hands. Light shimmered around him, and his strong muscled body seemed assured of protecting her. His face was all classic lines, his body honed from steel. He reached out to her as she ran forward. He held in his hands a dagger and raised it and as she stuttered to a frantic stop, too late, she realized he had not come to save her but to destroy her.

Emily cried out. She thrashed and moaned, trying to awaken before the sharp blade bit into her flesh.

Soft murmurs sounded in her ear. She felt a hard, warm body beside hers, a calloused hand gently stroke her brow. Someone was crooning to her in a language she didn't understand, soothing her out of her nightmare.

Her eyelids flew open. In the light of the waxing moon, she turned and saw him.

Raphael. He'd returned after all, to guard her sleep. Her angel of death.

She inched away from him. "Why are you here?"

"I told you I was going to stay with you to watch over you. Then you called out and I came."

He sat up, his muscled chest naked in the moonlight.

Raphael wore fleece pants and nothing else. Moonlight silvered his dark hair, reflected in the depths of his onyx eyes. "Emily, please, let me help you. I need answers as much as you do."

A hint of grief laced his tone. She wanted to trust him, reach out to him, but could not. Emily faced him down. "Your time is endless, unlimited. Mine is finite and short. You have nothing to lose. I have everything to lose. How can you even begin to understand my world and what I'm going through?"

"I want to understand. Let me in, allow me to see through your eyes. Work with me and let me see the ancient texts."

And what if he saw what she'd translated? Would he take it as a sign to fulfill his duty and execute her as planned? Would he give up on her as her own people had? Emily clutched the sheet to her breasts.

"Go away, Kallan," she whispered. "There is nothing here for you. You aren't like us, and never will be, so please, just go away."

Raphael returned to her living-room couch and the pillow he'd set there. As he sat, he punched the pillow with a hard fist.

Feathers exploded out of the casing as it split under the force of his blow. He coughed and gave a rueful smile as he blew feathers out of his face.

How utterly ridiculous he looked now. The powerful Kallan, Destroyer. Dealer of death!

Covered with fluff.

His smile faded. How he wished the dilemma before him was equally soft. No, it was a rock wall impassable to everything. Everything inside him demanded he protect his mate, tenderly care for her. He wanted Emily, wanted her body next to his as he guarded her in sleep. The feel of her softness against his tensed muscles had raised every primitive male instinct to roll her onto her back, mount her and make her his.

Instead, he'd focused on soothing away her fear and pain. In return, she chased him away again.

When would she open up to him and share?

He fingered the tiny gold dagger dangling from his earlobe, his guts twisting at the thought of using the Scian on his mate. He couldn't imagine using it to end Emily's life. Yet if he failed, he put Gabe's life in danger. The Burke pack wouldn't hesitate to kill his brother.

He would also fail in his duty as Kallan for the first time. Being Kallan was his sole identity, paralleling on a track with his Cajun roots.

Raphael set about cleaning up the mess he'd made. His body tensed as he remembered another time and place when he'd faced an equal mess.

Peach juice, pulp smeared on his face. The cruel sounds of laughter from the town boys as they pointed and mocked him...

It was in the past, he reminded himself as he brushed the last feathers from the bed and dumped them into the wood trash bin. He was Kallan now. Immortal, nearly invincible. The position elevated him above his lowly birth, gave him purpose.

Purpose lost now that he faced the inevitable horror.

And why did you become Kallan?

Introspection served no purpose. His responsibility was first to Emily. He had to guide her to what to expect if she died. *When she died,* he thought, his heart heavy. Prepare her for the inevitable, even as his own heart broke. Her needs came first. He could not allow his personal feelings and emotions to interfere with duty.

Raphael radiated power and command, despite his laconic posture as he leaned against the porch railing, regarding Emily with his steady, dark gaze. Instead of his usual attire, Raphael was dressed in a cranberry cable-knit sweater and neatly pressed dark trousers. Beneath the trousers his bare toes peeped out.

Like her, he was barefoot.

His dark hair was tied back with a leather thong. It accented the strong planes of his chiseled face and the firmness of his jaw. A flutter started in her belly as he gave her a slow smile.

He didn't resemble the males of her pack, but this ordinary dress came close. Her jaw came unhinged as he presented her with a single sprig of English lavender.

"It smells like you, so I picked it in your garden," he offered.

Emily took the flowers, inhaled their delicate fragrance, and opened the door to allow him inside.

He paced around her living room, his weight making the floorboards creak. She thought about her lonely bed and imagined him in it, only this time his big body on top of hers. She'd seen animals mate and knew what transpired. Emily imagined Raphael gently rocking back and forth atop her, thrusting into her and making the mattress creak. The odd flutter started in her stomach again.

He jammed his hands into the pockets of his trousers.

"Emily, I need to know something. As Kallan, I need to grant your last wishes. What is your heart's desire?"

The blunt question made her drop the sprig of lavender. It lay there, a splotch of color against the dark hardwood floor. Her heart's desire? Other than to live, and embrace life, she wanted much. A mate of her own. Raphael. A mate whose destiny was to cherish and love her, as her pack had once loved her. An ordinary life in an ordinary world.

It wasn't meant to be. Whatever wrong she'd done to invoke such a curse on herself, if she had, couldn't be reversed.

"Em?"

His voice held such tenderness, she could only gaze at him with abject sorrow. He truly wanted to make her feel good and see to her needs. Not the actions of the coldhearted but of proud and pureblooded Kallans in the ancient stories. Desire to draw closer, and share with him, bond with him in the flesh, warred with her natural self-preservation.

Emily used humor as a defense against his charm and her own instincts to mate and bond.

"Right now I have one wish. I wish you'd put some shoes on. You look like you're turning to ice."

The wide grin he gave her melted her heart. He looked so handsome. Raphael sat on her couch, propped a bare foot up on her coffee table. She liked his informality.

"I was in such a hurry, I left my boots in my cabin." He wiggled his toes, the mighty Kallan looking as boyish as a youngling.

Mischief filled her. Emily raced into her bedroom, fished through her closet and found the slippers she'd purchased for her father when she was eleven. They were lined with soft fur, and he'd loved them dearly, even though she suspected he'd only worn them to please her.

The slippers fell onto Raphael's lap. "Try these on."

Disbelief touched his face as he picked them up. "Bunny slippers? You want me to wear bunny slippers?" Raphael cocked an eyebrow at her. "Are you trying to push me off my mighty pedestal, *chere?*"

The giggle warbled up from her stomach and spilled out of her like water as he donned the slippers and pretended to attack his feet. "Prey, prey," he shouted.

Collapsing with laughter, she sank onto the couch, holding her stomach.

He fell onto the couch beside her, laughing as well. After a minute, they stopped, panting for breath, tears streaming down their cheeks.

His smile faded as he gave her a tender look. "It's so good to hear you laugh." He tweaked a stray red curl. "I would almost sacrifice my dignity again to hear it more often."

At the mention of the word *sacrifice,* her mood shifted. "I wish I could find it in me to laugh more," she said softly, her heart wrenching.

"Let's get back to why I'm here. What do you want more than anything else that I may do for you?"

Emily jumped up from the couch, hugged herself, the floral dress swinging about her ankles delicately. "It's silly, really."

"Nothing you want is silly," he said quietly. "Anything you wish for, let me try to grant it. It's part of my duty as Kallan to fulfill your wishes."

"I want to eat with my pack one more time."

He showed no surprise. "When did you last eat with them?"

Shame flushed her cheeks. Remembering how they had driven her away, she muttered, "It's been a long while. They will object, I warn you."

Raphael took both her hands into his, rubbing his long fingers over her mustard-yellow gloves. "Then I ask only this. Take off these gloves."

Dismay and shock filled her as he began tugging them off. The protest died in her throat as he removed the gloves, leaving only the thin layer of sterile surgical gloves. Raphael clasped her hands.

Breath caught in her throat as she waited for a reaction. He showed none.

"Emily, I told you, you can't hurt me," he said quietly. "I want you to eat with your pack wearing only these."

Misery filled her. The pack wouldn't allow it. They didn't want her near, even layered with protection. They'd chase her away again, only this time Raphael would witness her humiliation. Yet deep inside, she longed for one little bit of contact with them. *I just want to be like everyone else. Why can't I be like them?*

"They won't let me," she whispered, removing her hands and donning the heavy gloves once more.

"Then I'll insist."

The steely look in his dark eyes and the determined set of his jaw filled her with hope. Maybe Raphael could make them see her as they once had—not someone to be shunned, but someone who belonged and was part of their family.

A sound between a sob and a laugh fled her as she

pointed to his feet. "You'd best put shoes on, then. Urien won't take you very seriously in those."

The hard smile he gave her sent a shiver down her spine. This was the Kallan, a male who would not be brooked, whose power shone through no matter what he wore. "I think not. He'll take me seriously. Bunny slippers or not. Very seriously."

Sounds of silverware clinking drifted out through the opened door as they approached the house. The long-dead flower garden lined the house, and the rolling fields of green grass were waist high. It was such a pretty scene, but it had become a nightmare to her since her father's death. Potted geraniums flanking the steps were brittle with decay.

The wood bird feeders were empty. No seed had been placed there. The glassed hummingbird feeders were filled, but she saw no birds.

Raphael quietly ascended and stopped. He tilted his head, his expression concentrated. "Listen."

"I don't hear anything."

"Exactly. No birds, no squirrels, nothing. Not even insects." His eyes narrowed. "Odd. In the forest where your cottage is, there's plenty of birds and wildlife. But not here."

A shiver raced down her spine, but Emily shrugged it off. "The pack probably shapeshifts so much that their wolf forms have scared them off."

His touch made the hummingbird feeder swing. "Even hummingbirds? *Chere*, in the past has your wolf form ever frightened away the hummingbirds?"

Her palms went clammy, and she rummaged for an

excuse. "Life hasn't been the same since my father died. The animals probably sense it."

Raphael's jaw tensed. "Perhaps. Let's go in."

Emily hung back, her stomach in knots. He turned, held out a palm.

"Em? Come on. It's all right, little one."

When she hesitantly put her hand into his, he turned it over and brought her glove to his lips. She could not feel the kiss he brushed against her knuckles. How she longed to feel his mouth against her pale hands that never saw light, never felt anything but covering!

"One day, you'll trust me enough to take these off and know my touch," he said quietly.

He gave her hand a reassuring squeeze.

They entered the living room, with its hardwood floors, polished tables and vases of hothouse flowers. Lemon-yellow walls brought a touch of cheerfulness to the room, but the air seemed thick and heavy. She barely had a chance to wonder about it when Raphael steered her toward the enormous dining room. Seated at the lace-draped tables was her family. They dug into heaping platters of fresh sausage and chattered.

Emily swallowed hard as the entire pack stopped talking, turned their heads and stared. Raphael ignored their rudeness, drew her forward.

"I've decided to take you up on your offer of breakfast, Bridget," he told her. His eyes were stony, his jaw set.

Her draicaron resembled a warrior who could slay with a single icy glare. Surely they would not turn him away as they had done to her. Not the Kallan.

Urien paced over to them. A heartbeat of silence

passed as he approached, keeping a distance. He did not look at Emily. His gaze focused on Raphael.

"This is a bad idea, bringing her here."

Wincing at the fact that her own Alpha could not even call her by name, she stood her ground. Raphael didn't even blink.

"She has a name. Emily. And she will eat here."

The two males stared at each other, bristling with tension until Urien dropped his gaze, studying the floor. "The sun porch," he said curtly. "You may eat out there."

"No, we're not being confined to a section of the room where she can't interact with you. Emily is not a prisoner and she will no longer be treated as if she should be incarcerated. You're her family, and you will start treating her as family."

Emily didn't need Raphael to fight her battles, and she gathered her courage. She remembered one of the slang words Raphael had taught her. "Yes, Urien, get with the program and stop being such a tool."

A proud smile touched her dracairon's face as Urien looked shocked and the others looked puzzled. As Raphael guided her toward a table near the others, she heard Bridget whisper, "Did she call him a fool?"

Emily whirled. "No, I called him a tool. It's slang for *idiot*."

Inside her mind, she heard her mate chuckle softly, felt his pride in her. Emily sat in the chair Raphael pulled out. Even as he took the seat opposite her, his gaze focused on Urien near the lace-curtained window. The Kallan radiated such power and authority, even Urien seemed reluctant to cross him. Suddenly she realized what a champion she had on her side. With his shoulder-length hair, scrutinizing look and stern expression, he looked as if he could take on the world on her behalf and win.

The idea made her relax and look around with interest. But none of her family, even those who had expressed pity upon finding out her curse, looked her way.

She was as invisible as if she never existed. Emily lifted her chin. She pretended none of it mattered, even as her chest felt hollow with grief. Raphael had granted her dearest wish.

A wish that would never come true. Her own pack wouldn't accept her. Never again.

A pretty, solemn-faced woman with curly brown hair held out a plate of blood sausage to them. Maureen, a second cousin. Raphael helped himself and then nodded toward Emily.

Emily picked up the serving forks. She looked into Maureen's face. Her kin. Once, a friend who laughed with her and amused Emily with her whimsical stories.

"Hi, Mo." Emily smiled, using the familiar nickname.

No response. No friendliness showed now on Maureen's face. Maureen looked stricken as if Emily were a wriggling serpent ready to strike.

Emily helped herself, ignoring the lump in her throat. The food would stick in her throat, but she'd force herself to eat, pretending all was as it had been, long ago when she'd been welcome here.

As she replaced the serving fork, her hand brushed against Maureen's fingers. Her cousin gasped and staggered backward several steps. Her eyes rolled in the back of her head.

A heavy thud followed as Maureen dropped to the

floor, the platter of blood sausage spilling over her, the china plate shattering. She jerked violently once and lay still.

Shock rippled through Emily. She sprang to her feet to aid her cousin, but Urien blocked her path. Bridget shrieked, pointing a finger like an accusing judge.

"The death touch! She killed Maureen! She touched her. Even with the glove, she has killed our Maureen!"

"Stop blathering," Raphael said mildly, putting himself protectively in front of Emily. "She could be just stunned. I'll see to her."

Urien blocked his view. "No, Kallan. I told you this was a mistake. Leave us to our grief and our dead. Must more of our people die for you to realize how dangerous Emily is? How much more of this can we take?"

Anger glittered in his blue eyes. Urien's finger shook as he pointed at her. "Get out of our sight, cursed one. Leave us, before you kill any more of our family and bring your curse down on us!"

Emily couldn't bear it. She fled, hearing Raphael's cold voice. "We're leaving, Urien. But I warn you, I'll be back. Something isn't right here, and I intend to find out exactly what."

Chapter 10

The screen door banged behind her as she bolted out of the house, down the porch steps. Her heart was shattering, her grief too wrenching for tears. She tore across the meadow, racing for the protection of her beloved woods.

Ignoring Raphael calling softly to her in her mind, she ran, until she left the pack territory and crossed into the property of the abandoned farmhouse next door. She passed the house's sagging porch, the weathered and cracked windowpanes staring at her like ghostly eyes.

Emily, talk to me. Come back.

Go away, Raphael. I am nothing but death.

Sunlight dappled the few remaining leaves on the trees. She drew deeper into the forest. Pine mingled with the earthy scent of undergrowth. A crow called overhead and flew away as squirrels scampered up the tree trunks. The air was loamy with the scent of damp leaves. Insects hummed overhead in the trees, and she could glimpse the mountains peeking through the forest as gray clouds drifted overhead, allowing intermittent rays of sun to peek through.

Emily finally reached the oak tree where her aunt once planted mistletoe long ago. A twist of vine wrapped around an overhead branch, plump with berries. They might as well have been on the waning moon, for she had no means to harvest them. No gold knife.

Beneath the shady hollow, she sank to the ground. Her gaze lifted upward at the white berries dangling out of reach.

I killed my father. I killed Helen. And now Maureen.

Memories pierced like arrows. She and Maureen picking blackberries, their lips stained with purple juice. Hanging white cotton sheets on the clothesline and inhaling the fresh, sunny scent. Shifting into wolves, running with the moon. Her eyes squeezed shut as her mouth opened. A silent scream fled her lips as she rocked back and forth, hugging herself.

She must discover what the prophecy said. Why had she been accursed? What wrong had she done, what evil? All she'd ever wanted from life was to cherish those around her. Not hurt them.

For a long while, she sat on the ground, hugging her knees, holding her emotions at bay. Her throat squeezed tight as she tried to find solace in familiar territory. Yet it did not offer the comfort she'd found in the past. Clouds scuttled overhead, fully blocking the sun. Dismay filled her anew as she sensed the air shift. A sharp breeze tossed stray tendrils of her hair.

Emily hugged herself, shivering. In her thin cotton

dress, she'd dressed for the warmth of the homestead, not to seek refuge in the forest. She loathed wearing heavy clothing and wanted only to be free. Yet for the first time, she felt cold.

Or was it the icy knowledge she'd killed again, even inadvertently?

Leaves crunched in the near distance. Startled, she whipped her head around. Raphael's scent floated toward her.

"Em, come out. Talk to me," he said quietly. "I want to help."

She could not evade him. Emily stood and brushed leaves off her dress as he came into sight. In his trousers, scuffed boots, sweater and black leather jacket, he looked every inch the formidable rebel Kallan. But only gentleness shone in his dark eyes. In his arms, he bore a thick down quilt and a picnic basket.

"If you won't come to me, then I'll wait with you. Since you didn't eat, I brought breakfast for both of us."

His soothing voice lowered her guard. Raphael set down the quilt and the picnic basket. Suddenly all the fight went out of her. Hysteria rose in her throat.

"I killed my cousin. I loved her, and it's my fault. I only wanted to be with my pack again, but now someone else has paid the price. Why is this happening to me?" She gulped down a breath. He only watched her with his brilliant, steady gaze.

"I need to read the prophecies to find out why I am cursed and condemned to die, but I can't read them because you need to be calm and unemotional to decipher the language. If I had the mistletoe berries, I could smear them over the words and all would become clear, but the mistletoe, I can't cut it until nightfall, and it doesn't matter because I don't have a gold knife. I ruined the knife, like I'm ruining my life. Maybe I should just surrender, and let you execute me, for the good of the pack and our race."

Her voice broke. She bit her lip, fighting against the welling tears, wondering why she'd revealed so much to him.

Raphael shrugged out of his leather jacket. Gooseflesh sprang out on his bare arms as he draped it over her shoulders. "You're shivering."

Encased by the warm leather, she clutched the lapels. He couldn't tolerate cold weather, but he took care of her needs over his own. Maybe it was finally time for her to reach out to the one foresworn to be her mate and forget about her past, and those who had betrayed her.

He reached for the golden dagger on his belt. Silently he unsheathed it and handed it to her, hilt side first.

Emily could only stare at the sacred weapon.

"We'll wait for nightfall together. But you'll need this to cut the mistletoe."

"It's only fit for your hands. Not mine," she whispered.

He stepped forward, took her palm and opened it. Raphael placed the dagger's hilt into it. "You have a great need of it. Take it. Your needs are my own."

The words were formal, contrasting sharply with the gentleness of his husky voice. She took the Scian, tested its weight and with the dagger's heaviness, her spirits lifted.

Could she trust him enough with her life? Raphael looked down at her, his expression unreadable as a shaft of sunlight dappled his hair. His mouth was firm, unmoving, and he simply waited.

Sometimes you have to take a leap of faith, even when you're most afraid, Emily told herself.

She handed back the blade. "Thank you for the honor," she whispered. "It means more than you realize. But it's no use. The berries are ripe, but the moonlight is too weak and I'm too emotional to read the words they will reveal." A ripple of fear raced through her. "I can't foresee the future. Or read the prophecies. I don't know why I must die. What I did to offend Aibelle and suffer this curse."

He made no move toward her, but waited patiently, as if taming a wild animal who feared him. "You're not cursed, Emily. I seriously doubt you are, and I have my doubts about your family. If Maureen is dead, and I say if, it wasn't from your touch. I want proof."

"The only proof lies with our goddess, Aibelle. Only she has answers. I have none."

A deep sigh fled him. "Then I'll go visit the Other Realm and ask her."

Her breath hitched. "You would do that for me? Dare to risk it?"

His gaze was solemn. "You're my mate, the other half of my spirit. I only wish you would stop evading me, and trust me."

A heartbeat of silence passed. Finally she jerked her head forward. Tension seemed to ease in his wide shoulders.

"I wanted… I want to trust you. I'm afraid. So many of my family has turned against me. I'm all alone. Can I be sure you won't be the one who will hurt me most of all?"

"I would never hurt you, *chere,*" he said softly.

"My pack deserted me," she whispered. "I need my family, but they don't want me near them. I can't belong anymore."

Raphael looked away. "I no longer live with my pack, my family. My brothers stay with me sometimes, and I visit the family house, but never for long. My father loves me, but said the power struggle between us would be too great if I stayed. I know what it's like, *chere.* I once formed a pack of unbonded males, taught them how to fight, but it wasn't the same. It is possible to have your family about you, and love you, but still be apart."

"But your family doesn't fear your touch. They don't run away from you because they're terrified of what you've become." Emily's gaze dropped to the hated gloves covering her hands. "I wish I could touch someone and not be afraid of hurting them, or see the fear in their eyes. My touch is poison. Anyone I touch with my hands dies. Just for once I wish someone could reach out to me and not be afraid. Just for once I'd like to feel normal, like everyone else. You can't understand because people respect you. You're worthy of their respect."

His jaw tightened as he glanced away. "If I had knowledge, and could read the prophecies, I could help you. I can't read the ancient language of the prophecies. Those words are preserved only for the purebloods." A bitter laugh rumbled from his chest. "I'm worthy of respect only because people fear me because I can take their lives. I know spells and ancient words because I memorized them when Aibelle imparted me with the knowledge when I became Kallan."

For the first time, she saw past the guard he kept up, saw the shadows in his eyes. She saw him struggle with his pride.

"I'm not like you. I have no knowledge of the Old Ways, or the language, or traditions denied to my family because we were looked down upon as inferior. But I'll help you in any way I can, even if it means risking all and going to Aibelle to ask for help."

Her soft heart turned over. "Anyone can acquire the knowledge, Raphael. My family, and others, kept it secret to keep themselves elevated above other Draicon. They said they wanted to keep the hierarchy pure, the bloodlines clean, but they isolated themselves by doing so. And they lack something you have in every cell—courage."

Gulping down a breath, she continued. "I'm terrified of dying. You can't understand because you're so strong. I'd trade knowledge of the Old Ways for one ounce of your courage. All I ever wanted was to be like my family, fit in with the pack." She stared at the forest floor. "I see how they are, and I wonder if I've wanted the wrong thing all this time."

Leaves crunched like broken glass beneath his boots as he approached. Tenderness shone in his dark eyes as Raphael cupped her chin and lifted it. Mesmerized, she could not look away.

"I know how important family is, and the bonds of blood. But sometimes it isn't enough. You have to be yourself. Dare to be different, if that's what destiny calls for you."

She stared at him as he gently stroked his thumbs over her skin. "I don't want to be different. I just want to be one of them. An ordinary Draicon, living in the ordinary world," she protested.

"Em, it doesn't make you less of what you are. Sometimes you just have to go with what you're called to do. It's not easy being on your own and having a power others fear. It's the hardest thing I've ever had to do. But I'm here for you. I'll help you understand, and find out why you are so special."

His touch warmed her skin as he caressed her cheek, each stroke heating her blood. "Your life is meant for a purpose. Others fear you because they don't understand you or see you as someone who stands out from the pack. Stop running with them and trying to run away from who you are." A humorless smile brushed his mouth. "Besides, *chere,* your pack isn't so nice, so why be like them?"

He bent his head gently and touched her lips with his own. "Be with me. Run to me, Em. I will not turn away from you, I promise."

His mouth feathered over hers in a soft kiss. Emily closed her eyes, marveling in the firmness of his lips against hers. His hands held her steady as he deepened the kiss, his tongue coaxing her to open to him. She parted her lips and he slipped inside, tasting her, his tongue plunging and retreating, brushing the roof of her mouth, tracing every part of the moist cavern of her mouth. Emily sighed and shyly met his sensual advances. Breath escaped her as he lightly nipped her lower lip.

Raphael pulled away, his chest heaving, his eyes darker than the blackest night. Her own pulse beat frantically as she struggled to breathe, feeling the delicious flush of heat suffuse her entire body. The faint throbbing between her legs intensified.

She knew now what it meant, and she knew what he wanted. He wanted to mate, but he waited patiently for her.

She was ready now.

Chapter 11

As Emily telegraphed her desire to him, a wildness entered Raphael's gaze, a burning intensity of a beast who wanted to pounce and claim. But the barely leashed passion was held at bay. Raphael took her hands into his, studied them and brought her knuckles to his moist mouth to kiss. He closed his eyes, long black lashes feathering over his hollow cheeks.

Then he turned her palms over. "Will you trust me, *chere?* You can't hurt me. Let me fulfill what we both desire."

He was immortal. Her mate. Every instinct she possessed longed to touch him, cling to him and let no barricades come between them.

With a little sigh, she nodded. Panic filled her as he reached for her gloves. Emily quivered, but he brought her hands to his lips and kissed her knuckles.

"Take them off. It's time. Trust me," he said softly.

Emotion clogged her throat as Emily dragged in a deep breath. She peeled away the gloves, feeling as if she were shedding a layer of skin. Cool air washed over her whitened palms.

Raphael very slowly brought his fingers close to hers. Her breath hitched, and sweat dripped down her temples. He touched her bare hand.

He jolted, his head snapping back, then he smiled ruefully.

"It felt like a tingle, like when you touch an electrical wire, but I'm still standing." He touched her again, his dark gaze burning. "I think you need to touch me some more."

Her heart raced now with daring, not fear. Encouraged, she slid her fingers through his, clasping them. His grip was firm, comforting and strong, yet gentle, as if he knew his own strength. His skin was slightly calloused, the fingers long and lean, the nails neatly pared.

"You see? Your touch doesn't kill," he murmured.

He raised her bare hands to his face, turned one palm over and pressed a kiss to it. Emily trembled at the feel of his warm mouth against flesh that had not touched another in over a year. She yearned to touch him more, and when he released her hands, she brought them to his face. Hesitating only a little, she traced each angle of his jaw, the sensual curve of his mouth, ran her fingers over the thick, dark brows shading his enigmatic eyes.

When she slid a finger past his parted lips to investigate his tongue, a groan fled him. He sucked on the pale digit, lightly bit it.

Raphael removed her finger, kissed it again. Fierce intent burned in his gaze. "It's my turn now."

His hands traced a pattern down her throat, slipped down to her breasts. He cupped them in his palms and stroked his thumbs over the hardening crest of her nipples. Desire pulsed inside her.

"There's one part of me that will never die when you touch me," he said softly, a teasing light in his eyes. He brought her hand down to cup his groin.

Her eyes widened at the steely hardness straining beneath the fabric.

"I want you, Emily. Be mine."

Emotion overcame her. She could only nod.

As he spread out the quilt on the ground, she gazed around. The canopy of oak, loblolly pine and red maple sheltered them. Overhead, a crow called out as a bluejay squawked at a squirrel. It felt fitting they should come together here for the first time.

Raphael turned to her, touching a tendril of her hair escaping the tight bun. "Put down your hair for me. I've dreamed of this moment."

Fumbling with the pins, she plucked them free. A shower of pins fell to the ground and her hair, escaping the confinement of the tight knot, spilled downward in a cascade of red-gold curls. An inward hiss of breath came from him. He picked up a lock, rubbing it against his cheek, then touched the top button on her high-neck dress.

Emily unbuttoned the dress, feeling shy and uncertain but guided by her longing to become one with him. He had far more experience. Raphael stood, silently watching her, a hank of dark hair hanging over his forehead.

The dress fell open and spilled down to her ankles. She kicked off the sandals. Gooseflesh sprang to her arms. She was naked beneath it and shivered as cool air caressed her breasts. Self-conscious, she covered them. Gently, he placed his hands over hers and guided them to her sides.

"Don't hide yourself from me, *chere.* You're too lovely to hide."

Cold before, she felt suffused with tremendous heat as he caressed her breasts. Emily arched beneath his touch as Raphael brushed his thumbs over the cresting nipples. When he bent his head and took one into his mouth, the warmth and the shocking sensation caused a whimper deep in her throat. He lapped his tongue, swirling it over the taut peak, then suckled her. She was growing hotter now, a fire stoking inside her as the sweet tension braced her body.

When he stepped back and removed his clothing, arousal flared inside her. Breath caught in her lungs. He was stunning, hard, so different from her body. Even her pack. Muscles padded his broad shoulders, dark hair covered his deep chest. His limbs were athletic and sturdy, his abdomen ribbed and flat. She glanced down at his genitals and swallowed. Between his legs, his shaft jutted out, thick and long.

The thought of taking his hardness into her body filled her with anticipation and slight fear.

The blue-inked tattoo on his left biceps flexed as he stretched. "Like what you see?" he asked softly. "Come closer, *chere,* and touch me."

Emily ran her hands over the strong muscle beneath the tattoo. "Where did you get this?"

"My adopted brother, Indigo, runs an ink shop." Raphael closed his eyes, quivering beneath her strokes as she caressed his velvety skin.

She traced his body, the knobs of his narrow hips, his flat stomach, and then her hand shyly grasped the hard length of him rising from his groin. Raphael gave a low moan as her fingers danced along the soft skin, the rigidness beneath.

"Does it hurt?" she asked.

His eyes flew open, his gaze burning into hers. "In a good way."

When he kissed her again, they slowly fell to the blanket. A strangled sob escaped her as he slid his hand between her legs and began to stroke her wet flesh. Moisture seeped out of her and she arched.

"Doesn't it feel good?" he murmured. "I want to make you feel pleasure, little one."

Emily clutched his shoulders, squeezing the hard muscles as he thumbed her center, flicking over it. Raphael slipped a finger inside her, and her sheath squeezed around him.

He stroked and caressed, then circled her center, feeling her tense beneath him. Shudders wracked her as Emily cried out, caught in the grips of a climax.

He withdrew and mounted her, nudging her trembling legs open with his.

Bracing his palms on either side of her, he held her gaze with a fierce intensity. "Look at me, *chere*. Only me."

Lashed with desire, she focused on him. Raphael surged forward, breaking the barrier of her innocence. Emily went still with shock. Burning pain accompanied the odd fullness. She felt invaded, caught in a storm she was helpless to control. Instinctively she writhed, trying to pull away from him.

He held her face between his palms and kissed her.

"Shh," he crooned. "Just stay still. Trust me, little one, it will ease."

A bead of sweat dripped from his forehead down to her breasts. She felt him inside her.

"We are one now, Emily. Nothing, no one, can part us now."

He began rocking back and forth, a gentle rhythm, creating a delicious friction that pushed past the pain. Emily clutched his shoulders, feeling the muscles tense beneath her grip. She arched and pumped her hips, as he taught her the rhythm, rubbing against him, feeling the silky slide of the hair on his legs against hers, moisture sheening his body as he moved against her. His gaze held hers as he claimed her with every push into her soft, moist channel, with the soft words he murmured to her in his Cajun French.

Then she felt the tension in him build, and his big body went still and he threw back his head. Warmth spurted inside her, as cords on his cheek stood out in stark relief. Raphael cried out her name and then collapsed on her.

Gently she stroked his damp hair as his ragged breath thundered into her ear. For a moment he lay still atop her, his head pillowed on her shoulder. Then he nuzzled her neck, giving it a gentle kiss, and slid partly off her. He was still inside her, still rigid as a tree trunk. She felt the wet stickiness of his seed and her virginal blood trickle down her splayed thighs.

He rolled over, taking her with him so he was still nestled inside her, as if he didn't want to separate them. Perspiration plastered his hair to his forehead, beaded in the curly hairs of his muscled chest.

Experimentally, she rolled her hips and felt him twitch inside her. Emily tensed as he rolled her beneath him again. Raphael rose up on his elbows, giving her a small, private smile.

"Breathe, Em. Just relax and breathe. This time will be better," he promised.

She had trusted him before. Little choice now. Emily slid her arms around his neck, anchoring herself to him. He began to move slowly, and at first there was nothing but the slight burn once more. He kissed her, long, drugging kisses that coaxed her response. He raised himself up and began angling his thrusts, rubbing against the part of her that burned in a different way.

She ached, the tension building higher and higher. Emily writhed beneath him, wanting it, clawing for it. Her hands raked down his back as she hissed and twirled her hips, begging him with her eyes.

When he thrust even deeper inside her, she screamed and bit his shoulder, tasting the salt of his skin. Raphael groaned with pleasure as he cupped her bottom and drove hard into her. The tension shattered, burned her as she came apart, her inner muscles squeezing him tightly, and he followed her soon after.

Afterward, she lay in his arms, stroking the crisp hairs on his chest. Her hands traced his skin, reveling in the feel of muscle and sinew beneath her questing fingers. Emily rested her head on his shoulder as her fingers outlined his smiling lips. It was fitting they had made love here, in the woods she adored so much. It felt natural, unconfined, for her first time.

He kissed her temple. "Better," he asked softly.

Shyly, she nodded. Marveling at the ability to touch

him without fear, she fingered his streak of white hair, starkly contrasted to his dark, silky locks. "Where did you get this? Was it one of those Cajun traditions?"

Raphael raised his eyebrows at her teasing tone. "When I went to the Other Realm and became Kallan. The lock marks my status."

"What was it like, to take the test?" She raised herself up and studied her mate. "What did you have to do? Were you afraid?"

His eyes grew distant. "I had to make the journey and step into the mist off the cliff of the sacred mountain where all Kallans go to be tested. It was a long fall. Instead, I found myself in the Other Realm. Aibelle told me that to prove my worth and become our race's Kallan, I had to perform one simple task."

Silence descended over him. Absently, he began stroking her hair and then began talking again. "It wasn't so simple, but a test of courage and inner strength. I had already proved myself in the battles I fought with Morphs, and how many of the enemy I had defeated. Now I needed to know what it was like to die as the transitions whose lives I would take would die."

"You let yourself be killed?"

A humorless smile touched his mouth. "The elder Kallan whose place I would take did it. It was on a stone altar at the training place where all Kallans learn before assuming their roles. It was terrifying. I knew if my heart proved false and I was judged as unworthy, I would die and never return."

She traced the white lock of hair on his head. "But you didn't."

"No, I didn't. But it wasn't as simple as I'd been led

to believe. The elderly Kallan struck me with disease, age and wounds first. Before my eyes, my skin wrinkled, my bones grew fragile and I aged 1,500 years. The pain was…intense."

Her heart squeezed at the haunted look in his dark eyes.

"I resisted at first. The will to live came above all else. I fought the pain. I was proud, and nothing would fell me. The more I fought, the more the elder Kallan brought upon me. Then finally I realized it was time, and I begged him to end it."

"Why did he torture you so?" Emily hugged him, wishing she could have been there to ease his suffering.

"Because then I learned why the role of Kallan was so important and how to surrender to death." Raphael's gaze grew distant. "That's when he smiled, and told me, 'Now you are ready to take my place. You have the strength to endure pain and the courage to ask for it to end. You know what your transitions face and why the Kallan is vital to our people.'"

Emily caressed his beard-roughened cheek. "You are. And to me as well."

A shadow touched his face, but before she could question, he raised his head. His dark hair was tousled, and a small red mark flared on his shoulder from where she'd bitten him. "Let's get back to your cabin. It's getting too cold to stay out here, and though this place is safe, I'd feel better if you were surrounded by walls instead of trees." He gave her an intent look. "But first…"

Erotic shock rippled through her as he slipped his hand between her legs. Her virginal blood coated his thumb. Raphael walked over to a dead maple tree, split down the middle from a lightning strike. He wiped his thumb on the tree, causing her to blush.

"A blood offering to Aibelle, goddess of the earth, to sway her from demanding your sacrifice. And a warning to your pack that I've marked you as mine now, and I never let go of what is mine." His jaw was taut and the dangerous look came over him again.

Emily's eyes widened as her blood sank into the tree and vanished. She gazed upward as new bark began appearing over the scarred wood. From the tips of the branches, small green buds appeared.

Raphael's smile was tender. "You still have the gift to restore life, *chere*. This is why I harbor strong suspicions about your so-called death touch."

Emily slipped into her dress. Raphael wrapped her in his leather jacket and picked up the basket and the quilt. When she winced slightly at the soreness between her legs, he picked her up in his arms and carried her, despite her protests. Back at her cabin, he sent her inside while he walked around the outside of her cabin, iridescent sparks of magick floating in the air as he waved his hands and placed a strong shield around the perimeter. Raphael came inside, locked the doors and windows. "That should hold them."

"Hold who?"

"Whoever wants to come inside that isn't welcome." His gaze swept around the living room. "Show me the ancient texts."

Emily stepped onto the footstool and removed the book from its place on the tall wood armoire. With reverence, she laid the book atop her kitchen table and opened it to the page she'd been trying to decipher. Her trembling finger traced over the page, telling him the translation meant a huge risk, but he took a bigger one in offering to present himself before the goddess. Even though he was Kallan, Raphael might not survive such an intrusion.

"I translated part of the text. It says you must sink the blade into my heart to save our race. I could teach you to read the words, but it will take time."

"We don't have time. I'll have to resort to crossing over to the Other Realm and asking Aibelle."

Before she could question how, Raphael herded her toward the glassed shower enclosure and removed her dress. "You need to warm up," he murmured, twisting on the hot-water tap.

Twin jets of warm water cascaded over her. Emily lifted her face to the refreshing spray, laughing and dodging away from Raphael as he stripped and joined her.

Mischief overcame her. Emily stepped out of the spray, yanking the knob to cold. He yelped and ducked, giving her a mocking glare as he turned it back to warm. Then he leaned his head back, letting the water hit his face. Awe spilled through her. Magnificent, a rock-hard display of male, muscles rippling fluidly beneath tanned skin. Water cascaded down his chest, beading in the thick, dark hairs.

The bar of natural glycerin soap went into his hands. He lathered and then began washing her, soaping her breasts, teasing her nipples in slow circular strokes, and washed her belly and legs, then he slid the soap between her legs. A low moan escaped her as he pressed his slippery fingers between her folds. Raphael wrapped his left arm around her waist and with his other hand, gently slipped a finger inside her.

"Does this hurt?" he asked softly.

"N-o," she managed.

He guided her to the bench and made her sit. As the water cascaded over them, he dropped to his knees, splayed her thighs wide open with his hands and put his mouth on her.

The first touch of his warm tongue made her jerk backward in delighted shock. He slid his tongue between her folds in slow, steady strokes.

Raphael swirled and licked her, absorbing her scent into him, marking her with the taste of arousal. When she threw her head back and cried out, her nails digging into his shoulders, he did not stop but stayed with her until the shudders ceased.

Raphael looked up, wiping his mouth with the back of his hand. He gave her a slow, sexy smile.

They went to the bed, Emily curled into his arms. His hand stroked her head, relaxing her into closing her eyes. Suddenly his chest beneath her cheek vibrated. He was singing to her. A smile touched her mouth as she listened to the odd words in his language.

He wrapped his arms around her, hugged her so tightly she gave a small squeak. "Rest, Em. Just rest. I'll keep you warm, *chere.*"

A delicious languor stole over her. She dozed off and dreamed about Maureen, picturing her as she collapsed on the hard floor. The scream died in her throat as Emily stared at her cousin, lying still, so deathly still....

Helen had not been still when Emily touched her. She had jerked and writhed and then went motionless. It wasn't the same.

Her eyes flew open. Maybe she didn't kill Mo after

all, but had stunned her, as Raphael said. Emily writhed out of his embrace.

He sat up. "What's wrong?"

"I have to go to the farmhouse. I think maybe you're right. Maybe Mo isn't dead. I could have stunned her. It wasn't the same as with Helen."

As she reached for her dress, Raphael caught her wrist. Stone-cold eyes met hers. "I'm certain she isn't dead, *chere*. But you're not going back to them. You're staying here with me. They aren't safe. There's something your pack is hiding from you."

A pulse beat frantically in her neck. "What, Raphael? What would they hide? And why? They are my only family."

"They're lying to you, Em. They've been lying all along." His thumb stroked the inside of her wrist as if he wanted his touch to soothe her and prepare her for what he would say next. Raphael laced his fingers through hers and squeezed gently. "Urien wants you dead and out of the way. Your hands didn't kill anyone. They only want you to believe that."

He heaved a great sigh, his expression grim. "This isn't easy to hear, especially about your family, those who helped raise you, your own blood. But you need to know, *chere*. The birds no longer visit the farmhouse. The animals are too terrified to venture near your family. No woodland creatures would be that frightened by wolves. It would take something very dark to drive them away. When we were with your family at breakfast, I kept watching Urien's face. He always lowered his gaze to me before when I confronted him. I kept watching, knowing I'd eventually catch him if he didn't realize I was studying him. Finally he did it. He blinked."

Torment filled his dark eyes as he squeezed her hand again. "His eyes were pitch-black, without pupils, without irises. Your pack leader is a Morph."

Breath caught in her lungs. She couldn't move, couldn't feel, couldn't think. If he had kissed and then slapped her, she couldn't feel more shocked. "It's not possible."

Raphael caught up both of her hands in his and brought them to his bare chest, close to his heart. "I'm sure of it, *chere*. I had suspicions, and I know now I'm right. Urien is Morph, and that's why the butterfly Morph was on your land, and the same for the piranha that bit you in the river. There's no need to reinforce safeguards because this is their land. Not only Urien, but I think the rest of your pack is as well, and they want you dead."

Emily pressed her eyes shut as if to block out his words. "You make no sense. If they wanted me dead, they'd kill me and absorb my dying energy to feed. Why would they call you here to do it for them?"

"I don't know. I need more answers, and I can't get them here. But first, I have to make damn sure they can't get to you."

Panic wedged in her chest. "But the prophecy...I killed my father?"

Her eyes flew open to regard his steady gaze. "Did you? Or was it a ruse by them to make you think you killed him? And your aunt Helen?"

Believing him meant abandoning everything she'd known her entire life. Even abandonment by her pack hadn't cut the ties. Pain sliced through her as if Raphael had cut her slowly with his Scian.

"They're my blood. They can't be Morph." Caught between her mate and the family who raised her, she fisted her hands. "I won't believe you. Why should I? Maybe you're just trying to trick me."

Anger shadowed his eyes. "Emily, stop it. I'm not lying and have no reason to trick you."

"And if you don't execute me by midnight of the first night of the full moon, you sacrifice your own brother's life to my family. Your own blood. It's a good enough reason to me."

Bounding out of bed, she stooped and snatched up her dress, buttoning it rapidly as her heartbeat thundered in her ears.

When he caught her arm, fury snapped inside her. Emily whirled and removed his hand. "Leave me be. I need to go out and think."

"I'll go with you. It's too dangerous out there."

"I need to be away from you for a while, Raphael. Do you really think telling me my family is the enemy is something I'll just digest, agree with and go off with you as if you are my savior?"

"You said you trusted me."

"Maybe I was wrong." Emily blew out a frustrated breath. "Maybe I can't trust anyone anymore."

His mouth worked violently as if he struggled for words. Finally he jammed a hand through his long hair. "Emily, please. What's between us can't be broken. I'm your mate, and I want what's best for you. This connection between us, it's emotional and not merely physical. Trust me, not them. I won't deny you."

Caught in a lethal tug-of-war between her draicaron and her family, she shook her head. "Right now I can't be certain of anything. Least of all your feelings for me, the one you're foresworn to execute to save your own blood."

She left him in the cabin, his low, frustrated growl floating after her.

Chapter 12

Raphael shoved a hand through his hair again. The mighty Kallan, toppled from his pedestal by his feelings for his mate.

A mate who still disbelieved him. He closed his eyes, reaching out to her, but she'd shut him off as if slamming a door. They had made love and he'd fiercely claimed her in the bonds of the flesh. He'd marked her with his body, took her innocence and every primitive instinct raged inside him to chase her down, tumble her to the ground and bury himself deep inside once more.

Making love to her over and over, until she finally surrendered everything to him and would run no longer. Yet she reacted violently to his observations about her family.

All his suspicions about Urien and the pack were on target. He knew he was right. Why did she still embrace them and not him? Even after he'd tenderly claimed her body, she still danced away from him emotionally.

He knew how difficult it was to distance yourself from the pack and stand out. It had taken him years and discipline to achieve it alone. If only Emily would reach out to him, dare to believe he told the truth.

The truth was a hard pill to swallow.

Outside, he followed her scent, his senses tuned to track her. Emily's scent swam in his nostrils, strong, feminine and warm. True, she was angry and didn't want him around. *Tough,* he thought grimly. *I'm sticking to you like a damn mosquito.*

As he entered the meadow where the abandoned farmhouse sat, her scent grew stronger and alarm spilled through him. Raphael frowned. Why would she come here?

He didn't like it. A veil of darkness shrouded the farmhouse. Even if Emily hadn't told him her father had died here, his Draicon senses warned that bad things happened here. A slight stench of evil draped the area.

The scent trailed off. Lifting his head, he saw a female in the near distance. Red hair, spilling past her waist, delicate skin and a cornflower-blue dress. She was barefoot. Emily. Raphael heaved a deep sigh. Her wolf nature intruded on common sense. Because she hadn't shifted in over a year, her inner animal manifested itself in human form, wanting to be free.

But the human form wasn't fashioned for cold weather. He held out his hand, called in his most cajoling tone.

"Emily, come back. Let's talk. Or at least let me take you back to the cottage and put on warm clothing."

She raced into the farmhouse, fleeing from him.

The building was dangerous, rotting boards underfoot. Raphael cursed in Cajun French as he bolted toward the back door. Fear rippled through him. He, who feared nothing, now worried about his draicara, lost inside this crumbling maze.

Inside, he called out for her. Nothing, but he heard a faint cry coming from an opened door.

Raphael's heart squeezed at the pitiful sound, filled with pain and sorrow. He stopped, inhaled the air, and picked up her scent.

The door opened to a dark staircase. Raphael called out again. "Emily, *chere*, what happened? Are you injured? Please, talk to me."

A faint female voice called back. "My ankle, it hurts."

Caution warred with the instinct to race downstairs and aid her. He dragged in another lungful of air, catching her scent. Raphael broke off a piece of railing, ignited it with his powers and used it as a torch as he picked his way down the steps.

Sweeping the torch over the basement, he saw nothing, but her scent was stronger down here. "Em?"

A low, evil chuckle answered. Even as he turned to fight, he knew.

The clink of metal snapped over his right wrist. Silver. He could not shift. Raphael dropped the torch, whirled and kicked and heard a cry of pain. A heavy, metallic net fell over his head, draped his body. He staggered back. Weakened by the silver, he snarled and lashed out, fighting with all his strength. The heavy blow to his head sent a gray fog swimming through his mind. He struggled against it.

The last thing he saw in the torch's dim light was Emily's pack, standing in a circle around him, silently waiting for him like zombies from the electronic games he liked to play with Gabe.

Waiting to feast on him.

Raphael woke up to the grim knowledge that he was toast.

Blood streamed down his temples as he raised his head. He gave an ineffectual tug at the heavy silver manacles around his wrists and ankles, the length of chain secured to a ring on the wall.

All his suspicions about her pack were right. Too late now.

The Burke pack had stripped off his clothing, leaving him naked, and tied him up like a dog. They'd struck his head, then touched their fingers to the wound on his scalp and tasted his blood.

The thick stench of rotting evil filled the air, making him gag.

"You're a mixed-breed, a mongrel, Kallan. Had you been like Emily, a pureblood, filled with light instead of darkness, we could not touch you. Your blood would kill us, as Emily's can, instead of sustaining us."

That's why the piranha died, he realized. "Her blood killed your clones in the river," Raphael snapped.

Urien stepped closer, a contemptuous sneer touching his mouth. "We sent the clones after you, but they struck the wrong target and died. Now with your blood and the darkness inside you, we have the source of immortality. We shall live forever, with you as our nourishment."

His mouth went dry, every cell inside him screaming in denial as he watched them.

"You never wanted Emily dead," he realized, springing at them. Chains restrained him.

Bridget laughed. "It was a ruse. We tricked you into coming here to feed on you. There is something in the prophecies about Emily dying to save the race. Helen warned me of it, but I paid no attention." Her eyes narrowed. "Emily is an abomination. When her father told me what gift Aibelle had bestowed on her, the power of life, I knew we could not have such a powerful being amongst us. I killed Liam, Emily's father, to condemn Emily. She is so gentle-hearted, it was easy to convince her that the goddess had cursed her. I killed my own brother and gained a power far beyond yours. I told Urien, and those of us who protested, like Helen, who wanted Emily spared, died at our hands."

Sickening disgust raced through him. "You all became Morph because you feared Emily. How could you violate the sanctity of life?"

Urien pounded a fist against the wall, making the plaster crumble. "How could the goddess make her more powerful than us! She damned us and our existence. You are Kallan, but not pack—you have no family. You know this—a Draicon wielding a greater power than the Alpha cannot remain with pack. She gave us no choice. We had to do it to even the balance."

"You damned yourselves. All of you." Grief for Emily twined with fury. What a waste, her entire family.

Bridget eyed him. "We've had to be discreet and hide ourselves, foraging to feed in the mountains off other Draicon and in cities on stray, homeless humans who wouldn't be missed. Our energy levels need a greater source of power. It's time now, Kallan."

Cold dread gathered in him as he watched them, their mouths salivating, their eyes growing to pitiless pools of blackness. The entire pack suddenly shifted into vampire bats. Cold, dank air stirred with the beating of their wings. Fear raced up his spine as they flew at him. He waved his hands, trying to beat them off, but they dodged the blows. Raphael ran into the corner, protecting his back and snarling as he grabbed one and squeezed his fist. The bat screeched and died, but they were cloning themselves now, hundreds of bats, their wings beating the air, rushing at him.

They flew at the exposed flesh of his legs, his chest, torso and arms, tore his skin with sharp incisors. Strength fled him as the bats sucked on the blood flowing from the small wounds. One bat sank fangs into his jugular. Pain burned through him. He fought and struck at them, but they kept coming.

Roaring, he rattled the chains, but the movements only scraped his wrists raw. They sucked his blood until he felt drained. Then the bats retreated and shifted back.

Severely weakened, Raphael staggered back, not able to make his legs stand. He slid downward against the wall, feeling the burning in the dozens of cuts on his raw skin. Blood dripped onto the basement floor. His immortal blood.

One of the Burkes shifted into a cockroach, scuttled over to the crimson puddle and lapped it. Raphael dashed the hair out of his eyes and tried to stamp on it. It scurried back to the safety of the pack, shifted into human form.

Smirking at Raphael, the male slowly licked his lips.

They were feeding off his blood. Becoming immortal. He calmed his fury, willed his emotions into submission. Reacting would accomplish nothing. He needed to think, figure out a plan to destroy them.

Once they ingested enough of his blood, the Burke Morphs would become immortal. They could not be killed. The consequences for their race, and the innocent humans they would terrorize, were too terrible to bear.

Silver weakened him and subdued his powers, but the blood loss drained him physically. He still had enough strength to fight them one-on-one.

Keeping his thoughts guarded, he sank to the ground, pretending defeat. Inside, his brain was racing over a plan. He searched out for Emily, touched her thoughts. She was in the forest, but she sensed he was endangered. Raphael sent a soothing message to her, blocking her from seeing his pain. She must be kept safe. All his protective instincts rose to the surface.

"You're reaching out to Emily, your draicara," Urien noted.

He didn't look up, but he heard the sneer in the leader's voice.

"We know she's yours. You can't hide the fact from us. Now that we've had a little taste of your blood, we can sense who you truly are. What you are to Emily. It's programmed into your DNA. We are you, Kallan."

You will never be me. They could not know his thoughts, his mind. Raphael kept silent.

"This is pointless, Urien," Bridget said sharply. "We only need his blood, and to keep him chained here as our energy source. Nothing more."

"Oh, but there is so much more," Urien said softly. "He's very clever. I sense he's already working out a way to escape. And it's not enough to take his blood. I need to know what he's thinking. Put on the protective gloves."

Raphael backed to the corner and snarled as they came at him. They threw the netting of pure silver over his lower body, their gloved hands protected from the metal's effects. Ten of them held him down, forced him to lie on his side, his left side exposed. He writhed and fought but was too weakened. He felt a hand almost tenderly brush back the hair from his face and expose his ear.

He looked up to see Maureen, the one Emily thought she had killed, suddenly vanish. Urien held out his hand and bent down. Raphael could see nothing in the male's palm.

"Maureen has graciously volunteered to investigate your mind. She's now *Taenia solium*. The pork tapeworm. Usually the parasite is ingested and then develops into a worm that moves into the bloodstream and then the brain. It's nasty and causes seizures. In your case, I thought we'd expedite the process."

Urien's nasal voice became a buzzing in Raphael's ears. The male leaned over and put his index finger on the fresh scalp wound. Raphael bit back a moan as he felt the worm inch into the wound and enter his blood.

"The worm is usually harmless to the brain until it dies. Not this time. I need to find out what's happening inside that mind of yours, Kallan. I will find out."

The silver net lifted off his body. Dimly he saw the others shift back, saw the soles of their feet scuffle away. He tried to summon the energy to sit, not lie on the dirty floor like a kicked dog. Raphael pushed himself upright, the silver chains rattling.

Pain speared his head as if someone hammered into his skull with a sharp chisel. Moaning, he collapsed onto the ground again. Had to overcome it…he could do this. With the last ounce of his discipline and strength, he willed himself to ignore the pain. He sat in a cross-legged position and placed his hand on his knees to center himself.

Breathe in. Breathe out. He began to concentrate, the meditation soothing his mind.

More pain followed, then his entire body convulsed. He went into spasms, his body jerking.

Memories flashed by. Oh, dead goddess, that thing in his mind, that thing that once had been Emily's beloved cousin Mo, was piercing his temporal lobe, burrowing into the cortex that held the hippocampus. Invading his memories, making him relive. No, no!

He held his head, trying to fight the parasite, but the pain trebled as if Mo were cloning herself into hundreds of tiny worms burying into his brain. Tears gushed involuntarily from his eyes as he went into a fetal position. As the memories surged forward, Raphael moaned.

"Good," Urien said softly.

Raphael was endangered. Emily felt it in her bones, felt it in the spear of pain in her heart. She crept out of the forest, all her previous anger and grief evaporated like summer rain. Inside her head, someone was screaming.

Her mate.

Terror immobilized her. She touched his mind, felt waves of burning pain as if someone had laced her skin with a hot knife. Staggering back, she slumped against a pecan tree for strength.

She had to find and save him.

But how?

Raphael was in the dark place again.

Ten years old, cocky, whistling as he walked through the Vieux Carre. The French Quarter. Purebloods mostly lived here with the human populace. The outcast Cajun Draicon like his family stuck to the bayou. Today he'd ventured into town to buy fruit for his mother. They both adored fresh peaches.

Raphael turned a corner and went into the small store. He filled the wooden basket on his arm with plump, juicy fruit, paid the shopkeeper and left. As he ambled down the street, his mouth watered at the sweet smell. Maybe just one, now.

Halfway down a deserted alley, he stopped and bit into a peach. Juice dribbled down his chin. Moaning at the delicious taste, he took another bite, the scent swimming into his nostrils.

Until another, deadlier scent drifted into his awareness.

The half-eaten peach dropped into the basket as Raphael looked up to see five Draicon ambling toward him. Five mature males, at least ten years past their first change. Purebloods. He could tell from the aura they radiated of power. Their cocky arrogance, matching his own. The same ones he'd run into last week. They would not leave him alone this time.

Scanning the area, he realized it was too late to run. He'd look foolish and cowardly, and he was no coward.

Raphael set the basket down and drew himself up to

his full height. He was only ten, but he was tall already, though gangly. His father always teased him about how his change would make him widen as well as lengthen.

"Look what crossed our street. The mongrel from the bayou."

The tallest pureblood, with hair blond as corn silk, sauntered up to him. He kicked at the basket, spilling the peaches. "You're lost, Cajun trash. Get out of our territory."

"Not yours. I don't smell you, only the stink of garbage." Raphael wrinkled his nose. "Oh, wait, I'm wrong. It is you."

Crimson flushed their faces at the insult. The blond looked him over coolly. "I told you last time, if I caught you in town again, you'd pay. You're not welcome, mongrel. You contaminate our air."

Raphael snapped him a rude gesture, hiding the hurt deep inside. Why did they always treat him like this, just because his blood was less pure, and he was Cajun? He could be just as good as they were. Equal.

Better, even.

Drawing up his fists, he prepared to fight.

They rushed at him in a pack, their moves swift and coordinated. One kicked at his legs, while another jumped him from the side. He fought his best under the assault of furious blows, but they outnumbered him. Outweighed him.

He fell with a grunt, holding his hands up against his head to ward off the blows. How he wished he could shift! The wolf could hold them at bay. But he was two years away from the change.

The blows ceased. He opened an eye and saw Blondie fish something out of his pocket.

The collar was snapped around his neck. He struggled and fought, but they held him down and attached a length of chain to the dog collar. Tears of pain surged in his eyes as Blondie yanked at the leash.

"Come on, doggie, let's go for a walk."

If he acquiesced, they'd never leave him alone. Deep inside, he knew he had to fight, even if it were a losing battle. Raphael jumped to his feet.

"Go to hell," he snarled, lashing out with his fists.

The punch caught Blondie by surprise, landing on his lip. Blood streamed from the cut. The male wiped his mouth, his eyes narrowing.

"I'll teach you to behave, mongrel."

A hiss sounded as the switchblade popped free of its casing. Terror surged through Raphael as he struggled in the arms of the two who held him.

Had they cut him, he could have borne it. Instead, they sawed at his hair, his pride. Until nothing was left but tufts. Then they took the basket of peaches he'd loved and cut them open, squishing them over the lacerations and bruises. Fresh cuts stung from the juice. The tangy scent of peaches mingled with the smell of his own blood.

Blondie kicked him in the groin, sending him crashing in agony to the pavement. They tied a rope around his midsection and tugged at it.

"Now we can go for a walk. Now, mongrel," the pureblood said with satisfaction.

As they dragged him down the street, whistling to him with mocking laughter, his body battered, bleeding and bruised, he curled into a ball and cried. He did not want to cry. He wanted to be strong, like his brothers, like his father. But he could only weep and let the rough pavement scrape his exposed arms raw as they paraded him through the Vieux Carre, like the mongrel dog he was....

Raphael opened his eyes and suppressed a moan. He could not let the Burke pack see his disgrace. With everything he had, he fought the memories. Sharp pain lanced his head. He bit his lip, tried to ward it off. Could not.

Laughter rose around him like smoke ascending to the heavens. He felt something large and itchy crawl along his cerebrum, invade his blood and exit through the wound on his scalp. Wiping the blood from his eyes, he looked up to see Maureen shift back into human form. She threw out her arms and chortled.

"I've seen what he hides, Urien. I know what he hides. My clones are still inside him and can torment him if you wish."

"I wish," Urien said softly. "But for now, I am hungry again. Aren't you, kin?"

He could not even summon the strength to groan as they shifted into vampire bats and flew at him again to feast.

Chapter 13

Raphael was hurting, and the pain he felt was screaming at her. She'd sensed he'd shielded her from it, but now he was too overcome to keep it barricaded. Emily bent over as a seizure grabbed her body. Pain burned her from inside out.

Fresh horror filled her as she entered his mind. The low moan spilling from her was a cry from her spirit. She hadn't believed him, trusted him, and now Raphael paid the ultimate price. Her pack was feeding off him. It had been a trap all along.

She stood upright, warding off panic, thinking fast. All her senses reached out to him, to find him. Aid him. Her nostrils flared as she picked up a faint scent.

Emily raced through the woods, her heart pounding hard. How she wished she were a warrior, a strong male who could overcome them. She was nothing but a meek, gentle Draicon. A misfit among their people, a female who refused to shift because she was too afraid to kill.

Realization forced her to grind to a halt. She had no weapons at her disposal.

Her wolf did.

Emily fisted her hands. Did she even remember how to shift?

And what then? Her pack was strong and could easily subdue her if she rushed at them as wolf. She knew nothing of sneak attacks, how to battle a force far greater than herself.

I'm a lone wolf. The thought coaxed a grim smile to her mouth.

So was Raphael. But he was a warrior, one who had fought and killed many Morphs.

Sucking in a breath, Emily slid gracefully down to the ground and sat. She closed her eyes and reached out, touching his mind.

Screaming pain invaded her senses. It felt like waves of burning, searing heat. Emily gasped, but kept going. She entered his mind, barreling past the flashes of agony, seeking out his memories.

Buried deep in his cerebrum, she saw hundreds of tiny worms feasting on his brain cells. Feeding his memories. Anger welled inside her, cresting to a flood. She sought her inner self, thought of pure, undiluted energy and directed pulses of white light at the creatures.

They burst like soap bubbles beneath the force of her thoughts. She sent soothing light to replace the worms, crooning words to ease the torment Raphael had suffered. But the emotional damage had been done.

Later, she'd address it. For now, she must find his knowledge.

She traveled swiftly through her mate's memories, pulling free past battles, attacks with his brothers on Morphs and solo ventures alone against the enemy. But it wasn't until she touched an alien part of him that curiosity flared.

Knowledge of battle plans, culled from things called electronic games he played with his brother Gabriel. Emily turned the memories over, absorbing them. A smile touched her lips. When she finally fled his mind, sweat dripped down her temples.

Determination filled her.

Tugging off her dress, she closed her eyes, reaching out to her own memories. Touching upon happier times with her father, when she ran wild and free beneath the silvery moonlight. When fur had covered her body and joy filled her heart and wolf was not a beast to maim and kill but a creature of the earth she adored.

Emotions warred with each other. Fear wrestled with resolve. Grief battled with her feelings for Raphael. *I can do this. I will change. I remember.*

Bones lengthened. Muscles shifted. It had been too long since the change, and pain grabbed her with meaty fists as her body contorted and her face became a muzzle. With all her might, she fought past the pain to reach for the wolf inside her.

Emily opened her mouth. A long howl rippled out of her throat.

She opened her eyes, her vision sharpening. Wind ruffled her fur, and scents and sounds teased her senses.

The best means for a lone wolf to defeat the enemy

was stealth. Cunning. Hiding in places the enemy could not see. Blend into her surroundings so they thought she was like the wind. Like an assassin in the dark night, creeping into the enemy's stronghold to slay them in their sleep.

Her pack would pay for hurting her beloved draicaron.

She ran toward the abandoned farmhouse.

Raphael was lost in a black maze. It felt like white-hot fangs constantly scraped open his wounds. The agony in his head was worse. He slumped over, dimly smelling the stench of his own vomit and old blood. A hank of dark hair, crusted with blood, hung over his forehead. Tossed carelessly to the side was the sheath containing the Scian. The Burkes had not wanted to touch it—they seemed afraid of the sacred weapon.

They were not as fearful of using and torturing him. He could only breathe and dully endure.

Another seizure hit, and he moaned as his body contorted from the worms infecting his brain, eating and releasing his memories. His body slammed hard against the concrete floor and rose up again.

The torment continued until suddenly he felt a gentle presence. He hissed out a breath, tried to warn Emily to stay out, to protect herself. He could protect her no longer.

And then, like a cloth wiping away a dark stain, the spasms ceased and the pain in his head stopped. He felt the worms vanish, replaced with white, pure light. Emily. She touched his memories. Ashamed, he pulled the darkest and grimmest away from her.

Instead, she fled to his other memories, searching them like a shopper picking up items and replacing them. He did not question. He remained huddled in the comfort of darkness.

Many minutes later, or perhaps it was hours, Raphael heard a noise. He forced his eyes, crusted with blood, to open. The basement window, cracked and grimy, edged open. Something dropped to the floor with a soft thud.

He sensed a presence of light, yet the stench accompanying it was Morph. It made no sense. Still, hope hammered faintly inside his heart.

Raphael remained motionless and watched.

A wolf, its coat grimy with dirt and decaying leaves, approached noiselessly. It loped over to him and whined as it licked his face. Then the wolf stepped back and began to change.

Shocked awe spilled through him as the muddy wolf shifted, transforming into a petite woman with flaming red hair, shining like the sun. His eyes watered from the brilliance of her, the purity shining in her green eyes. Her beautiful pale skin was smeared with dirt, her eyes shining with moisture. Tears spilled down her cheeks as she studied him. "Oh, my brave Raphael, what have they done to you?"

He wanted to hope, wanted to believe his beautiful Emily was here. It was a mirage, a vision born from desperation. His head lolled forward again, but he dared to peek upward.

Emily scrubbed her face with one glove. She fell to her knees gracefully. "I came to save you. Tell me now what I must do. Are the chains silver?"

Raphael tried to struggle to his feet but could not. He lay on the floor, watching her through a fog of agony. "Silver. Use…gloves. Key…far wall," he rasped.

Chains clinked together as Emily unlocked them from the ring attached to the wall, then unlocked the manacles about his wrists and ankles, using her dress to touch the silver. Raphael winced as he rubbed the raw, bleeding wounds from the bindings. He tried to stand but collapsed again.

Reaching out with his senses, he felt the enemy was not far now. They were returning again to feed on his blood. Resignation filled him. He had no strength even to stand. Emily came first.

"Just leave me. Save yourself," he whispered. "It's too late."

Instead, she reached for the Scian. Emily swallowed and drew the dagger across the inside flesh of her arm. Blood welled up.

With her left hand, she tipped his head back, forced his lips open. Raphael felt the blood drop onto his tongue. She closed his mouth.

"Swallow," she ordered in an authoritative voice he'd never heard her use.

He did. Strength flooded him as he felt wounds close, the blood racing through his veins, cleansing him, renewing his life. Deep inside, he knew something else important was at hand, but he could not concentrate. He closed his eyes and let Emily's healing magick restore what had been lost. Physical strength surged inside him, but the darkness remained, gray shadows hovering in the background.

Raphael ignored the emotional darkness, concentrating on flexing his unused muscles. He carefully stood. *Not exactly überwolf,* he thought humorlessly, *but this will do.*

Mindful of the grime and blood still covering him,

he turned to his draicara. Raphael longed to touch her, feel her softness against him, but he didn't want to darken the shining purity of her. "Thank you."

She tilted her head up to regard him, her eyes luminous in the faint light. "Did you think I would run away from you again? When you needed me most? I needed to face facts, and because of you, I had the strength to do it."

He marveled at her inner resolve, displayed in a stubborn tilt to her chin he'd seen from his first glimpse of her. There was something very special about Emily. Emotion made his hands tremble like a elder's. To disguise it, he pretended to sniff her and managed a faint grin.

"You stink," he murmured.

Her petite nose wrinkled. "I should, it's Urien's scent. I cloaked myself in his scent and then coated my fur with mud so the pack couldn't differentiate." Her lower lip trembled. "I got the idea from your memories of electronic games you've played, to disguise yourself among the crowd. I couldn't bear the thought of you alone here, what they did to you...."

"Em, it's all right now," he told her softly.

Warmth encased him as Emily hugged him gently. He relished the softness of her sturdy body, the silk of her hair spilling over his arm even as he shrank from it. He was contaminated. Dirty. Didn't want his darkness touching her. Reluctantly, he pulled away.

"Let's get out of here." His voice was stronger even to his own ears.

The beaming grin she gave him melted the ice inside him a little. "I think we both could use a long, hot bath."

Senses restored by her blood surged to full awareness. He whipped his head around, scenting the enemy even before the basement door opened. Raphael gave Emily a gentle push toward the space beneath the stairs. "Shift again and hide," he ordered.

He retreated to the hateful little corner and crouched down, pretending helplessness.

The steps creaked as Maureen plodded downstairs. He glanced at his captor, who bore a bowl of raw, bloody organs in her hands. Dinner for him.

Suddenly a muddied wolf loped out from beneath the staircase. Maureen seemed disinterested in the four-legged newcomer.

"Urien? I thought I smelled you. Hungry again?" Mo yawned. "It's my turn to feed him and keep watch, though it's a waste. Emily will never come for him. She's too afraid of her own shadow."

"Wrong, cousin. Emily isn't afraid. No longer."

Mo opened her mouth, her eyes wide as silver dollars at Emily in human form. Raphael sprang out from his corner, but Emily acted first. She whirled and grabbed the Sacred Scian still coated with her blood. The Burke cousin made no sound as his draicara swiftly stabbed her in the heart.

A bubble of blood frothed on Mo's lips as she staggered back. Dread speared Raphael. Mo was immortal now, thanks to his blood. The wound felled her as she gasped and toppled downward.

But it would not kill her.

The Scian tumbled from Emily's outstretched fingers and clattered on the floor. A low laugh spilled from her lips.

"I guess I have truly killed Mo now," Emily whispered. "I didn't want to risk it with my hands, because I'm no longer certain I have the death touch. I couldn't risk it, not if I came here to do what my heart urges me to do."

Raphael picked up his dagger, studied the blood on it. Maureen's blood mingling with Emily's. Something nagged him, but he dismissed it and used Maureen's skirt to carefully wipe the blood from the blade. He tugged his earlobe, and the Scian appeared on his left earring. Raphael nudged his draicara.

"Emily, she's not dead, just temporarily stunned, as I was when you stabbed me. She can't be killed. We need to get out of here." The urgency of his voice seemed to penetrate the fog of her misery. Emily nodded.

Together they shifted, and as wolves they fled out the open basement window. But something nudged Raphael to look backward, into the basement.

Grime coated the window. Surely it was the dirt, and his imagination, for the body on the basement floor that was Maureen had vanished. In its place was a pile of ash.

And a wolf stood next to it.

A day later, the Morphs that once were her pack had fled. Raphael sensed it in his blood.

They would return and try to capture him again. *Let them try,* he thought grimly.

On the back porch of her cabin, he rocked in the chair, watching Emily feed the birds by hand. Her sweet, lilting laughter floated up to him. He'd showered alone, the cold water mingling with hot to erase the pall of dirt still clinging to him, to try to banish the darkness. He'd then gone outside, tormented by the sounds of water running, Emily in the shower, and images flashing through his mind of her supple body, water cascading down her breasts, beading upon her taut nipples.

His hands gripped the armrests. Depleted of energy, his body had been nurtured by the restorative powers of her blood. Physically, he was well. Mentally, he hungered for her touch. He needed the emotional comfort, and his body sang out for her. The sexual drive was stronger now, the need to mate and achieve a mating lock with her overwhelming.

Her hips swayed gently. The enticing scent of female, Emily, drifted toward him.

The beast inside him roared to life.

When he'd been mired in burning pain while in the basement, he'd clung to thoughts of Emily. Emily's spunk, her kindness, her intelligence and warmth. Her hunger, how she'd clung to him when he'd driven into her again and again, her white, satin limbs draped over his hips.

He burned for her, his body craved her, feeling her writhe beneath him with her own wild hunger. Raphael fisted his hands, wanting to crush her against him, bury himself in her sweet softness, the scorching heat of her, the innocent purity and goodness of her. Taking her goodness into himself and erasing all the smothering darkness, filling himself with Emily as he emptied himself into her.

He needed her as a Draicon needed his mate. He craved, hungered, the heat building to an inferno, scorching him, needling him to forget all else and just jump off the porch and take her. On the ground, her white limbs spread wide, her pink flesh glistening in welcome, he'd ride her until she writhed and screamed, until he screamed with her, flooding her with his seed, his damn, inferior seed.

Breath heaved out in ragged pants as he stared at her, and he made a strangled sound low in his throat. She was his salvation, his anguish.

She was his, and damn it, he'd have her.

Now.

Emily felt the heat of his burning gaze centered on her back.

She turned, and her gaze collided with Raphael's. The ferocity of his look, the darkness of his expression, froze her into immobility.

Never had she seen him this intense, this maddened, driven by sheer sexual need. She swallowed hard, his clear message arrowing straight through her body. Moisture gushed between her trembling legs, and her heart raced in response. Warmth suffused her, searing as the intent look he gave her.

His big body trembled, and he clenched his fists. A dark wildness swam in his eyes as if he were close to losing control. She sensed the power inside him welling up, the raw, primitive male demanding they bond in the flesh.

She'd barely cleared the steps when he reached for her and took her mouth in a deep, crushing kiss. Her mouth was fire, and he was nothing but gasoline fueling it, kissing her, muttering against her lips as he took and teased and stroked. Emily gave a little moan, clasped him, fumbling beneath his shirt to touch warm, velvet skin.

"Can't wait," he rasped.

Raphael swung her around, pressing her against the door, reached for the hem of her skirt and pushed up. He unzipped his jeans as she wound her limbs about his hips sinuously, still giving him those frantic, begging kisses. He cupped her soft bottom in his hands and lifted her.

The first touch of his shaft to her moist female flesh felt electric. She shuddered, and then he surged forward, driving deep inside her. Shock rippled through her as her flesh shrank back from the raw, primitive force. He was a sudden storm roaring through the forest, shaking all in its path. She could only wrap her arms around him, hold on like a leaf trembling upon a tree.

Raphael raised himself up and she saw the hardness in his eyes as he began thrusting inside her. Behind her, the door rattled on its hinges. Pleasure as spearing as agony pierced her, gripping her as she pleaded, her back arching, hips pumping in desperation. She sought his skin beneath his shirt and dug her fingers deep into his muscled flesh.

He understood and pumped into her harder and faster, penetrating deeper. Emily screamed and dragged her nails down his bare back. Rocking back and forth, he thrust, rasping aloud in Cajun French, until she convulsed with pleasure. He shuddered, went still and shouted her name.

His breath bellowed in her ear as she gulped down air, heard the violent hammering of their hearts. Emily's legs quivered with the effort to keep them wrapped about his hips.

Finally he lifted his head, the torment faded from his dark eyes. A hank of dark hair hung in his face as he gazed down at her. "Emily. My Emily. Be one with me."

She caressed the stubble darkening his strong jaw. "Always yours."

He carried her inside then, still locked within her.

Raphael set her down on the bed and began making love to her again, slowly, gently.

For a long while after they'd both reached completion, Raphael held her close, stroking her hair almost absently.

"Peaches," he muttered. "I hate peaches. I didn't, once. They…forced it out of me."

Raphael's eyes were like dark glass as he stared up at the ceiling. She stroked his hair, weeping inside at his pain. Pain he would not share with her.

She wondered if he ever would.

A while later, Raphael lay in bed, watching Emily sleep. Face flushed from arousal, her lips parted like a child's, she looked languidly satisfied.

Instinct demanded he achieve a mating lock and exchange powers and emotions with her. How could he? The darkness inside him would swallow her whole. He could not let her see that part of him he most despised, the weakness that had shattered him as a youngling. The weakness that enabled the Burkes to capture and use him.

Raphael felt the grim irony of his fate hang on his shoulders like twin weights. If he were pureblooded and better suited for Emily, the Burkes could not have used his blood. It would have destroyed them.

Instead, he had nurtured them into becoming immortals like himself.

For the first time since he became Kallan, he loathed the powers he'd been given. His own pride and desire to become mightier than purebloods could be the downfall of their race.

I am truly the Destroyer, he thought bitterly. *Because of me, our race can be destroyed.*

He needed to get her the hell out of there. Knowing how powerful her family now was, and what danger he and Emily faced, made him feel as vulnerable as a fish to the deadly caiman.

Awakening her with soft kisses, noting ruefully the scrape on her jaw from his rough beard, he watched her sleepily open her eyes. "*Chere,* we need to talk. It's too dangerous to stay here. I can't defeat your family." He dragged in a deep breath, hating to admit it was his fault. His mixed blood that gave them strength. "They have enough of my blood inside them, and they're immortal now. They can't be killed."

Anger shimmered in her emerald eyes, and then they flashed to a tempestuous brown, mirroring the twist of her pretty mouth. She sat up, the sheet spilling to her hips, her satiny breasts pale in the dim light.

"They used you, enticed you here for this. Somehow we have to find a way to defeat them. They hurt you for their own means, their power."

Something was off. If Emily didn't kill her father or Helen, why had they both collapsed after she touched them? He gently grasped her palms. Frowning, he turned them over. "Yet the prophecies state your touch is to be feared," he mused. "If it were a ruse by your family, why would the texts say that?"

"I don't know. Maybe by the next full moon I can find out."

The next full moon, in less than two weeks.

He sprang out of bed, made calls on the landline, summoning the cavalry. Five of the strongest, baddest Draicon he knew.

His brothers.

"Now what?" She looked at him expectantly as he hung up.

"We're leaving, tomorrow. By the time we return, my brothers will be here."

Danger lurking in the shadows outside still threatened. Even with his mighty powers, he could not see how he could stop what the Burkes had become. They were immortal. Invincible.

When her family returned, all hell would break loose.

Chapter 14

Later that day, they departed on his bike. Raphael rode through the national park, wind whipping past them. Pine and oak trees flanked them as they wound through the mountains.

After a while, Raphael stopped for a break, parking the bike on the side of the road. He removed a small canvas bag from one of the saddlebags, slung it over his shoulder. They walked in silence, absorbing the sounds of the wilderness until arriving at a meadow. Thistle-wood, Queen Ann's lace and goldenrod blossomed among the meadow grasses. Pine trees and oak ringed the meadow. They avoided the meadow, sticking to the trees, coming across water gurgling in a small creek. He bent down and cupped his palms and drank, then offered her some. She drank from his hands, droplets sliding down her chin.

They sat on small rocks by the creek and Emily opened the sack Raphael had set down. She drew out a peach and an apple, offering them to him.

Raphael looked at the peach as if had a worm wriggling in it. He selected the apple and bit into it with his strong white teeth. She ate the peach, juice sliding down her chin, and she licked her mouth.

Raphael finished the apple and stared at her mouth. His nostrils flared.

"I've hated peaches for a long time," he murmured, tossing aside the apple core.

Emily licked her lips again, set aside the peach. "Maybe it's about time you tried one again."

A shadow darkened his eyes, reflected an inner torment. Guided by instinct and need to chase away his ghosts, Emily leaned forward and kissed him.

She licked his mouth, tasting him, letting him taste the peach juice on her lips as she flicked her tongue past his lips. Raphael closed his eyes and drew her closer, deepening the kiss.

Then he swiftly moved and was tugging off her jeans, shimmying down her panties. Raphael spread her legs wide and put his mouth on her. Emily cried out in shock at the smooth, warm slide of his tongue between her moist folds. Her hands fisted in his dark hair as he kissed and licked her. Holding her legs open with his hands, he stroked until she bit back a scream and convulsed with pleasure.

She sensed the desperate need in him when he drew back. His body tensed, his eyes were wild as his breathing grew ragged.

She felt him behind her. She heard the rasp of his

zipper sliding down, felt his warm hands clasp her hips.

"Bend over and place your hands on the rock," he said roughly.

The rounded knob of his penis touching her soaked, hot entrance made her go still. Raphael gripped her hips and then surged deep inside her. Emily cried out as her palms flattened against the rough granite. He went absolutely still.

She understood his need, the urgency. He needed to bond with her in the flesh, sink deep inside her and lose himself. Emotionally he was remote and haunted, so he reached out to her physically. She arched her hips in welcome, signaling to him her own need and her acceptance of his demands.

He increased the speed of his thrusts, his flesh slapping against hers, then he wrapped a strong arm around her and touched her center. Emily flew apart with a cry and felt his seed spurt deep inside her.

After, he held her in his arms, burying his head against her shoulder. She wanted to cry.

She did not.

They hiked back to the bike and resumed the ride through the park. When they reached North Carolina, she sensed his eagerness mingling with apprehension.

After a long while, they came to a narrow path winding up a remote mountain. The path led to a small gravel opening. The house was larger than her cottage, and its tall peaks seemed to soar into the sky.

Raphael turned off the bike and kicked down the stand. He slid off, turning to watch her expression.

A riot of wildflowers lined a rough rock bed, giving

way to a smooth expanse of emerald green. To her left came the sounds of a small brook trickling down to a pond. Rough-hewn pine benches sat before the pond.

"Where are we?"

"It's called Sanctuary."

Peace suffused her as they stepped inside. The house welcomed her with its natural wood setting and furniture carved from white pine and stuffed with thick cushions. A large wool area rug with a dark green floral print covered the hardwood floor. The wingback chairs, love seats and wood tables scattered about the living room gave the room a welcoming feeling. Cream walls set off the wood-framed picture windows. At the room's opposite end, built-in bookshelves invited reading at one of the chairs with brass reading lamps.

He hauled their knapsacks into a large bedroom with colorful rag rugs, an acre-wide bed covered with a soft ecru down quilt and wood dressers. She investigated and found modern facilities, including bathrooms and a kitchen with a gas range and a fully stocked refrigerator.

"The house is a training ground for all Kallan, but it also serves as a refuge for other Draicon who need to escape threats from the Morphs. A female acts as housekeeper and stocks the kitchen with food once a week. It's a retreat for anyone who needs to feel sheltered and safe," he explained.

They made thick sandwiches of rare roast beef and slabs of white cheese and held an impromptu picnic on the table outside as the sun slowly descended into the mountains. When they finished, he cleaned up as she unpacked. Emily went to the living room and found him studying a book as thick as a railroad tie.

Emily sat down on the leather sofa, watching him. He seemed absorbed, almost as if engaged in a ritual, and she didn't disturb him.

When he went outside, she followed. A large expanse of sloping meadow greeted them, the silvery grasses leading to a rough trail up the mountainside. Raphael glanced at her. "Come with me, Emily. Let's change and run."

Raphael needed to howl, be free and run. He needed her by his side, as well.

But Emily stepped back, hugging herself. Raphael studied Emily, troubled by her pallor. A lemon wedge of moon hung low in the sky. Inky blackness draped the sloping meadow. Raphael held out a hand.

"Come, Emily. The night is lovely. Look at the moon." She hung back.

"Come, change and run with me. You don't have to hunt. Just run. You did it before when you saved me, and it's safe here. No Morphs can infringe on this land. There are hundreds of acres for us to explore," he coaxed.

"I can't."

"You did before."

Night vision showed fear flickering in her eyes. "That was different. You were in trouble. I'm scared, Raphael. Scared of turning. I just can't."

He gentled his voice and touched her arm, needing the contact between them. "*Chere,* why are you afraid?"

"You wouldn't understand." A short, sad laugh followed. "You of all people. Immortal. Powerful."

"I understand more than you know."

Rubbing her arms, she remained silent. He reached

out and tipped her chin upward with one finger. "Em, I'm not leaving this spot until you tell me."

"All right!" She jerked away from him. "It's not just trying to impress my pack with the fact that I refuse to kill. I'm afraid of running in the dark."

He stared, totally flummoxed.

"I'm afraid because the darkness—it must be what death is like. Empty blackness. Nothing after."

The small whisper jerked his heart. Tenderness mingled with sorrow. "Ah, *chere,*" he said softly. "You are wrong, so wrong. This is where I can help you."

"With stories of happily ever after?" She dodged his outstretched arms. "Don't. Just don't."

"The truth," he said quietly. "Trust me, I know death and what it's like. How it feels to die, and what happens afterward, in the Other Realm." He closed his eyes, remembering the moment the previous Kallan had sunk the blade into his chest. The sharp flash of pain, the draining feeling and the white mist surrounding him...

"What's it like in the Other Realm?"

"It's peaceful, serene, beautiful. Endless forests and glades. Friends who have gone before you to greet you. No pain. No hunger." He touched her cheek, running his thumb over her soft skin. "Emily, it's wonderful. I wouldn't lie, especially not to you. There's nothing to fear."

"But you came back. And the others can't."

Raphael acknowledged this with a slight nod. "I did. I experienced death, though, the same as others."

"But it's not the same. Even if you were afraid, and had to have total trust, you knew if you were brave enough to risk it, you'd come back. Be immortal.

Never again fear death, until you were too old and weary to continue. It's not the same. How can you even think what you went through is the same? You're different."

"You are as well," he said quietly. He held out a hand, silently looking at her and using their unique telepathic connection. *Be with me. Run with the night, and be free. I will watch over you. No darkness will harm you.*

She studied his palm and shook her head. "No. I have to do this by myself. If I don't, I'll always be afraid. The fear will always rule me."

Respect washed over him. Raphael marveled at her inner strength, her gritty resolve. He stepped back and watched her shimmy out of her clothing.

Iridescent sparks shimmered and then turned into pure white light. Awestruck, he stared as the cloud of white surrounded Emily. He'd never witnessed anything like this.

Then suddenly a white wolf appeared where his mate once stood.

A white wolf. The significance slammed into him as the wolf, its eyes shining bright, turned to him. Dropping to his knees, he reached out and ran his hands over the luxurious, thick pelt. The wolf nuzzled his cheek. Then it turned, pawed at the ground, lifted its head and released a long, mournful howl and silently loped toward the forest.

Every instinct hammered at him to run after her. He did not. Instead he headed for a flat boulder to wait for her return.

Raphael sat on the rock, staring up at the mountain. Tonight he would make love to Emily, giving her pleasure again and again. And by the week's end, he would go into the mountain and ask a favor of another. A chill shuddered down his spine. He recognized and acknowledged it.

Fear.

They spent the next few days lazily in the lodge, reading, making love, talking. On the fourth day after they dozed in a light nap, naked in bed together, Raphael stalked toward the window and lifted the curtains with the back of his hand.

He was ever protective of her, even here in this place that held all the protection.

Her hungry gaze took in his long, muscled body, the athletic limbs dusted with dark hair, the pads of muscle on his back, the tautness of his buttocks. Suddenly he swung around, his dark intense gaze meeting hers.

A hot blush covered her cheeks. Emily hugged her knees. "I like watching you," she confessed.

A slow smile touched his mouth. "Watch all you like. I enjoy it."

Her eyes rounded and she released a slight gasp as her gaze dropped to the nest of dark hair at his groin and his genitals. His penis, which had hung slack between his legs, now began to grow hard and erect. Beneath her fascinated and astonished gaze, it grew longer and thicker as it rose until it practically touched his belly button.

Raphael's gaze intensified. "So you see, I do indeed like watching you watch me."

He joined her on the bed. *"Ma belle petite,"* he murmured, kissing her. "My beautiful Emily. Love me again with your hands. Let me feel the touch of your fingers upon me."

She traced a pattern on his chest, swirling her fingers in the dark, thick hairs upon his chest.

One by one he kissed her fingers with reverence. Emily closed her eyes.

Raphael flexed his powerful muscles. His look was intent, an odd shimmering in his dark eyes. He slowly caressed her, then his big hands touched her lower belly. Taking his time, he aroused her to a fever pitch. Her skin felt flushed, hot, and she was in desperate need of him.

"Please," she begged, tugging at him. "I need you inside me now." She spread open her legs wide.

Raphael gave her an intent look and mounted her. In a deep voice, he murmured words she didn't understand and then entered her hard and fast. His thrusts were deeper than ever before, his strokes pounding into her with a hungry ferocity. She climaxed first, screaming as she clutched at him.

He followed after, his entire body going rigid as he threw back his head. Cords and tendons in his neck strained as he cried out her name and his body shuddered as he kept coming.

At last he fell atop her, spent. Then still joined, he rolled her so she lay atop him. They lay like that for a few minutes, then he gradually separated their bodies.

Resting his head atop her lower belly, he gave a drowsy, sexy smile.

She wished it could be like this forever.

In the morning, Raphael awoke to the delicious feeling of a soft female body lying in his arms. Her musky, floral scent flooded his senses. He studied the long sweep of golden lashes feathering Emily's cheeks, her slightly parted lips.

She was beautiful.

She was his.

And he must kill her.

His heart twisted. *Must not think of that now.* Gently, he kissed her and slipped out of bed to shower.

By the time he finished and began to shave, Emily was awake. Wrapped in a sheet, she sat on the bed, swinging her bare legs. Raphael tried not to look through the open bathroom door. This was intimate, cozy, a scene shared between bonded mates.

Bonded mates meant to remain bonded, not torn apart as they were destined. He scraped the razor over his thick whiskers, noting with rueful amusement the approaching full moon. His beard was always heavier during that time of the month.

"What was the hardest assignment you've ever had to do?"

Her sweet, melodious voice softened the blunt impact of the question, like a mortar cloaked in velvet. He set down the razor, wiped soap off his face. Bracing his hands on either side of the sink, he regarded the male in the mirror.

You, Em. I can't do this. How can I take your life, even if the prophecy says I must? I'd rather take my own.

He glanced sideways at her. "An elderly female. My first assignment. She was so happy to leave, and relieved to see me. Very grateful."

Emily slid off the bed and came toward him, her hips swaying gently. He tensed against her approach, the beguiling innocence in her green eyes, the concerned look on her lovely face.

I am darkness. Death. You told me your hands killed with your touch, you contaminated. You're wrong, chere. I am the one who is shunned, and feared. Except for you and my family, all others of our people regard me as an outcast. You're goodness and light.

I am death.

"Why was it so hard for you if she was so eager to go?"

Silence hung in the air for a minute as he lowered his head. Little bits of dark whisker lay there dotting the white porcelain sink, like tiny insects blotching a landscape of snow.

"I think because she was so grateful. She made me feel guilty for doing it."

"What was it like for you, that first time?"

Fear darkened her eyes. Emily clung to the doorjamb, hanging back yet so close. He picked up the razor, turned it over and over in his hands.

"I was terrified. Either the knife would slip or I would lose my nerve. It took far too long for me to say the words and do the deed. I'll never forget the look in her eyes turning from trust and joy to doubt and then terror."

He set down the razor, his voice a bare whisper. "The terror was the last thing I saw before I did it and closed her eyes. I will always carry that weight of knowing had I been quicker and more efficient, as a Kallan should, I would not have given her time to fear."

Raphael could not meet her gaze. His chest felt hollow with grief.

If Aibelle didn't grant his request, what could he do?

How could he terminate the life of his beloved mate?

Chapter 15

In the morning, just before dawn, Raphael awoke. He very gently slid his arms from Emily. She stirred in her sleep, murmuring as if missing his warmth. Brushing a kiss against her temple, he whispered words of love.

Naked, he padded to the door and slipped outside.

Rose and violet light streaked the sky. Cold air slapped against his flesh. Wet earth and pine scented the air. He headed straight for the grassy meadow, leading to the path. Raphael began to climb the mossy, needle-strewn path, following the sounds of the brook paralleling it.

Fallen logs demarked the edges. The going was slippery from dead leaves and the previous night's rain, but his steps were sure. About a mile up the mountain, he came to a dead end.

The path ended at a silvery waterfall spilling down granite rocks. A sheer cliff rose one hundred feet upward, its mossy, slick edges forbidding access. Pine and oak trees above stood like silent sentinels. Water cascaded down the rocks, pooling in a small pond, then tumbling down the mountain.

Sacred, the waterfall was forbidden to other Draicon. Only the most courageous and purest of heart could ascend. Only those the goddess deemed worthy could climb.

Raphael sucked in a breath and plunged into the pond beneath the spray. Icy needles stung his skin. He took the natural soap resting on a rocky ledge and scrubbed his body for several minutes. Pine scented the air as he lathered and rinsed beneath the waterfall. His skin was raw and red. He opened his lips, letting water gush into his mouth. The mystic falls tasted of whatever emotion was reflected in the person drinking. When he'd last visited, the water was sweet and refreshing. Today it tasted bitter.

He stepped out of the spray. Wet, naked, he shook himself and bowed down in silence. After a moment he uttered the sacred words.

To the left of the waterfall, stone steps magically appeared in the cliff.

Raphael shifted into wolf.

Wolf senses flared to life. He scented deer droppings, a rabbit hiding nearby. His wolf ignored these smells and bounded up the barely visible path. Up he climbed, following the scent trail of others who had gone before him.

For one hundred feet he climbed, his paws nearly skidding on moss-covered rocks. Leaves drifted silently downward, caught by a slight wind rustling through the oak, pine and maples. Finally he reached the rise.

The clearing boasted a supreme view of cloud-shrouded mountains, brilliant splashes of gold, crimson and orange leaves. Raphael shifted back to his human form. Naked he walked over to the stone circle and knelt in supplication. Motionless he remained, centering his thoughts, his arms crossed over his chest. He ignored the piercing chill racking his body.

One did not ask for such a tremendous favor while complaining of the cold.

A voice spoke in the hushed silence.

"What do you ask?"

He kept his eyes closed. "In this sacred spot, great and wise one, I seek wisdom and guidance. I am Kallan, come to ask of you."

"Then enter my realm, and be welcome. Walk into the mist."

Raphael stood and squinted at a veil of brilliant white fog shrouding the edge of the cliff. He steeled himself and gathered his courage. To leap into the mist required a leap of faith that one would fall into the Other Realm and not to his death.

He was immortal, but it was a long way down.

He closed his eyes, thought of his feelings for Emily, and jumped. A soft bed of moss cushioned his feet as he landed.

"Open your eyes, Kallan, and see."

Doing as he was asked, he glanced around. The mist lifted, revealing the green, soft images of the Other Realm. The deep forest, cheerful chirping of birds overhead and scampering of animals seemed to be of earth, but to his senses, everything smelled cleaner, looked more serene. It was as if someone had scrubbed away all the pollutants and darkness and left only the purity.

Aibelle, the earth goddess who created their race, stood in a pool of white light, clad in a forest-green gown. A nimbus of red-gold hair flowed down past her hips. He dared to lift his gaze and glance at her brilliant green eyes. He remained standing but dropped his gaze.

"You have served the people well, Kallan. Your loyalty, courage and strength have marked your duties. What troubles you?" Her voice was soft, lilting as a crystal stream.

Shame crept over him as he thought of the dangers his blood had unleashed on the world. He kept his gaze downward as he told Aibelle what had transpired.

"I know, Raphael. I see all things. There is a great evil force at work that can destroy the Draicon." Her voice was soft, contrasting to the darkness of her words. "All things will unfold as they will."

Raphael couldn't help a small shiver as he summoned his courage. He dropped to his knees, kept his thoughts centered, but ringing through them was a single image. His beloved Emily.

"I came to ask a favor. Please release me from acting as Kallan to terminate the life of Emily Burke."

Aibelle's green gaze grew distant. "It is your destiny, Raphael Robichaux, son of Remy. You are Kallan, and you are foresworn to execute Emily Burke, the Chosen One."

His hands fell to his sides. "It cannot be." He dared to protest. "She is my draicara, my mate."

She studied him with calm indifference. "Do you love her?"

Emotion clogged his throat. Love her? Admit to what

he himself could barely acknowledge. But if it saved her, saved him from this awful fate, he would shout it out. "Yes," he said in a strong voice. "More than my own life. She is the missing half of my soul."

A shadow passed over her face. "I cannot spare you what you must do. To save the Draicon, you are called to do what the prophecies demand. At midnight on the first night of the full moon, you will take the Sacred Scian and plunge it directly into her heart. With her blood on the blade, the Draicon will be saved."

Hands fisted at his side. "I cannot."

"You must."

"How can you ask this of me?" he demanded.

Light shimmered around Aibelle, but the clouds overhead grew angry and dark. A wind blew at him, cutting him to the bone. Raphael dropped his gaze. "I apologize for my forwardness."

"Remember your place, Raphael. Remember who you are." The icy breeze faded. He felt her drift over to him and the warmth of her palm resting atop his head. "You were chosen as well. Your blood, and the darkness inside you, has called you for this task. No other will do."

"My mixed blood." Bitterness laced his tone.

Her tone was gentle, though the words were not. "You are not pureblood, but you have the powers your pedigree brethren do not possess. It is the reason you were selected by destiny for this."

He was chosen because he was a mongrel. Inferior. Raphael wanted to protest, to plead. He swallowed hard and thought of his life, his family, his brothers.

He thought of Emily, whom he loved. Her life mattered more.

Raphael bowed his head. "Then I beg a favor of you, great Aibelle. Make me mortal, and no longer Kallan. And trade my life for hers."

"You wish to sacrifice yourself to save Emily, your mate?"

Words failed him. He could only nod, squeeze his eyes shut, silently plead. He had a good life and had served his race well. He had known the greatest, sweetest love in those precious few days with his mate.

He would die for her, if Aibelle allowed it.

"No." The goddess's voice was gentle but firm. "I cannot allow this. You will not escape your fate this way, Raphael. See not with your eyes, but your heart. Hear not with your ears, but your mind. You possess great intelligence and wisdom. It, and the tremendous depth of your heart, is what made me chose you for Kallan. Do not let emotions cloud your judgment of what must be."

It felt as if his heart had been ripped out of his chest. He could barely breathe.

"Why can't you save her?" he dared to whisper.

"I cannot interfere in free will. Events will unfold as they must. But if you and Emily are willing to make the greatest sacrifice of all for each other, and your race, you both can save the Draicon."

It made no sense. He heard a tremendous buzzing in his ears, her voice growing dim as if Aibelle were retreating.

"Go now, Raphael, son of Remy. Bond with your draicara in the flesh as well as the spirit and be one with her. Then fulfill your fate on the first night of the full moon and the reward will be greater than you can imagine."

A protest died in his throat. He felt the atmosphere

shift, a roar sounded in his ears and he shuddered from the force of being caught in a wind as fierce as a tornado. Raphael squeezed his eyes shut, surrendering to the powers.

When he dared to open his eyes, he was curled in a fetal position, lying on the soft, lush grass outside the chalet. Like an elder, he slowly got to his feet, standing on trembling legs. He gazed upward. Gray clouds covered the sky. The forest was utterly still, as if stricken with silence from the mighty power that had delivered him from the Other Realm.

A slow, steady rain began to pour down as if the sky itself were weeping. Droplets splashed on the green leaves, plunked on the stones wreathing the expanse of grass. Fog drifted over the mountains, turning their blueness into mist.

His chest feeling as if crushed by boulders, Raphael raised his face to the rain. He tried to speak, to shout, to say anything, but he could not. His body shuddered and his fists clenched and unclenched. Grief felt like a white-hot arrow thrust into his heart.

As if it split in half, the pain was too horrible to endure.

He opened his mouth once more and tasted something rolling down his cheeks. Salty, wet. Not raindrops.

His tears.

"No," he said hoarsely. "Don't make me do this. I can't kill her. Please."

Only the hush of wind brushing against the trees answered. The rain fell faster and harder, like small bullets hitting his naked, shivering body. He remembered the vision seen in Emily's eyes and suddenly everything inside him broke.

Fisting his hands, Raphael raised his arms to the sky and the mountains. He opened his mouth.

"No, no, no. No, please, no."

He screamed and sobbed, tears running down his face to mix with the pure, clean rain.

Raphael remained in the rain a long, long time.

Emily woke to the enticing scent of bacon frying in the kitchen. She rolled out of bed, donned the red Chinese silk robe Raphael had bought for her. Barefoot, she walked to the doorway and observed him.

Rigid as the stones on the retraining wall, he stood at the stove. A baseball shirt and a pair of worn, faded jeans covered his body. His feet were bare.

"I thought I'd wake you up with something good to smell."

His voice was dull, as if it were a struggle to speak. She went to him, touched his arm.

He turned and caught her in his arms, crushing her to his chest. Emily laughed and put her hands around his neck. "You're acting as if you'll never see me again."

Raphael rested his cheek against the top of her head, stroking her hair. He said nothing. Alarm sluiced through her. "My love, what happened? What did Aibelle tell you?"

His jaw worked as he released her. Raphael turned down the heat beneath the frying pan and went to stare out the window as he braced his hands upon the sink. "I asked Aibelle to make me mortal again."

"But why? Why would you?" She cupped his cheek, feeling faint stubble beneath her fingers.

He turned, his eyes closing as he leaned into her

tender touch. "For you, Emily. You're right. I've never had to face death as any of my transitions have. I've never been truly afraid because I know I can't die. I asked her to remove my immortality." He fell silent. "And then I asked her... I asked if I could trade my life for yours."

Breath caught in her lungs. "No."

"That was her answer. She told me if you and I are willing to make a sacrifice, we can save our people." His gaze grew haunted as he looked at her. "But I don't know if I can, Em. I just don't know if I can do this any longer. But I have no choice."

Raphael closed his eyes. "Damian, my pureblood French brother, had words for a dilemma like this. Sometimes, life is just a damn case of *que sera, sera*— whatever will be, will be."

Rage replaced the bitter sorrow as he twisted out of her embrace. Raphael picked up the pan of bacon and smashed it against the wall with a snarl. His hands gripping his hair, he bellowed out his emotions. She watched the storm of rage with a broken heart.

"Oh, my love," she said softly. "Just let go. Let it go."

Spent, he slid down to the floor, burying his face into his hands. When he told her he needed to be alone, she felt an odd turning in her stomach.

Emily went outside. It was time to do a little bargaining of her own.

Other Draicon whispered of this place, where the Kallan came to be purified and made immortal. The goddess living atop the mountain might take pity upon her and release her from the curse for Raphael's sake.

The pathway was clearly marked. She began to

climb, hope fluttering in her chest. Surely Aibelle would listen.

When she reached the waterfall, she realized all access had been cut off. Heart pounding, she approached the rock and tried to climb. She slid back down, and rough rock cut her feet, blood pooling in the clear stream and spilling in the brook. Emily grappled for purchase, trying to climb, desperate now.

"Oh, please, please, let me up. I can't bear to see Raphael like this. Don't make him do this. Spare him," she cried out.

Tears she'd held in check spilled out. Through her blurry vision Emily saw the unrelenting rock, the impossibility of her task. Still, she tried, her fingers torn and bleeding as she ascended only a few feet, only to slide back down. Her knee ached from where she'd scraped it.

Finally she went to the small pool and waded in. Icy needles stung her naked flesh. Emily let her tears flow freely as she ducked her head beneath the spray to rinse away signs of her crying. She tasted the water.

Salt. Like her tears.

Emily closed her eyes, lifting her face to the hard rock cliff. "I understand. I'm not worthy enough. I'm cursed. I'll go. Please, just one small request, I beg you. Free Raphael from being the one. I'm willing to die, but please, don't make him do this. It will break him. I just want him—" her voice dropped "—to be happy. I love him so much. I can't bear to see him in pain."

She set her trembling palm against the rock. It seemed to warm beneath her flesh. Startled, she hastily stepped away.

Overhead, the trees rustled their leaves. Gold and yellow leaves floated downward, showering her. A lilting voice whispered in the wind. Emily suddenly felt enveloped in a comforting warmth as if someone hugged her tenderly.

The feeling left as she heard Raphael's faint call. Emily hastily scrubbed at her face, dressed and put on her shoes and began climbing back down.

Near the entrance of the path, she saw him. Her heart beat faster. Worry etched his expression.

"*Chere,* I've been searching all over for you. Where did you go?" Even as he spoke, he glanced upward at the path.

"I wanted to see the waterfall, and then I couldn't resist a quick dip in the pool. It looked so serene."

Tenderly he stroked her cheek. "You were crying."

She managed a small smile. "Just a spring shower."

Lines ravaged his handsome face. He jammed a hand through his hair. "I'm sorry I lost it. I thought I had better control. Once I did."

He looked ashamed, as if baring his emotions had weakened him. Tears burned in the back of her throat. "You have control, but you have something greater as well. You gave me a great gift, Raphael. No one has ever offered anything so dear to save me. Everyone else has turned away." She picked up his fingers and kissed them. "Nothing else I can do will ever come close to repaying you for what you offered on my behalf. I love you."

"Emily." Raphael gathered her to him. As she rested against him, he kissed the top of her head and buried his face in her wet hair.

For a long while they remained in each other's arms.

She cherished the contact between them, knowing with sorrow it would not last.

They spent the day together, quietly making love, reading and talking of everything. Everything but the inevitable.

After eating a delicious dinner of roast lamb, they retired to the living room. Raphael added logs to the fireplace. A side table had a collection of carved wolves. She went and picked one up, cradling it in her palm and marveling at the intricate craftsmanship. The wolf had a playful expression.

"Mine," Raphael said, prodding the logs with the metal poker. "I carved all of them. I was here for about two months last time, and passed the time."

"You're very good with the wood."

A boyish grin touched his full mouth. "There wasn't much else to do at night. No radio or television, and I wasn't permitted to shift and run with the moon. When Aibelle made me the Kallan, she arranged it so I'd never worry about money, nor would my family. It's part of the gift of being Kallan, so we can concentrate on our duties. So to indulge my art, I carved, and Alex, my brother, sold the pieces. He's an art and antiquities dealer."

He sat on a love seat and she joined him. Raphael draped an arm about her as they stared into the crackling flames. The log snapped and popped as sap trickled into the fire.

Emily snuggled against him, relishing his warmth. She pushed aside the underlying sorrow threatening to steal over her. Tonight was for each other.

Tomorrow would come soon enough.

"What did you do for two months while you were here?" she asked, running her fingers over his chest.

"Meditated. Waited. Wondered. Since I was the youngest to be appointed Kallan, my time here was longer."

Most Draicon who were Kallan were at least six hundred years old before they assumed the duties. Curiosity filled her. "What made you decide to undergo the test?"

His dark gaze grew somber as he gazed at the fire. "It was after Damian's family was killed. We had taken Damian in, taught him everything about survival and fighting. One day we were out in the bayou and Grandpere was teaching him how to hunt for game Damian had never tasted."

"Nutrias, the big rodents you told me about that resemble mutant beavers?"

Raphael grinned. "Yes, those. We ran across a Draicon who had barely survived an alligator attack. He was quite old, about 980 years, and in a great deal of pain and couldn't move. He begged and begged us to just end it. I asked Grandpere, but he told us it was forbidden. Only the Kallan had the power over ending a life. Grandpere took the elderly Draicon back to our cabin and called upon the Kallan. It seemed like only hours later the Kallan arrived. He spent a few hours with the Draicon, and immediately after his arrival, the elderly man seemed at peace. He was happy to go, and grateful.

"I was so much in awe of the Kallan. He seemed wise, immensely courageous and yet he had compassion and allowed someone in so much pain to pass through to the

Other Realm. He was more respected than anyone I knew. I thought he was invincible. I wanted to be just like him.

"And later, I found out, he wasn't invincible. Because every Kallan has a breaking point when he wishes he were invincible. And he finds out the worst way that he isn't. There are some situations where he is totally helpless."

"And how does he feel about it?" Her voice was the barest whisper.

His jaw seemed set in stone. "He wants to die inside."

Flames danced in the reflection of his dark eyes. He seemed to struggle with something to say.

Raphael removed his arm, studied his hands. "The basement, back at the abandoned farmhouse. When your pack was torturing me, it wasn't the physical pain that undid me."

She waited in silence, holding her breath, not wanting to distract him. Tension thickened the air between them.

"It was the damn memories." He glanced at her, a tic visible in his cheek. "I thought when we first met, you shied away from me because of your bloodlines. Your superior lineage."

At her headshake, he continued. "I know it now. But it's always been a shadow in my past. Dodging my footsteps wherever I went. When someone made the mistake of calling me mongrel—" he reached for the Sacred Scian, flipped the blade into the air "—I showed them the unfriendly side of my knife."

A shudder raced through her at the grim set of his jaw.

"There was an incident that happened to me as a child. It forever marked me, and though I put it behind me, it was reason for me to strive to be the best. Prove to others I was stronger, more powerful."

Horror pulsed through her as he slowly relayed the details. She could smell the sweetness of the peach juice, hear the jeers of the pureblood French Draicon, feel the young Raphael's deep shame. Emily gripped her hands together, knowing that if she showed pity he would break.

"It's the main reason why I became Kallan. To show others I could not be bested and no one would ever do anything like that again. I suppose I came to the job with bad intentions."

When he fell silent, staring at the fire, she told him what was in her heart.

"When you came here, I wasn't afraid of you, only suspicious and angry. And then when I realized who you were, and how you acted toward me, what you were willing to do in giving me the Scian, the symbol of your power, I realized something else. I knew you were the greatest Draicon of all. It had nothing to do with the depth of your power. It had everything to do with the depth of your heart."

Her voice dropped to a bare whisper. "That's the greatest power of all—to know others' needs and put them before your own. It was this ability Aibelle saw in you, Raphael. And that's why she made you Kallan and gave you this honor. Nothing else."

Something seemed to lift from his shoulders. He turned to her solemnly and held out his arms. She went to him and hugged him, feeling his fingers tunnel through her hair.

"Tell me about your brothers. Are they much like you? What do they enjoy?"

He talked about everything—from how they liked

playing basketball, football, baseball and electronic games to the close bonds they shared. The cuckoo clock ticked as he spoke. Marking time, each second slipping away like sand pouring through opened fingers. Emily swallowed past a lump in her throat. No sadness. She wanted to take tonight and hold it close, cherish it as a precious memory.

For a few moments they let the crackling fire break the silence. Relishing the solitude and peace. Emily glanced outside. "Let's walk."

The night was cold, crisp, scented with applewood smoke and balsam pine. It was so still she could almost hear the haunting echo of a train whistle far in the distance. Stars glittered overhead. Silver light from the moon glinted on the river rocks lining the property.

Raphael threw back his head as if to howl in protest at the moon. The anguish etching his face echoed her own agony.

Not like this. She would not have their last night here, alone, extinguished like the last log on the fire. Emily clasped his hand.

When they returned inside, the fire had died. Gray ashes littered the hearth, and a lone spark glowed on the remaining log. She watched it, in quiet desperation, as it sputtered and winked out.

"Come, Emily." Raphael held out a hand, his look intent.

She took it, following him to the bedroom. Raphael studied the fireplace there and stretched out his hands. A fire roared to life.

"Tricks of the trade," he murmured. "Sometimes power has its advantages."

"Yes."

Her soft reply drew his attention. Raphael pulled her to him, kissing her deeply. They undressed, taking time, as if memorizing each other. He tumbled her onto the bed and they made long, slow love as if he wanted to draw out every single moment. Murmuring to her in Cajun French, he loved her as if sharing a lifetime's worth of memories.

Deep inside, she sensed they were. The end would come soon enough.

Days later, they returned to the Burke farmstead. In her blood, she felt the approach of the night's first full moon.

The grounds were still and empty. Wildlife that had returned to the area had deserted it. Emily sensed her pack would return soon, to try to capture Raphael again.

They ate lunch on her back porch, propping their feet up on the railing, gazing into the serene forest. As they placed the dishes in the sink, a vehicle rumbling down the gravel drive broke the peaceful silence.

Raphael looked alert. "My brothers are here."

He slid an arm about her waist as they went outside. A large, shiny vehicle pulled up into the circular drive before her cottage and five males jumped out. Emily's breath hitched. The Draicon were tall, muscled, swaggered with confidence and looked menacing.

His brothers. She recognized the resemblance, but for a shorter Draicon with piercing green eyes and an enormously tall, slightly dark-skinned male with long black curls tumbling down to his waist.

Raphael introduced all of them. Etienne, the oldest, wore conservative dress and had kind blue eyes. The tall, imposing Draicon was Indigo, his adopted brother, she remembered. Bearded Alexandre had a quiet, deadly air about him, but his smile for her was kind, and sad. Damian, the pureblooded brother, had the natural authority of an alpha male.

Gabriel, the brother whose life was forfeit, was dressed all in leather and wore his dark, thick hair past his shoulders. He bore the strongest resemblance to Raphael but was slightly taller, and beneath his friendly, relaxed demeanor lurked something darker. Dangerous. She studied him, wondering what secret he hid inside.

They were different, stood out from her pack just like Raphael did. Emily drew in a deep breath. She had only wanted to belong with her pack, to fit in. She hadn't.

Could she fit in with his pack, his family? Emily's heart lurched.

Raphael drew her forward and took a deep breath. "This is Emily. She's…my transition, as I told you over the phone." He waited a moment, then said deeply, "She's also my draicara."

Silence draped the males. They looked stricken. Gabriel's jaw tensed and he looked away. "Oh, *merde*," he said softly. "You didn't tell us that."

"Your mate. Your draicara is the one you have to execute." Blood drained from Damian's face. The others muttered darkly and looked upset.

Damian jammed a hand through his dark hair. To her shock, tears sprang to his eyes. "Oh, Rafe, your draicara, you have to…and you can't revive her using your blood, your gift, you gave it to Jamie that one time, you saved her life with your blood, you gave it to my mate, and now…"

He turned, and she heard sobs wrench from the man.

Her heart turned over. Raphael gave her a reassuring squeeze and went to his brother, murmuring quietly, taking him by the shoulders as they walked away.

She understood. Raphael selflessly gave his one gift to his brother's mate, to save her life. And he could not use it to save her, his own mate.

Distress filled her at the guilt radiating from Damian. Her courageous, strong mate had spared his brother endless pain, and now Damian felt broken about it.

She realized the strong bond between all the brothers. Raphael might have been turned out of the pack because of his enormous powers, but love still forged all of them together. Maybe it was possible to be different, stand out from the pack and walk a different path and not be alone.

Her heart squeezed at Damian's obvious distress. The other brothers shuffled their feet, looking upset. When Raphael returned with Damian, the other Draicon looked wounded, but he no longer wept.

Emily knew she had to do something. She went and hugged Damian, careful of her gloves. "It's all right," she whispered to him. "It's not your fault, and my Raphael has a good, kind heart. I'm glad he gave the gift to your Jamie."

Damian suddenly crushed her in a hug. "There has to be another way," he said fiercely.

Surprise filled her as she inhaled his scent. Emily angled a smile up at him. "Your scent is unique. Your Jamie…her scent is mixed with yours. She is carrying a child."

His brothers whipped their heads up. Raphael stared. Damian sighed as Emily stepped back. "I was going to tell all of you at dinner."

Amid the hearty round of congratulations and back-slapping, Damian looked morose again. He glanced at Raphael. "I'm ecstatic and so is she. If not for you, Rafe, we wouldn't have had all this. I wouldn't have my Jamie." His jaw tightened as he stared into the distance.

The others fell silent. She wanted to cheer Damian. Emily wracked her brain for a way to pull him free of his misery and shock him into smiling. She squeezed his hand. "Congratulations. I suppose this means playing with your balls isn't your favorite pastime."

The others sputtered with laughter. "He told you that?" Damian asked, his eyes widening.

Emily nodded and beamed. "He said all of you enjoy it. It's your favorite game. Perhaps after dinner you all can show me how you do it."

Gabriel scratched his stubbled jaw. "Ah, maybe Rafe can show you. He's always doing it."

Gabriel ducked as her mate scowled and swung a mock punch at him. Emily returned to her mate's side, slid her arms about him.

"No, Raphael hasn't done it once since his arrival. All he's shown me is what he can do with his wood. He's very skilled."

Raphael made a choking sound. Alex studied her mate's pallor. "Hey, Rafe, man, are you blushing?"

Damian burst into laughter. The others whistled as Raphael muttered in Cajun for his brothers to do something. Emily turned to him, considering.

"Isn't that anatomically impossible?" She aimed a teasing smile at him. "Or are you confusing your metaphors like I usually do?"

His dark eyes widened as he gently touched her

mind, saw what she meant. "You little minx…you knew what you…"

Of course I knew what I was talking about. I did it to break the tension. Your brother Damian needed a distraction. He is hurting badly. She looked at his brothers with an impish smile. "I forgot. We have no *basketball,* no *football,* or *baseball* here. You'll have to improvise. And I expect you'll show me exactly how you play the game when all this is over and I can get to know you, and your families, much better."

Now his brothers blushed. Raphael laughed. He pulled her close and stared solemnly down at her. "I love you," he said aloud. "And I'm not about to let you go. We'll find a way."

"We will," she replied.

Then he kissed her deeply, and Gabe chortled, "Hey, Rafe, man. Before you get too involved, think you can show us where we sleep?"

Emily blushed this time as her mate laughed softly. He kissed her again and regarded his brothers. "Let's get all of you settled. All the cabins are free. A little musty maybe, but you guys remember how to clean."

"That's what females are for," Damian said with a straight face, and then he laughed again at Emily's scowl. "Don't tell my mate," he added, with a mock look of horror.

She felt Raphael finally relax beside her.

"Then what, Rafe?" Etienne asked.

His jaw tensed as he stared into the forest. She knew he sensed what she did. Evil was soon approaching. The air felt thick with the stench of raw, abused power.

"And then we fight," he replied grimly.

Chapter 16

No answers had come to Raphael during the night. He'd spent a sleepless night trying to think of a solution and arrived at nothing. They'd all spent the day talking, trying to arrive at solutions. No one had any.

He slipped through the woods now, sidestepping the crunch of pecan shells beneath his bare feet. Green moss coated the dirt pathway, making it slick, but Raphael's tread was sure and light. Overhead, a mockingbird, ever protective of its territory, scolded him. The damp, enticing scent of forest surrounded him. Tonight was the first night of the full moon.

Raphael paused by the small glen where the stone altar sat, the grounds humming with unseen power. With reverence he approached the altar, put a hand upon the stone. He called forth all his magick, all his strength.

Closed his eyes.

No visions came to him.

He thought of what Aibelle told him—to see with his heart, not his eyes. To use his intellect, not his strength.

Raphael opened his eyes and saw the altar. Saw Emily lying upon it, her red-gold hair spilling about her, her delicate, nearly translucent skin glowing with health and vitality. She was like nature herself, strong and endless, one with the earth, the source of her power. He envisioned her gentle heart giving life, but her hands causing death.

He saw her eyes shifting color, blue with passion, gray with grief or fear, amethyst.

He envisioned her, fertile in the springtime, growing sad and distant with winter.

The vision slammed into him with the force of a hurricane. He staggered back, driven into mute shock. How could he have been so damn blind?

No wonder Emily was different. "Different like me, and just as alone because of it," he mused aloud. "It was meant to be."

The realization slammed into him with the force of a Category 5 hurricane. Neither of them was destined to blend with the pack because of who they were. Raphael felt overcome by a feeling of deep peace and acceptance—and forgiveness of those who wronged him in his childhood.

Now he knew what Aibelle had meant. His eyes, and his heart, were opened.

Giving a little bow of his head, he murmured thanks to the place of sanctity. He turned and headed back to the cottage where Emily waited, summoning all his inner strength.

For surely he was right.

If he were wrong, he risked much.

Her life.

When he returned from the forest, Raphael sent his brothers to secure the property with a powerful shield. He could tell that Emily liked them. Their casual yet powerful air and their loyalty to each other were appealing. They had treated her with courtesy while her mate was gone, but she'd brought out some bottles of beer Raphael claimed they liked, and soon they had loosened up. They told her stories about Raphael, joked about him, yet beneath the teasing air lay tremendous respect and almost a worshipful air.

She was glad she and Raphael were alone now, though the reason for it made her heart heavy.

A full moon, the size of a half dollar, hung low in the sky. Emily braced her hands on the railing, staring at the silvery light filtering through the forest.

Her beloved woods. She had lived here, nurtured the earth with tender care, loved the land with a fierceness and relished the freedom it gave her.

Tonight, her blood would be shed on the earth she cherished.

The screen door slammed. Raphael stepped onto the porch. His gaze was filled with warmth, understanding, and yet she sensed the tension inside him.

In his hands he held the ancient texts. "Are you ready?" he asked.

Unable to speak, she nodded. They climbed down the steps and ventured deep into the forest to the stone altar. Set on the slab was a bowl filled with ripe mistletoe berries.

Emily took a deep breath as Raphael set the book down, and then she smeared the ripe berries over the sacred words.

Beneath the ghostly, pale glint of light, words appeared. She craned her neck and pointed, her finger shaking. Her heart pounded as sweat trickled down her back. Raphael gave her a questioning look. She didn't want to tell him, couldn't bear it. Emily strained to read the rest of the words, but they blurred once more.

He must know.

Her voice trembled as she spoke, the words sounding on a moan like the wind.

"It says, 'The Destroyer, Raphael, must shed the Chosen One's heart's blood on the sacred altar on the first night of the full moon by plunging the Scian through her heart.' It names you, Raphael. Tonight, you must kill me."

Too emotional, Emily couldn't read the rest of the text that followed. Raphael tried to soothe her fears, but she trembled in his arms.

"How can you do this? It's too much to ask of you," she told him.

Illiterate in the ways of the Old Language, he couldn't read the book. The knowledge was denied to him because he was of an inferior lineage. Raphael didn't know what followed the sentence Emily read. If there were instructions or specific directions on how to shed her blood, he was ignorant of them.

All he had was gut instinct and his heart to guide him. He drew in a deep breath, hoping it was enough, and turned her around to face him. Using their telepathic link, Raphael poured all his love, all his trust and belief in her.

Emily, I know now why Aibelle said what she did. Texts and traditions didn't hold the answers. You do. I saw you with my heart's eye, and I know now. He touched her red-gold hair, his hand straying to her face, cupping her chin.

Your eyes shift color depending upon your mood. They turn brown when you're angry, gray when you are sad, and— a faint smile touched his mouth *—various shades of purple when you are aroused. Your hair is a rich, vibrant color, like autumn leaves touched by sunlight. You're fertile only in the spring. Four drops of your blood, representing the four seasons, restore life to the dying. No other Draicon has this ability. Everything about you is unique, special. Different.*

"I don't want to be different. I never did. I only wanted to be ordinary, and belong," she cried out. "What good is it to be apart from everyone else, and be alone?" His heart broke at her next words. "Wasn't I ever good enough to be loved for who I am?"

"You are. I love you and I always will. Those who once loved you, and abandoned you because you are special, let their fears and their resentments crowd out their ability to love you for who you are. They turned to embrace evil because they couldn't bear someone being more powerful than they were, as you are. It's the essence of why Draicon turn Morph. Their fears and their quest for power leads them to embrace evil. Yet some Draicon are called to walk alone and be different. I was. And you are as well." He caressed her skin, savoring the silky touch of her. "You will never be anything other than special because of who birthed you."

As she stared blankly, he forged ahead, knowing she must believe in him for this to all work. "Your mother,

Aibelle. The goddess. You're her daughter. And because you are, you are immortal, as I am."

Emily's lips parted as her huge green eyes went wide with shock. "Which is why when I do what I am called to do, sink my blade into your heart, you will not die," he continued. "This is the sacrifice Aibelle told me that you and I must make to save our people. I don't know what will happen, but we have to believe it's for the best."

Immortal. Aibelle was her mother. And she could not die.

Emily, who had trusted few, who had been taught to be wary of growing close with anyone, now must trust Raphael with her very life. Trust that he was right.

Raphael was different. His strength, courage and mixed blood set him apart. He had lived alone, as she had, had walked the solitary path, as she had.

His was a choice. He made the choice to become Kallan. She had no choice in what she was given.

And now he asked her to step out in complete faith and trust.

It was too much to absorb. She wanted to dance away, retreat and think over what he'd said. They had no time.

In the pale moonlight, he watched her. Keeping a little distant, but his expression filled with love and concern.

"What you ask of me, it's very difficult," she managed. "What if I'm not? What if it's all not as you think?"

"You have to trust me, *chere*. Trust in my love for you and what we're both called to do." A heavy sigh fled his deep chest. "It's like when I stepped off the mountain into the mist. It was damn scary, and all my instincts protested. But I took the leap."

"A leap of faith. Just as I am supposed to do with you."

If he were wrong, she'd die. If he were right, and something wonderful did happen, then they had a means for defeating the most powerful Morphs of all.

"There is a reason for the gifts you were given, *chere*. Just as there was a reason for my being different." Raphael's body tensed as he stared at the book. "When I was younger, I only wanted to be like the proud French, the Draicon who looked down at me because I was Cajun. They called me mongrel, but I see now that perhaps there was a reason for what I was. I was already different, and this enabled me to become stronger, and be willing to step outside the pack. Because to be Kallan, I had to be alone."

Her heart lurched at his sad but resolved tone. "It was difficult, always having them loathe me for my impure bloodlines. I was separate from most when I was younger, and when I became Kallan, I became even more so. I see now why I took this path. Because it led me to you. For all the pain it cost me, I wouldn't do it any differently, as long as I have you."

His eyes closed. "And I have to trust that what my heart, as well as my intellect, tells me is right. We're called for a special purpose, to do this. Trust me."

For years, she had felt different, hated standing out from her pack. Could there be a reason for all she'd endured? Was she truly the daughter of a powerful goddess?

She thought about her love of the earth, how she always felt comfortable and welcomed by natural surroundings. How she coughed at the exhaust of cities and needed to be close to the land to restore her strength.

Emily stretched out her hands, seeing them as gifts. Her gaze flew to Raphael.

Her mate. The one who loved her, despite all her attempts to turn him away. The one male who knew what it was like to walk alone and have all others turn away.

Her missing half of magick.

Her love, who offered his life for hers.

Called for a special purpose. It was hard to believe, yet Raphael sounded so convincing. He truly believed in this. Emily sensed he asked her to do more than just trust in his words.

He wanted her to trust in him, as well. Believing what he said meant a very large leap of faith. Suddenly she wanted more than anything in the world to believe what he said, because it meant she was no longer alone. She had someone at her side who fully understood the trials she'd undergone, because he'd suffered the same.

Pulse racing, she placed her hand over his, feeling the tensile strength in his hands. Remembering how tenderly they had caressed her, how they had shielded her.

"I love you. I have a hard time believing what you're telling me, but I trust you. I'll place my life in your hands because it's the best place to be," she whispered.

Raphael hugged her, tunneling his fingers through her hair. When they broke apart, she touched his cheek. "In the words of your brother Damian, *que sera, sera.* Whatever will be, will be."

Raphael bent his head and gave her a slow, lingering kiss. She felt his sad smile against her lips. "So let it be."

The midnight hour had arrived. The time had come. Rapahel knew what he must do. He wanted to stroke

Emily's face. Upon the altar in her white gown, she lay still and pale, no fear shadowing her features. It was as if she were dead already.

His brothers gathered around, watching with unease. When he had explained to them, they accepted, but he sensed their disquiet and more so, their intense worry for him. Yet they trusted him enough to leave him to his duty. Anguish had crossed Damian's face as he glanced at Emily. He, more than the others, sensed what this cost.

Silver light stroked the short blade of the Sacred Scian. Raphael closed his eyes and uttered a short prayer for strength.

As he opened his eyes, he saw Emily looking at him. Love shone in her emerald eyes, not fear.

At the final hour, she'd opened her heart and poured all her faith and trust into him.

His hands trembled slightly. He only hoped he was worthy enough of it.

Raphael poured all his strength into her mind. *Forgive me, my love,* he said silently.

Raising the dagger, he spoke the ritual words. His deep voice rang out through the still woods. "In accordance to the honored ways of the Ancients, I, the Kallan, release you, troubled spirit, into the Other Realm to dwell peacefully forever in the lands of the ones before us."

The blade shimmered in the moonlight as he held it, quivering, above her breast.

"I love you," he told her. *I will always love you.*

She gasped as he plunged dagger down, sinking it into her heart. Blood gushed from the wound in a small fountain, spilled over the stone.

Emily's eyes fluttered closed as he withdrew the blade.

Something splashed from his face onto the altar. He brought his left hand, the hand not covered with her life's blood, to his face.

The tears rolled down his cheeks. He could not stop them. A low moan rumbled in his throat.

Take a leap of faith.

But had he leapt too far and wide, assuming in his arrogance that he held the answers? Raphael bent his head, his blurred vision scanning Emily's still face. She looked asleep.

What if he were wrong? His hands went cold and clammy as he set down the dagger and wiped his hands against his shirt. Tenderly he stroked her hair back, willing her to breathe again.

No movement showed as a heartbeat of silence passed. Nothing.

He'd killed her. Assumed she had been immortal, the daughter of Aibelle.

"No," he whispered.

"Rafe, man." Behind him, Gabriel's voice broke. "You did your duty. You had no choice."

There's always a choice, and I made the wrong one.

"It's my fault," he yelled, tipping his head back to shout at the sky. "I was too arrogant, too proud, and assumed I was right. Damn it, why did I do this? Maybe it was the wrong time, the wrong place. I don't know! If I had been able to read the damn texts, if I had the knowledge, I could have deciphered the rest of them and saved her. Why did you pick me, when I don't have the knowledge she needed to live? I'm supposed to be the one who cherishes and keeps her safe, and look what I've done."

His voice cracked as he smoothed back silky strands of hair from her face. "Look what I've done to my beautiful Emily," he whispered.

Anguish lashed him as he gathered Emily against his chest, her blood trickling onto his shirt. He picked her up in his arms and kissed her pale, still lips. Holding her body, Raphael marched around the altar, her arms dangling down. He could not speak or make any noise. She needed quiet, his beautiful Emily. His courageous, trusting draicara. Around and around he circled, the tears on his cheeks cold with the night air.

"Rafe, Rafe." Damian's anguished voice came from a great distance. "Look, Rafe. Look at the dagger!"

He could not look at the blade that had sunk into his beloved draicara's heart. Stealing away her blood, her essence.

But a faint light shimmered in the ghostly shadows in the little glen. The light pulsed white and grew stronger.

It came from the Sacred Scian he'd dropped on the altar.

Hope sprang up in his chest. Carefully he laid Emily down on the altar and studied her blanched face. "Breathe, just breathe. C'mon, *chere,* you can do it. Breathe for me," he whispered, caressing her cheek.

He bent over and sealed his lips to hers, sending a warm breath into her mouth.

She sighed and opened her eyes.

Behind him, his brothers dropped back, muttered in Cajun, even Damian. He ignored them, his gaze affixed on his Emily. Her rosebud mouth parted, and color flooded her cheeks. Deep emerald eyes filled with tender love studied him.

"You're crying," she whispered, touching his face.

"Just a spring shower." He let her wipe the tears from his cheeks, his heart lurching with joy.

Carefully, he helped her sit up. Already the terrible wound in her heart was healing, the blood vanishing from the altar. Raphael helped her off. She seemed stronger, more vital. Magick shimmered in the air, sparks dancing in the silvery moonlight.

The Scian still pulsed with white light. He picked up the blade and tested the edge with his thumb. Power surged through him. He turned to Emily, helping her off the altar. Raphael picked up her hand.

"Now. Touch Gabriel. My brother. With your bare hands."

"Ah, can't you pick another volunteer?" Gabe protested.

Emily did as he asked. Gabe staggered back and collapsed on the ground. The others stepped forward, rumbling with anger and shock. Raphael held up a hand.

"Wait," he told them.

His brother lay still, as if dead. A heartbeat of silence passed. Two. No movement. After what seemed like an hour, but was only minutes, Gabriel stirred. He got to his feet, passing a hand over his pale face. Gabe flashed him a wry look.

"That's some handshake your draicara has, Rafe. Remind me to keep my hands off her."

"How do you feel?" Raphael asked.

"As if someone shocked my insides with a 220 line. In a good way, though. I feel stronger." Gabe frowned. "Like I've been pumped full of power."

It made sense now, the tingle he'd felt when Emily first touched him with her bare hands. Jubilant, he flipped the Scian into the air and caught it by the hilt. "You have. Emily's power. Aibelle's power, of the earth. For Draicon, her touch is not death but inner strength. It overcomes you, because your body is too weak to receive it. Shocks you. But when you regain consciousness, you're stronger." His tender glance fell on his mate. "She isn't the cursed one but the one who will save us."

Emily held out her hands. "Then why, why did I kill my papa?"

The broken tone nearly undid him. Very gently, he picked up her hands. "I doubt you did. You stunned him, as you did to Gabe. Urien killed your father. Not you. Urien realized your newfound powers spelled the end for his rule, and he made it look like you killed your father, in order to condemn you with a curse that would result in your execution."

He bent his head to her, tenderly embracing her and fusing his mouth to hers. He didn't care if his brothers watched. The moment was only for her, a celebration of life. His and hers.

"Ah, Rafe, man, we've got company," Etienne said softly.

The moment shattered like glass against rock. He lifted his head, protectively shoving Emily behind him. The stench of rot and raw sewage nearly overpowered his senses. Shuffling noises sounded in the forest as the enemy neared.

Emily's pack had returned.

Chapter 17

Once they were her family. Her pack. They had carried her on their strong shoulders, helped to raise her, showered her with kisses and adoring hugs. Emily, their hope, Urien called her. The only youngling born among them in more than fifty years.

Now they were the enemy.

They would kill her, if they could.

Emily watched Raphael, wind ruffling his long hair. Moonlight touched the streak of pure white in his head, glinted off the earring in his left ear. Once she thought him different, a loner like herself, and feared him.

Love poured through her. He was different, like her. She embraced the difference in her heart and slipped to his side.

Looking up at him, she clutched his arm. "Not behind you, protected, but beside you. This is what is meant to be, my draicaron. We will fight in this form."

Still, his brow was furrowed with worry. "Stay low," he warned, as his brothers growled, shifted and prepared to fight.

The attack came like thunder rumbling down the mountain. Her pack rushed forward, shifting into their true Morph shapes, yellowed fangs shining, saliva dripping from their reddened, twisted mouths.

She recognized Urien's tall form as the leader snarled and attacked the first Draicon he encountered: Gabriel, who went for his throat. Raphael's brother sank his teeth into Urien's skin and ripped. Acid blood flowed, burning Gabriel's muzzle, but the Draicon bravely kept attacking Urien. Yet each time he feinted forward and his fangs sank into the Morph's skin, Urien healed. Cruel laughter echoed in the valley as Urien pointed a finger at them.

"You can't kill us," sneered the thing that had once been her uncle. "We're immortal, invincible."

A melee broke out, Raphael's brothers pouncing on the Burkes, who kept healing each time the Draicon attacked them. Then Urien sprang forward and aimed for Gabriel.

Talons extended from his fingers. He slashed at the wolf's throat. Blood spurted and Gabriel fell, howling. Shivering, he shifted back to his human form, clutching the crimson pumping between his fingers.

Emily saw her pack stop, lean forward to inhale the Draicon's fear and dying energy.

Feed.

"No," Raphael said, stricken. He started forward, but she laid a hand on his arm, staying him. She took the Scian from her mate and slashed her wrist.

Emily raced to Gabriel's side. She dripped her life-giving blood into his mouth, forcing him to swallow. His eyes closed, then flared open, shining with renewed strength and determination.

Glaring at the thing that had been her uncle, whom she once loved, Emily let all her anger surface. "It's your turn now, Urien. You're not invincible. You're toast."

She pounced forward, touching him just once.

Urien screamed and dropped down. All around them, everyone went still, even the Burkes.

A heartbeat of silence passed, then the incredible happened.

Urien twitched, and his body contorted, writhed and then split into two halves. A gray wolf emerged from the writhing mass, shook itself and stood by the screaming, bubbling mass.

The bubbling mass went still, then turned into ash.

She understood then and sent her thoughts to Raphael.

Her mate, glowering with fury and power, charged forward. He was beautiful, this Kallan, his long hair flowing behind him, his muscles working as his long legs pumped furiously. Raphael sprang over the wolf that was now Urien, slashed at Emily's pack with the glowing white blade.

The Morphs began to scream and fall. One by one, each cut from the sacred dagger made them drop, writhe and split in half.

Their good Draicon selves stood by silently as wolves.

The evil Morphs were left as writhing masses of wet flesh, which bubbled, died and then turned to ash.

Emily raced forward to assist, touching those Raphael could not reach. Soon it was over.

More than two dozen gray wolves stood before them,

mute and staring with yellow eyes. Docile as lambs as they huddled in a mass before the Draicon.

Raphael's brothers shifted back into their human forms and clothed themselves. Gabriel went to Emily's side and picked up her hands.

He touched them with reverence, moonlight showing the awe on his face.

"It was you. The Chosen One, not the cursed one. Your blood gave me back life, and your touch gave them new life as well."

Raphael bounded back to her side, sheathing the blade even as its light died and it became golden once more. He swept her off her feet in a hug, crushing her to him.

Setting her down, he smoothed back her hair. *You okay?* he asked with his eyes.

She nodded, leaning against him, trembling and overcome by what just transpired.

The light from the Scian had faded, but the altar suddenly began to glow with a brilliance. They shielded their eyes, all but Raphael and Emily. As she lay her head against his muscled chest, listening to the steady, comforting beat of his heart, she knew what was coming.

It was about time to meet her, she reasoned.

The white light expanded from a small circle to encompass the entire glen. It became as light as if the sun itself shone in the clearing.

The red-headed goddess, draped in a forest-green gown, shimmered into form. Raphael's brothers dropped to their knees, bowed their heads, but Raphael remained standing. Strong, proud.

A tender smile graced Aibelle's rosebud mouth. A mouth Emily had seen in the mirror.

"Mother," she said, her voice strong.

Aibelle held out her arms, beckoning to her. Still, Emily hesitated, looking at Raphael. He nodded and released her.

"My daughter, my lovely Emily," Aibelle whispered. "How proud I am of you, child."

Warmth suffused her as the goddess wrapped her arms around her. She felt something wet drop atop her head. The goddess, creator of their race, was weeping.

Emily looked up, her heart twisting. "Why didn't you tell me? Why all these years, leaving me to think I was without a mother? Alone, after Papa died?"

Aibelle smoothed back her hair, her green eyes wet.

"I could not interfere in your free will, your right to choose your own path. After I birthed you, and gave you to your father to raise, in the purest pack of all, I told him never to reveal your secret. You needed to be free from all influence that you were immortal and my daughter. Your destiny was your own, to reject or embrace."

"My father." Her own eyes were wet now. "Your lover."

Aibelle told her. She had met Emily's father while he walked in the forest one day and they became lovers. The goddess's gaze grew troubled. "I foresaw a great evil ahead for the Draicon, and knew they needed a tremendous power to even the balance and fight the Morphs. Evil and good must always be in balance. Thus, I conceived you."

Continuing to stroke her hair, Aibelle looked at Raphael. "You were in her destiny as well. Her mate, a male of tremendous strength and prowess. A male whose courage and strong heart would spell the redemption of Morphs and become a new weapon in the battle against evil. A good match for my daughter."

Raphael looked away, his strong jaw tensing. "I am not what you say. I'm not like Emily, a pureblood whose heritage is superior."

"You are far better, Kallan," Aibelle said, her voice gentle yet firm. "It matters not what your heritage is, but the size of your heart and the depth of your courage. Urien was a direct descendant of the first Draicon. Yet he was weak. He feared Emily and contrived a means to terminate her life and siphon off energy from you to become immortal. His greed and fear did him in."

Raphael bowed his head and tension fled his big body. Emily sensed the relief coursing through him, along with renewed strength. "What of the Burkes?"

Aibelle hugged her again and then released her. She walked over to the wolves milling about, the white light pooling about her. Bending over, she stroked the head of the largest. Urien.

"Your touch, Emily. It splits the Morph in half, separating the evil self from the lingering bit of Draicon deep inside, the wild wolf that is a creature of nature but misdirected by the Morph guiding it. When Raphael sank the Scian into your heart, it was coated with your lifesaving blood and performed the same function. The Burke pack is wolf now, unable to communicate except as a wild animal. Yet they are able to redeem themselves by living out their last days in the wild as wolves. When they pass, they will pass to the Other Realm and be at peace, as are all my children who are Draicon. Your touch did not kill, but saved them, as will Raphael's Scian from this moment onward."

Aibelle waved her hands, gesturing to the wolves.

"Go, flee into the woods and live in the mountains, off the land as you are aught. Remember this night, when you were set free by the Kallan and his mate."

The wolves dispersed into the night. Emily felt a heavy load lift. She went to Raphael, who encircled her waist with his arm. He kissed the top of her head.

Aibelle's gaze swept over Raphael's brothers, still motionless, in the posture of respect. "Stand, brothers of the Kallan. Your bravery has been well noted. Your rewards will be plenty."

Slowly they rose. Gabriel's gaze was astute as he looked upon the goddess.

"Emily's mother. I suppose that makes you Rafe's mother-in-law. Better watch your step, *t'frere.*"

Silence descended. His brothers looked stricken, as if Aibelle might slay him with a lightning bolt. But the goddess merely smiled, mischief dancing in her eyes. *That's where I get my sense of humor,* Emily realized, squeezing Raphael's hand. He laughed.

"I have a feeling my mother-in-law won't be a frequent visitor. She has other things to do. Still, it would be nice for Emily to get to know you better," he murmured. "You are always welcome. Just do me a favor and give plenty of loud, advance warning."

Thunder crashed in the quiet glade, lightning sizzled. Raphael's brothers yelped and Raphael grinned. "I guess that's loud enough."

The goddess looked serene as her gaze rested on Emily. "Your father wishes you well, and he wants to see you again."

"Papa?" Emily stepped forward as Raphael released her.

Into the pool of white light, another form appeared. A tall, well-formed Draicon, clad in the traditional clothing of the Burke pack.

She rushed forward into his embrace, not caring that he was now of another life force. His arms around her felt strong and corporeal.

"Emily, my Erin," he whispered, kissing her cheek. "How grieved I was to see your loneliness. But I knew your destiny would work out in the end."

"I didn't kill you?"

It was a question, yet doubt rang in her tone.

He hugged her, love shining in his eyes. "Just as Gabriel did, I dropped down from the power of your touch. By the time Urien arrived, I was on my feet again. I told him what happened, told him you were Aibelle's daughter." Sorrow touched his face. "I had sensed a darkness in him and Bridget, but I thought they were merely struggling with the reality of your true heritage, and I couldn't believe my beloved brother would turn against me. Urien killed me and turned Morph and began the chain reaction in the pack. The only one who held out was Helen. In the end, he killed her as well."

They clasped each other for a long few minutes. Then he released her and bid her to return to Raphael. Her mate. Her love.

As they stood, their arms about each other, Aibelle clasped each one of their hands. "I think it is time you both were mated."

The ceremony Aibelle performed was poignant, and the blessing she imparted filled Emily with peace and renewed resolve. Emily turned to Raphael, sliding her arms around his neck, and kissed him deeply. Their mouths fused in electric contact, a promise of passion to come.

"Go now and seal in the flesh the bond that has been created in the heart and the soul," Aibelle solemnly proclaimed. "When the two are one, you will be the weapon that will help defeat Morphs. With your Scian, Raphael, and your touch, Emily, you will redeem what was lost to evil."

Light shimmered around them as Aibelle embraced Emily's father. Then it faded slowly, and with a small wink they both vanished.

They were left with Raphael's brothers, standing in the small clearing, moonlight shining upon their faces. The wind whispered through the tree limbs, as if her mother said goodbye.

"Well, I'd say a celebration is in order, but I think *t'frere* has a little catching up to do." Gabriel nudged Damian, whose white-toothed grin flashed in the moonlight.

"Lots of catching up. I think we should leave them alone," drawled the normally quiet Indigo, the half vampire, half werewolf.

"Let's retire to the farmhouse for the night. Far away from any sounds we might hear in the night. We'll leave in the morning. Besides, I'm missing my own mate," Etienne drawled.

"That's all you ever think about—sex," Alexandre grumbled, giving the older brother a good-natured cuff. "That and food."

Raphael grinned at his brothers, but Emily sensed that his mind was already in the bedroom. A blush raced across her face, and she was glad of the cover of darkness.

With promises to reunite in New Orleans, the

brothers ambled off. Raphael kissed her again, cupping her face. Erotic heat shot through her.

They raced up the path to her cabin.

Inside, he paused in pulling his shirt over his head. Doubt flickered in his gaze as Emily placed a hand on his muscled chest.

"What is it, my love?"

"I don't know how easy our life will be, *chere,*" he told her. "I'm constantly on the move. I travel across the country as needed, and with our new powers, we have new obligations. You've always lived here, on the land, which nurtured you. Will you be happy if we have to visit a strange city, a new town, and you seldom see your beloved forest?"

"It wasn't easy for me to always be different from my people and have them shun me. Now I know other Draicon will always look upon me with fear and hold themselves back. I will never belong to a pack, and leaving this land will feel like losing a part of my heart. But I can handle it, as long as you're with me."

He pulled the shirt over his head and gathered her against him. "You belong to me. We are one with each other. It was meant for both of us to be different and be alone for a while. But no longer. We will always have each other, in our hearts." He touched her heart. "And our spirits."

"And the flesh," she whispered. "You are my missing half, Raphael. The other half of my magick, my strength. Give me your strength now, your courage, and I'll never again be afraid of what lies beyond."

They made love slowly, tenderly. As she felt him harden and widen inside her, the shimmering magick of the mating lock overcame her as she absorbed his powers, his emotions. His love and strength, and she gave back to him equally.

Light and darkness became one, as her mother had foreseen.

As she clung to her mate, opening her heart and pouring all her love into him, Raphael tenderly smiled down at her.

She was different and would always stand out from the pack. She was special, like Raphael.

Emily knew she would never walk alone again.

* * * * *

This November,
Silhouette Special Edition®
brings you

NEW YORK TIMES
BESTSELLING AUTHOR

LINDA LAEL
MILLER

At Home in
Stone Creek

Available in November
wherever books are sold.

Visit Silhouette Books at www.eHarlequin.com

REQUEST YOUR FREE BOOKS!

2 FREE NOVELS PLUS 2 FREE GIFTS!

⊽™ *Silhouette*®

nocturne™

Dramatic and Sensual Tales of Paranormal Romance.

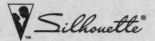

Romantic
SUSPENSE

**Sparked by Danger,
Fueled by Passion.**

*Blackout
At Christmas*

Beth Cornelison,
Sharron McClellan,
Jennifer Morey

What happens when a major blackout shuts
down the entire Western seaboard on Christmas
Eve? Follow stories of danger, intrigue and
romance as three women learn to trust their
instincts to survive and open their hearts to the
love that unexpectedly comes their way.

*Available November
wherever books are sold.*

Visit Silhouette Books at www.eHarlequin.com

SRS27653

Silhouette *Desire*

**FROM *NEW YORK TIMES*
BESTSELLING AUTHOR**

DIANA
PALMER

THE
MAVERICK

**A BRAND-NEW
LONG, TALL
TEXAN STORY**

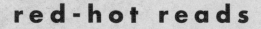

Silhouette®

nocturne™

TIME RAIDERS
THE PROTECTOR

by *USA TODAY* bestselling author

MERLINE LOVELACE

Former USAF officer Cassandra Jones's unique psychic skills come in handy, as she has been selected to join the elite Time Raiders squad. Her first mission is to travel back to seventh-century China to locate the final piece of a missing bronze medallion. Major Max Brody is assigned to accompany her, and soon Cassandra and Max have to fight their growing attraction to each other while the mission suddenly turns deadly....

Available November
wherever books are sold.

www.silhouettenocturne.com
www.paranormalromanceblog.com

SN61822

Silhouette

nocturne™

COMING NEXT MONTH

Available October 27, 2009

#75 TIME RAIDERS: THE PROTECTOR •
Merline Lovelace
Time Raiders

Cassandra Jones's psychic skills—and her need to escape her past—led her to the Time Raiders. But as she prepares to make the jump back to seventh-century China disguised as a Viking, she has no idea that her partner, sexy Major Max Brody, knows of her past…and may very well be a part of her future.

#76 THE VAMPIRE AFFAIR • LIVIA REASONER

Wealthy and handsome Michael Brandt tried to fight his attraction to Jessie Morgan, the reporter who uncovered his double life as a vampire hunter. But with his immortal enemies plotting to sink their fangs into her, he'd battle the ultimate evil to keep her safe and in his arms.

SNCNMBPA1009